BUSHWHACKED!

The shot clipped the saddle horn, then sizzled his side like hot iron.

Clint Ryan flung the reins and lead rope, then plunged from the saddle as Diablo, his big palomino, sidestepped and threw its head. His extra mount and the pack mule hump-backed away, fighting to shed themselves of their loads.

Before the echo of the shot quieted, Ryan was deep in the brush, his Navy Colt revolver in his hand. Hunkering deeper into a thick blanket of wild grapevine, he let his eyes scan the oak- and buckeye-covered canyon wall above, without making any other motion. The shooter must have been far up the west canyon side, for it had been a split second from the time the shot shattered the saddle horn until he had heard the report of the rifle. Had he been any closer, odds were he'd already be drawing flies.

Why the hell would anyone be taking a potshot at him?

<u>BOOK YOUR PLACE ON OUR WEBSITE</u> <u>AND MAKE THE</u> <u>READING CONNECTION!</u>

We've created a customized website just for our very special readers, where you can get the inside scoop on everything that's going on with Zebra, Pinnacle and Kensington books.

When you come online, you'll have the exciting opportunity to:

- View covers of upcoming books
- Read sample chapters
- Learn about our future publishing schedule (listed by publication month *and author*)
- Find out when your favorite authors will be visiting a city near you
- Search for and order backlist books from our online catalog
- Check out author bios and background information
- Send e-mail to your favorite authors
- Meet the Kensington staff online
- Join us in weekly chats with authors, readers and other guests
- Get writing guidelines
- AND MUCH MORE!

Visit our website at
http://www.pinnaclebooks.com

CONDOR CANYON

L.J. Martin

PINNACLE BOOKS
Kensington Publishing Corp.

http://www.pinnaclebooks.com

PINNACLE BOOKS are published by

Kensington Publishing Corp.
850 Third Avenue
New York, NY 10022

First Printing: July, 2000
10 9 8 7 6 5 4 3 2 1

Printed in the United States of America

One

The shot clipped the saddle horn, then sizzled his side like hot iron.

Clint flung the reins and lead rope and plunged from the saddle as the big palomino sidestepped and threw its head. His extra mount and the pack mule hump-backed away fighting to shed themselves of their loads.

His revolving Colt's rifle rested in its saddle scabbard—trotting away with the palomino—but he had his Navy Colt revolver strapped to his side, and before the echo of the shot quieted, he was deep in the brush and had it palmed.

Diablo, Clint's mount, headed away, back down Grapevine Canyon; the extra horse, a dappled-blue roan, and the roman-nosed bay pack mule followed.

Hunkering deeper into a thick blanket of wild grapevine, the namesake of the canyon, Clint let his eyes wander over the oak- and buckeye-covered canyon wall above without making any other motion. The shooter must have been far up the west canyon side, for it had been a split second from the time the shot shattered the horn until he had heard the report of the rifle. Had he been closer, odds were Clint would already be drawing flies without blinking his eyes.

Why the hell would anyone be taking a potshot at him?

Why the hell would anyone be taking a potshot at anyone, this hell and far gone from anywhere?

As he let his eyes seek anything that was out of the norm

on the hillside, he felt his own left side to see how much damage the shot, or the chunks that flew from the saddle horn, had done to him. Only a scratch, he decided, but it burned like hell. Must have been the hot ball that creased him after it careened off the horn.

Flies and gnats began to hone in on him, and he wanted to brush them from his eyes, but didn't. He would stay stark-still and give the shooter time to worry about if he had hit his target, or if his target had crawled away in the deep vines and was circling to get above and behind him.

Yes, let him worry.

He knew the big palomino wouldn't go far. They were 120 miles south of his barn and pasture on the banks of central California's Kaweah River, and besides, the big horse had never run off and left him yet—unless he was in sight of the barn and ready for a handful of oats.

The sweat began to trickle down his back; seeping blood left worm trails on his side, and the palm of his gun hand was lined slippery from the heat. Still, he didn't move.

He was sure the shot had come from above him on the same side of the canyon on which he rode. The far side, only fifty paces away, rose as steeply as the side he hugged, its ravine bottoms lined with live oaks and a few buckeyes— and a few patches of green wild grapes—and almost barren on the crowns between except for deep grass, now gone golden.

Clint carried a heavy pouch of gold, for he was on his way to buy some new breed stock for the ranch. But he hadn't seen a white man—and bushwhacking was a white man's trick—since he had crossed the Tule River, except for a lonely one-burro, one-blanket prospector and his mule, and that was forty miles back on the banks of the Kern. No, he doubted if this shooter was after his money. He probably wanted to scare him away. Maybe he had a gold strike up on that hillside.

But this canyon, Grapevine Canyon, was fast being established as the main route between Los Angeles and what was becoming known as the San Joaquin Valley—California's great central valley of swamp, tules, and prairie. The Valley Indians had long used Grapevine Canyon to ride into the San Fernando Valley just north of Pueblo de Los Angeles and raid the rancheros for horses.

The shooter was probably some crazy Yocuts who had learned white man's tricks, telling him to stay away from his stolen-horse string.

Finally Clint decided to give the shooter a target. He was getting nowhere lying in this pile of twisted grapevines; the bugs were driving him crazy and he had three days of hard riding ahead of him if he was going to make Los Angeles.

Eyeing an outcropping of granite twenty paces back down the trail, Clint took a deep breath, then broke from the vines and ran—half expecting a lead ball in the back for his effort. But he slid into the shade of the outcropping without incident. He lay quiet for a while. A blue-belly lizard appeared, then did lazy push-ups on the sun-warmed rock face nearby before disappearing again into a vertical fissure. Clint waited, hearing the screech of a red-tailed hawk, but no sounds of an approaching back-shooter. But this time he lay still only until the flies and gnats found him again; then he broke and scrambled forty paces to a small clump of sandpaper oak.

Still, no shot.

Wearily he moved out of the scrub oak and strode off down the trail to recover his stock, his eyes trained up the slope, searching for the shooter, still half expecting to attract another lead ball. It took him an hour to recover his animals. Diablo was grazing in the first small, flat meadow with green grass; the other two had moved on. With the big horse under him, though, he caught up with them before they reached the valley floor. Then, hardheaded as the mule he led, he turned back up the canyon. It was a hell of a long way around to another

pass, and he wasn't going to ride two days out of his way for
any back-shooting bushwhacker.

Only this time he would be watching.

Big Jory Mortenson broke brush in a hurried trot a mile
west of the canyon, dragging his own laden pack mule, long
before Clint Ryan had run out of the clump of grapevines.

He had seen the rider far below, and just for good measure,
had discouraged the man from coming on up the ravine he and
the old ranchero had taken west. Jory had no idea if the rider
was one of those he knew was looking for him, and he cared
less if he hit the man or not. So long as the rider kept his distance.

He knew that when he got to Condor Canyon, none of them
could follow him. And Condor Canyon lay only a few miles
to the west.

The old man on the mule behind groaned.

"Shut up, you ol' coot, or I'll tie you belly down again,"
Jory snapped.

"I *am* old, señor . . . too old for this kind of treatment. If
you will only stop here, my family will be along and will
give you the money you seek."

"I said shut up, old man."

"Sí, señor," the old Mexican said warily, but he sat straight
in the saddle. Old but proud, even with hands tied behind him.

For the first day this crazy gringo had kept him tied belly
down across the saddle. This was the third day, and he was so
sore he could barely breathe without crying out—but Don Carlos
Diego was not the kind of man to cry out, for any reason. And
he did not do so now, even though every joint in his body ached
as if he had been beaten with a stubby ax handle. But at least
he was upright in the saddle, as a caballero should be.

At seventy-two years of age, Don Carlos had not sat a horse
for almost eight years, since the last one he had ridden had
sidestepped out from under him and one of the old man's
brittle legs had broken when it met the hard ground beneath.

It had taken him almost two years to be able to walk again, much less ride. He had since been relegated to the carriage and the use of a cane—but it was no matter; he had many vaqueros to do his riding for him.

And a fine carriage it was, he normally rode in, for Don Carlos was among the richest men in the San Fernando Valley.

Yes, my family will come, Don Carlos thought with what pleasure he could garner. *They will come, and they will take your gringo hide to dry on my* establo *wall. They will cut your* cojónes *from you with a dull knife and let you bleed to death like they would the chicken for the pot.* Don Carlos continued to stare at the broad back of the big gringo who rode in front of him, and to silently condemn Jory Mortenson as the rough-gaited mule fought for a foothold on the steep canyon side. He would live through this; he had lived through worse. The thought of what his sons and grandsons and vaqueros would do to this man would sustain him until they came.

He had to live through this, for if he didn't, all would be lost. His family did not know what he had done. And what he had done hurt him more than this torturing ride.

But come his family would.

Clint reined up as they crested the steep narrow canyon and a wide, mountain-rimmed flat opened before them. The horses and mule blew and shook off the hard climb, flinging lather in the process. Giant live oaks covered the flat, and the bright green of a strip of river willows advertised the probability of a creek.

"Water ahead, ol' horse," Clint said quietly. The big palomino's ears pivoted and he shook his head as if he understood the man who had sat astride him for more than seven years, then flipped them in irritation as gnats gathered and pestered him. Clint had been given the horse by a grateful Santa Barbara don not long after he had landed on the shores of California, the result of the wreck of the hide-and-horn brig upon which he had come around the Horn.

And they had crossed this canyon one time before, shortly after the Bear Revolution, before California had become a state. Clint remembered this flat for two reasons. First, it was a broad meadow with grass-covered mountains on either side and a good creek—and he had been a man looking for land— second, because there was a big live oak with the words "Peter Lebec—kilt by a X bear" carved deeply into it. The first time he'd seen the crude eulogy he'd sat studying it for a long while, then began to laugh when it dawned on him that the carver had used an "x" in lieu of the word "cross." Clint remembered wondering who Peter Lebec had been—probably a French trapper with the Hudson Bay Company—and how he had come to get in the grizzly's way.

"Let's find that creek," he said absentmindedly and gigged the horse forward. But Diablo needed no encouragement. There had been no good water since they left the San Joaquin Valley, and the big animal could smell the opportunity ahead. It was late afternoon, Clint deduced, checking the sun. He searched his mind, trying to remember how far the next water lay. Then he decided to camp here, with plenty of water and graze. It had been a hard pull up Grapevine Canyon; then they had to retreat and repeat it, and the mule carried the better part of two hundred pounds and the spare horse a light pack of a hundred. And Diablo carried Clint's own two hundred pounds.

The stock had earned its rest, for they had started at day-break from a camp on the shore of a big lake, one of the largest along the banks of the Kern.

Clint turned the stock out without trepidation, knowing they would have no interest in leaving the belly-deep grass of the meadow, the shade of the stand of live oaks, nor the sweet water of the little creek—and if one of the grizzlies the area was famous for came along, he wanted them free to protect themselves. The ferocious thousand-pound animals were a constant threat, and all California lived in the shadow of the grizzly—even though meat hunters, supplying the mines, were rapidly decimating the population.

Clint had been on salt pork for three days and decided a brush rabbit would suit him tonight. He pulled the revolving Colt's rifle from its scabbard and walked away from camp—where he had dropped the tack from the animals, rolled out his bedroll, and pulled his coffeepot and frying pan from the mule's packsaddle.

"No one will find us here, unless I want the beggars to find us," Jory Mortenson growled as he reined up near a trickle of water.

"This is Rancho San Emigdio, gringo. There is nowhere in Alta California where my vaqueros will not find you."

"This ain't Alta California no more, and it ain't no rancho, ol' man."

"Rancho San Emigdio, and my sons will find us."

"Your sons won't be findin' us till I want 'em to. And when they do, they better have a satchel fulla money."

"They will have a knife to take your head—"

"Shudup, unless you want me to cut your worthless old tongue out."

Don Carlos remained silent.

Jory dismounted and untied the thongs with which he had bound the old man's legs to the cinch rings, then jerked him roughly from the saddle.

Don Carlos sank to his knees, unable to remain on his feet. He glanced up, angry and embarrassed that his old legs would not serve him.

A trickle of water ran down the bottom of the ravine that the gringo had decided to use as camp for the night.

"Cut me loose, gringo, so I can clean myself."

"When I get 'round to it," Jory mumbled as he dropped the saddle from his horse, then the mule.

"Only a coward would keep a *viejo* tied . . . an old man who could do him no harm."

"Shut up, old man, or I swear your family will get you

back mute . . . if they get you back alive." Jory jerked a ten-inch knife from his belt and stomped forward.

For a fearful second Don Carlos thought he had pushed the big, ugly gringo too far as he saw the knife's blade flash orange in the setting sun, but Jory Mortenson bent and cut away the knot on the leather bindings on his wrists.

Don Carlos slowly managed to get to his feet. He stood for a moment, rubbing his galled wrists. First his hands tingled, then pained him terribly as blood surged through them. Jory went back to arranging the saddles; then he pulled free his bedroll and spread it on the ground.

"Clean up, ol' man. I gotta tie you again a'fore we turn in."

Don Carlos found a flat rock and sat beside the trickle. He removed his flat-brimmed hat and slowly bent to allow the trickle to fill it, then set it in his lap and, very slowly, began to wash.

Darkness came quickly to the meadow near Peter Lebec's tree.

The rabbit lay skewered on a river-willow branch across a small fire, its odor beginning to entice Clint. His hat lay aside, full of watercress gathered from the banks of the little creek, and wild mustard and meadow onions filled the little frying pan to the brim and were already boiled soft in salted water.

He poured himself another cup of coffee and leaned back against the broad trunk of a live oak as the night sounds began to replace the day. He would sleep away from the fire tonight, deep in the brush, for the shooter might still be in the area, and Clint intended to give him no invitation to slip into his camp. He was exhausted from the long day's pounding ride, and sleep would cover him heavily.

In the growing shadows crows had gathered in a stand of live oaks across the meadow, and the rookery had been raucous and loud, but was now quiet—even the crows respected the night.

A lone big-eared owl launched himself silently from a digger pine, swept low over the meadow and made a furtive pass at a white-footed mouse, missed, and continued on, beginning his night of hunting. The mouse whistled shrilly, berating the owl and awaking the rest of the night creatures. In the distance, officially welcoming the night, coyotes barked, then began a melancholy song.

Clint sighed contentedly. He had a thriving ranch left behind him in the capable hands of two good friends and employees, its pastures full of prime Andalusian horses and its hills covered with several hundred head of cattle. Hogs, over two hundred now, rooted in the scrub oak along the creek and riverbeds, even though he continually harvested and sold barrels of salt pork for prime prices to the growing cadre of gold miners. A band of sheep now over five hundred strong roamed in the high country, far up the south fork of the Kaweah, under the care of two fine young Yocuts and a half-Yocuts/half-Mexican shepherd who had learned his trade well at Mission San Jose.

Clint's life was good, and was made better by the succulent smell of roasting rabbit.

It was the best of times—and the shooter was probably miles away by now.

Clint closed his eyes for a moment, then snapped them open as Diablo neighed loudly and stamped his feet.

Cautiously Clint studied the night sounds, but heard nothing. The shot that had clipped his saddle horn had him wary, but he was also weary.

"A wild mare on the wind, ol' stud," he said quietly, placating the horse. Reaching over, he turned the rabbit a half rotation, then went back to dozing, sipping his coffee, and awaiting the pleasure of a quiet meal and a good night's sleep.

His arms were pinned, and the blade pressed deeply into his throat before he could cry out.

Two

Three vaqueros knelt around him. Two restrained his arms roughly, the other pressed the knife to his throat. He must have fallen completely asleep.

"You are a dead gringo!" one of them snarled.

"Ease that blade, señor," Clint managed.

"Yes, I will ease the blade from your gullet, then open your gut. . . . It will be better to have you watch your entrails drag before you die."

"*¿Donde es Don Carlos?*" another of them asked, and grabbed Clint by the hair, slamming his head back into the rough bark of the live oak hard enough to send a shock of pain down his spine.

"Turn me loose, muchacha . . . let me up and face me like an hombre and I will stomp you like a cockroach," Clint said quietly, giving the man a look that would wilt most men.

"Let him up, amigos," another voice demanded from out of the darkness.

The men stepped back and allowed Clint to climb to his feet. Five other men, dressed in the *calzones* and *charros* of the vaquero, and covered with the dust of a hard day's riding, stepped forward out of the darkness into the flickering light of the small cook fire.

Clint eyed them, each in turn, with a casualness he didn't feel, then reached down to pull his rabbit, now perfectly browned, off the fire.

The vaquero who had grabbed his hair, a wide-faced man with a scar across his cheek, stepped forward and booted the rabbit as Clint reached for it. It spiraled away into the darkness. The man put his hands on his hips and guffawed.

In a step Clint smashed a hard right hand to the man's open, laughing mouth and he dropped like a sack of flour, his head angled up against the trunk of the same oak he had smacked Clint's head against.

The others were on Clint, beating and pummeling him to the ground until a tall man pulled them away. "He can do us no good unconscious. Stand away," the man shouted.

Clint struggled to his feet, bleeding from nose and mouth, but smiling wryly. The wide-featured broad-shouldered Mexican he had managed to punch lay unmoving, bubbles of blood covering his lips. The blow had been a good one, Clint decided, well worth the ones he'd taken in return—even though his hand ached as if a mule had stomped it.

"You are too brave for your own good, gringo," the tall Mexican said quietly. "Will you be so brave after we drag you behind our *caballos* for a league or so and the skin is scraped from your hide?"

The two men doing the talking were dressed better than the others, but were young—a half-dozen years younger than Clint, he guessed. In their very early twenties.

"That *maldito* had it coming," Clint said with a smirk.

"That is not the reason you will be dragged, and you know it."

"I have no idea why you are in my camp uninvited. Had you called out like *hombres de razón,* you would have been welcome."

"Enough of this, Emilio," the other well-dressed, tall Mexican said, stepping forward. He jammed a .50-caliber Aston into Clint's belly. His eyes bulged wild, his hair spread askew, and he was clearly worked into a fit of anger. "You will tell us now, what you have done with Don Carlos, or I will kill you where you stand."

"You tell me who Don Carlos is, and I will tell you if I have done anything with him."

The man drove the barrel of the Aston deeper into Clint's gut, making him give a step.

But he narrowed his eyes and growled, "You, like your *gordo* friend there, will be very sorry if you don't stop jabbin' me with that old blunderbuss."

The first of the two tall men, the one who had been called Emilio, stepped forward again and laid a hand on the shoulder of the man with the Aston.

"Stand away, Enrique, let me give this gringo one more chance to atone himself before he dies."

"Was that your rabbit I took?" Clint asked sarcastically. "For that's about the only live thing I've seen for the last hundred miles."

The Mexican began to have a glimmer of doubt in his eye. "Where have you come from?"

"From the north, from my ranch on the banks of the Kaweah."

"How long have you been at this camp?"

"Since late this afternoon. Last night I camped on the shore of the big lake at the south end of the San Joaquin Valley."

"What you gringos call Kern Lake?"

Clint shrugged. "It's fed by the Kern River. It's in the south end of the Ton Tache as the Indians call it, the Tules or Tulare as it is known to the Californios."

"And have you seen any other riders?"

"I have seen no white man since the banks of the Kern."

"Two riders, one a Californio; one, we think, a gringo?"

"I've seen no one."

Emilio's eyes softened. "Their tracks led here, but we lost them in the darkness. We hoped . . ."

"Who are these men you seek?" Clint asked, his own voice losing its hard edge.

Again Emilio's eyes narrowed. "One of them is my grandfather, and the other is the scum who has abducted him. A goatherd saw it happen. Don Carlos Diego is our grandfather and the patron of several ranchos. He was on his way home from Los Angeles, on the trail, minding his own business."

"What would a gringo want with your grandfather?" Clint asked.

"We do not know."

"This gringo is lying," the one Emilio had called Enrique said, stepping forward and again shoving the Aston into Clint's belly, but this time Clint was ready and he spun to the side, grabbed the man's wrist, and using the man's own momentum, hip-threw him. The tall man flipped in the air and landed hard on his back, one booted foot in the fire. The others were on Clint again, but this time they merely clasped his arms, while another encircled his neck and jerked his head back roughly.

Enrique scrambled back, slapping at the leg of his *calzones* and gasping for breath—his face reddened, not from the effort but from embarrassment and anger.

He climbed slowly to his feet and recovered the Aston from the dirt. Clint could not see the man, but he could clearly hear the ratchet of the hammer as he cocked the big-bore pistol.

"I will kill him now," Enrique said. "I know he is part of this."

"You will collect yourself," Emilio said with finality. "We will kill no gringo for merely being on the trail . . . we would be no better than them . . . and it might give their courts a chance at us again." Emilio had moved between Clint and Enrique as he spoke. He reached out and pushed the muzzle of the Aston down. "Let the hammer down on that *pistola* before you do something we will be sorry for later."

"There was someone up on the canyon side when I rode up," Clint said, appreciating Emilio's intervention and understanding these men's attitude if one of their own had truly been taken. The man who throttled his throat released him, but his arms were still pinned to his side by the others.

Emilio turned away from Enrique and eyed him.

"You said you had seen no one?"

"And that *es verdad* . . . I saw no one, but unless the rabbits, the *conejos,* have taken to defending themselves by bushwhacking, there was a man up there. He fired a shot at me. Take a look at that saddle." Clint motioned with his head, for the men still had his arms held to his side. "The bastard ruined the pommel of as fine a working saddle as was ever made."

Emilio walked over and crouched by the saddle and inspected the shattered horn, then he reached and lifted the leather fender and studied the maker's mark beneath.

"Who did you steal this fine work from, gringo?" Emilio asked, striding back to face Clint.

"That saddle was made for me by Ramon Diego, who is with me on Rancho Kaweah."

It was a long studied moment before Emilio spoke again. "Ramon Diego, of Santa Barbara?"

"The same."

"He is the son of my great-uncle, Don Alfonso Diego."

"God rest Don Alfonso's soul," Clint said. "I was there when Don Alfonso died at the hands of a Yocuts band. Ramon and I rode together to avenge him."

"Release him," Emilio snapped.

The men released Clint. Emilio extended his hand.

"I know of you. You were called 'El Lazo' in Santa Barbara, were you not?"

"I was," Clint said, and slowly extended his hand and shook the man's slender but strong offered hand.

"I am Don Emilio Diego."

"And he is still a gringo," Enrique snarled, but the pistol now hung slack at his side.

"He is El Lazo, of Santa Barbara, and he is an amigo, a *compadre* of Don Ramon." Emilio eyed each of the other seven vaqueros in turn, including the one Clint had knocked cold and who still remained unmoving, then turned back to Clint. "I am sorry about your *conejo,* Lazo. You will join us for supper."

"Accepted," Clint said.

Two of the other vaqueros knelt by their still unmoving

comrade, then pulled him into an upright position. His jaw
hung slack, and out of line. Blood ran from his mouth. The
men shook him and he began to come around. He groaned
and lifted a hand to his face.

The jaw was broken badly and lay askew. His teeth would
probably never fit together again.

"He is hurt badly," Emilio said sadly, then faced Clint. "No
one has ever knocked Morengo from his feet, much less unconscious. Is there something we can do to straighten his jaw?"

"I am no médico, Don Emilio, but I would imagine it is much
like an arm or leg. I saw it happen on shipboard one time. We
had better straighten it now; set it before it begins to heal."

Clint thought he had never met a man so strong, as seven
of them tried to hold the man called Morengo still while Don
Emilio tugged the jaw outward and forced his shattered bones
back into line.

To the echo of his moans, they bound it with rags around
his head, but Clint still feared the man would never again
gnaw a haunch of beef.

Don Emilio Diego, his brother Enrico, and the six vaqueros
were from Rancho Del Robles Viejo in the San Fernando Valley, not far from where Clint was bound. They explained their
background as they shared their dinner of cold beef and salsa
wrapped in tortillas. And since they were continuing on in
search of the patriarch of the rancho and would find no place
to replenish their supplies, Clint shared his ample pack with
them at breakfast. By the time they had arisen, Clint had a
frying pan full of fried salt pork and a pan of biscuits ready—
and a pot of very strong coffee.

They ate hurriedly and prepared to ride out.

Don Emilio walked over and extended his hand to Clint.
"I am sorry, but I know you understand."

"I have an auction to attend . . . but it is unimportant compared to a man protecting his family. I will ride with you, Don Emilio, if you wish."

"Seven of us are enough to handle this matter," the tall, young, straight-featured don said. "But there is a favor I will ask of you, if the auction you seek is that of Andalusian horses . . . it is near our home."

"Anything I can do to be of service."

"Morengo is of no use to us in his condition. The sale of the horses is at Rancho Agua Caliente, is it not?"

"It is."

"It is the rancho just west of Rancho Del Robles Viejo. Would you deliver Morengo there, where he can be properly cared for?"

"That's the least I can do."

"*¡Vaya con Dios!* Maybe we will meet again, El Lazo."

"Good luck finding your grandfather."

"We will make our own luck . . . and the *maldito* who did this will pay."

They rode off in a swirl of dust; Morengo was still prone in his bedroll, unmoving.

Clint sighed deeply, watching them leave. It had been a hard time, the last five years. The Californios had been obliged to watch the country—a sublime country they had been a part of for generations—overflow with hard men from all over the world, and watch it become the thirty-first state of a country they knew little about. They had to live under a legal system of which they knew nothing and, more important, alongside many men who did know the system but had little or no scruples and used the system to their advantage.

John Clinton Ryan had been a part of the force who rode against the Californios at San Pasqual, at Mule Hill, and at Rio Los Angeles, and he was proud California was now a state—but he had not been so proud of how his countrymen had since treated the Californios. The Californios had been right to be against the seventh flag flown over Alta California, the Bear Flag.

Clint packed the mule in silence, attended his other morning business, then walked over and gave the large lump that was Morengo's bedroll a prod with his toe.

The man groaned, rolled over, then immediately reached up and massaged his swollen jaw, keeping his eyes tightly closed. With effort, he sat up and finally opened his eyes. They flared in anger when he saw the camp empty and only Clint Ryan staring down at him.

"Get up, amigo," Clint said quietly in Spanish. "I have some coffee left if you can get it down; then we are riding back to Rancho Del Robles Viejo."

Morengo tried to speak, but then winced and remained silent. So Clint continued.

"Don Emilio and the others rode on to find his grandfather. He has asked me to accompany you back to your rancho."

The man eyed Clint warily as Clint moved over and poured him a tin of coffee and extended it to him. He waved the coffee off, refusing it, so Clint flung it aside, dumped the grounds from the pot, and packed it while Morengo sullenly rolled his bedroll—grudgingly accepting his escort. Morengo then went to the creek, and as if his face was as sore as a boil, which Clint was sure it was, he gently washed the caked blood away, then tried to drink from his cupped palms.

Clint walked to where Don Emilio's vaqueros had left Morengo's horse tied and began saddling it, but the big man strode over and shoved him away with a rather ineffective scowl.

Clint smiled at him. "Only trying to help."

"Gonup callouph." The man mumbled some complete gobbledygook that Clint had no possibility of understanding.

"You're gonna be great company," Clint said in English as he moved away to put his string together.

The big Mexican mumbled again, but was mounted and ready to ride by the time Clint had the string lined out and was astride the big palomino.

"Vamanos, amigo," Clint said.

"Humph," the man managed, as Clint led the way south.

The big Mexican had an old cap-and-ball musket in a saddle scabbard, and a foot-long pigsticker in his belt. Clint was glad they had his spare horse and the mule between them, for the knife was vengefully silent.

And what the big Mexican didn't know—although he carried a big grudge for the gringo who rode ahead of him—there was no load in the musket. Clint had seen to that the first thing after Don Emilio had ridden out of camp.

Still, he would have to watch the man. It was three days to Rancho Agua Caliente at the slow pace Clint would have to take to keep the Mexican from passing out in the saddle from his broken face that would be throbbing with every step of the animals.

But that wouldn't keep the big man from trying to slit his throat in the night.

It had been a while since Clint had had to sleep with one eye open.

It wasn't going to be the most pleasant trip, from here on.

Three

Doña Angelina Diego LaTour, her eyes ringed with dark circles, the lines in her middle-aged face even deeper than usual, wrung her hands and paced the floor behind her husband, Don Jacques LaTour, who sat at the long dining-room table, calmly finishing off a roasted half chicken. Even in middle age, Angelina could be strikingly beautiful, but now her face was lined with worry and lack of sleep.

"Please, Jacques," she pleaded, "send the rest of the vaqueros, all the vaqueros, to find *mi padre.*"

Jacques reached over and lifted the mug of wine and finished it, then dabbed his mouth with a linen napkin before answering. He was still as handsome as he had been when she married him, twenty years before; maybe even more so, now that his temples had gone gray and his former gauntness was fuller. He centered his gray eyes and flashed a white-toothed smile at his wife from over a perfectly tied cravat. "Don't give me indigestion, my sweet. I've told you repeatedly, *ma chere,* your father will be found by the boys. Your nephews are capable, and God knows no one can outride them—"

"They should have returned by now," the gruff voice rang out from outside the door, which opened onto a small courtyard that was planted with a variety of spices between the main dining room and the *cocina,* the kitchen, which was a separate building to the rear of the expansive main hacienda.

Don Juan Diego filled the doorway, shoving his flat-brimmed

hat back so it hung from the woven horsehair lanyard around his thick neck, now lined with sweat and dirt from the morning's review of the fields. "I should have gone myself," he muttered as he entered and took a place at the head of the table—a chair normally reserved for Don Carlos, who had now been missing for four days.

"That is Don Carlos's place," Angelina chastised quietly.

"Don Carlos is not here!" her brother, Juan, said harshly, his heavy jowls quivering, and his thick graying brows lowering.

She started to speak, but rather brought her hands to her face and covered it, then spun on her heel and ran from the room.

After her footfalls disappeared, Don Jacques began to rail at his brother-in-law, but an Indian servant hurried into the room with a platter heaped with another roasted chili-smothered half chicken, and tortillas and beans—the midday meal.

Jacques calmed himself and waited until the woman disappeared through the doorway; then somewhat calmed, he began again. "You are a hard man, Don Juan, sometimes too hard for your own good—"

"And you are sometimes a fool, Jacques," the barrel-chested Juan snapped. "In fact, too many times."

"We have coexisted on this rancho for twenty years, Juan, and I have not killed you yet, but don't press me . . . I am still as good with a blade as I ever was."

Don Juan Diego laid the half chicken down carefully, not taking his eyes from his brother-in-law, while wiping his hands on the cloth napkin. "You were not welcomed by me when you came to this rancho, Jacques, and you are still unwelcome, and still a man—a sniveling opportunist—who enjoys too much the sound of his own crowing. I have tolerated you only for my sister's sake—"

"That's a lie. You have tolerated me because Don Carlos insisted you do so. And I have refrained from skewering you with my blade only for your sister's and father's sake."

"Only for my sister's sake? When Don Carlos dies, and that may be soon, even if he survives this abduction, you had best be off this rancho before I and my vaqueros *lazo* you and drag you off, and *that* would be for the good of my sister."

"Talk is cheap, Juan," the Frenchman said coldly.

"And drag you off, I will, if I find you here one hour after the news of Don Carlos's death. He has made provisions to bequeath the Santa Paula rancho to Angelina, and if you wish to go there in some manner other than at the end of my reata, be gone before my father's body is cold . . . in fact, why don't you go today. I will have the women begin packin—"

"Rancho Alimitos is a very small property," Jacques said, his eyes narrowing.

"Far too good for you, Frenchman . . . far too good."

Angelina's footsteps could be heard returning. She entered the room, and the men resorted to a respectful but reluctant silence. Her lace handkerchief strained in her hands, entwined in them as she held them in front of her at her waist, but she had stopped crying. With quiet deliberation, she began again. "I think you, both of you, should gather all the vaqueros from all the ranchos and ride to find Papa."

Don Juan slapped the table so hard with the flat of his hand that it sounded like a gunshot. The silver candelabra in the massive table's center quaked and Angelina jumped back a step. Even Jacques flinched.

"By our beneficent God, I will decide who rides where and when on this rancho—"

"With Don Carlos gone, you decide," Jacques said coldly. "But when he returns . . ."

"Don Carlos has not made a major decision on this rancho since his accident." Don Juan rose and flung his linen napkin into his half-eaten plate of food. "I have made, and will continue to make all decisions, and the matter of who has gone to find Don Carlos was settled four days ago. Emilio and Enrique and the vaqueros I sent will bring him back. It was only one gringo who abducted him."

"But—" Angelina began.

"It is settled!" Don Juan roared, jumping to his feet.

"Do not yell at your sister," Jacques said coldly.

And Don Juan did calm himself. The redness flowed out of his cheeks, and his look at his younger sister turned to a loving one. Finally he rounded the table and placed his wide callused hands on his sister's shoulders, then gently lifted her face to where she was forced to look into his eyes.

"You know how much I revere our *padre, mi hermana.* Let me handle this. The rancho business must go on; that is what Don Carlos would want—"

"But what has happened to him?"

"We shall know soon," Don Juan promised his sister for the hundredth time. "Soon." Then he spun on his heel and left the room via the outside door, his voice floating back over his shoulder. "I must ride into Los Angeles. I will not be here for supper."

Don Jacques waited until Don Juan's footfalls faded, then rose and took his wife in his arms. "I am so sorry, *chérie,*" he whispered into her ear. "Keep hope, keep hope."

She pushed away from her husband. "You should have gone!"

"Chérie, you know I am a man of commerce. These matters are for men of the land to handle."

"You are a coward, Jacques!"

Jacques's face reddened and he cocked a hand as if to slap her, but then collected himself and spun on his heel, facing away from her, his hands clinched at his sides. Then he relaxed slowly as her voice softened.

"I am sorry, Jacques. I-I am so distraught."

He turned back and a tight smile crept across his face. "I know you did not mean that, Angel. I know you do not think such a thing." He was silent a moment, then questioned, "Why is Juan going to town?"

"I have no idea," Angelina answered wearily. "No idea. I am going to lie down now. I have hardly slept a wink since . . . since Papa . . ." She quietly walked from the room and headed down the hall toward their sleeping quarters.

"A coward," Jacques said under his breath after she had

gone. "I will show them all who the coward is." He reached for a pitcher of wine and refilled his crystal goblet, then downed it with a single gulp.

Clint was well into the second day with the big broken-jawed Californio dogging his trail. The night before had offered little in the way of sleep, but the big man had done nothing to make Clint believe he had any evil intent.

Morengo had slept badly, if at all, and had eaten little since his jaw was broken—and probably would not be able to eat anything solid for more than two months, if ever again. Clint had cautioned him not to try to talk or open his mouth, if he wanted the bones to set properly. The lower left side of the jaw was badly swollen as was the joint on the right side, a situation that made the lower right side look as if it was smashed in, but that was not the case. Clint surmised the jaw was broken in two places. The night before, Clint had boiled some jerked venison until he had a broth, and he had actually received a somewhat grateful look from the big Mexican when he had handed him the tin of fragrant liquid. It took Morengo an hour to press the hot cup to his swollen jaw to comfort it and then bring it to his lips, but he managed to sip it until it was drained.

The country had changed, becoming drier as they descended out of the mountains known as the Tujungas toward the San Fernando Valley. But it was beautiful with the tall blooming Lord's Candles spotting the hillsides, their two-foot white blooms dwarfing the rest of the wildflowers that had just begun to fade in the growing dryness.

Clint remembered a river, the Santa Clara, and hoped to make it by midafternoon. From there, it was only a few miles down the San Fernando pass into the wide valley, and only a few more to Rancho Agua Caliente.

They plodded along a narrow trickle of water that Clint thought was named Castaic Creek, and the gait of the horses was slow and swaying. Clint was so convinced that the man behind him meant no harm that he was actually dozing in the saddle when Diablo sidestepped nervously and snorted. Clint then heard the ratcheting of the hammer on Morengo's musket.

Clint turned slowly in the saddle, sure that the big Mexican's rifle was unloaded and that he was safe, but disappointed that the man would lay down on him.

But Morengo had reined up, and the musket lay aimed at the ground on the side of the trail. Clint reined Diablo around and rode back. Morengo aimed carefully, and the hammer of the musket clanked down—and as Clint knew it would, only the cap fired. Clint had carefully unloaded the weapon's powder charge two days before. The big Mexican looked perplexed, then disappointed as a four-foot rattlesnake slithered away through the brush. He eyed the weapon and shook his head in disgust, then it dawned on him what had been done. He gave Clint, to Clint's surprise, not an angry look but a disappointed one.

"*Rallesna*," he mumbled, resheathing the weapon.

"Right," Clint said, trying not to smile at the man's mumbling, as well as the fact the big man had meant him no harm. He reined back to the lead and picked up the pace. If he made Rancho Agua Caliente by midday tomorrow, he could be on his way home to his own ranch, Rancho Kaweah, within a fortnight.

He was looking forward to that.

Don Carlos Diego, even more weary and more worried, sat astride the rough-gaited mule and looked at the narrow trail they were about to descend into a very desolate and uninviting canyon.

The man who called himself Jory had been pushing hard to stay ahead of the riders they had spotted behind them the day before. Jory had grumbled that almost a dozen men pursued them, as Don Carlos knew they would, and he knew the number would be closer to thirty-five, all of his vaqueros from all four of his ranchos.

His son, Don Juan Diego, a man among men, the *segundo*

of Rancho Del Robles Viejo and all the other ranchos, a rider who surpassed all—even at forty-eight years of age—would be leading them. His very clever and able son-in-law, Jacques La-Tour, the man his vaqueros called 'El Coyote,' would be at his side. His two grandsons, Juan's fine sons, Emilio and Enrique, would be next in the pack, and all his vaqueros would be close behind—the finest group of caballeros in all of California, and men who would stop at nothing to avenge their jefe.

Jory Mortenson eyed the narrow steep trail in front of them and glanced back over his shoulder. "You better hang tight, ol' man. It's better'n six hundred feet down there, and you could be nothing but a grease spot, you ol' greaser, if'n yer skinny butt fell off that mule." He paused to guffaw, enjoying his own crude humor, before continuing.

Don Carlos was not worried about falling off the mule, even as exhausted as he was, for the gringo had tied his legs to the cinch rings. He was concerned, however, about the mule. He had noticed that the animal's gait was slowing and the mule was beginning to favor a right hind foot. Only slightly, of course, and a man who had not spent most of his life in the saddle would not notice it, but Don Carlos did. No, *he* would not fall off the mule, but the mule . . . ? It was a very steep trail, and most of it on hard, gravel-slick, crumbling sandstone.

Don Carlos raised his eyes to say a silent prayer. He was not reassured by the sight of a pair of giant condors circling high overhead. "Not yet, great birds," he said under his breath. "I will live to see my sons and grandsons draw and quarter this scum of a gringo—and to solve my small problem with 'El Boticario'—then you may feed on this gringo's miserable remains."

The thought of the great birds ripping the flesh from his abductor made him stronger, and he girded his courage as the gringo spurred his horse ahead. The animal moved forward carefully and the lead rope tightened. Don Carlos could sense the mule's hesitation, but the animal followed.

Carefully picking each step, they began the dizzying descent into Condor Canyon.

* * *

Morengo slept the second night without moving, the sleep of the exhausted. Clint knew what it was like to have serious injury, for he had had more than his share of hurt after a dozen years at sea, a revolution, a time in boomtown San Francisco, and just getting by in a rugged, untamed country. He carried the scars of more than one bullet and blade, and more than one accident. He understood well how a man needed sleep to begin the repair process. Morengo slept without moving, and his steady breathing kept pace with Clint's own good night's sleep, having been reassured by Morengo' s pointing the musket at a rattlesnake and not at Clint's back.

Morengo had managed not only two tins of soup, but a tin of coffee at the evening meal.

So Clint handed him another at breakfast.

"Gracias," the big Mexican managed.

"You're welcome," Clint replied. "We're what, six or eight hours from Rancho Del Robles Viejo?"

The Mexican held up three stubby fingers.

"Only three?"

He nodded his head.

"Bueno. You can be home with your señora and I can be at Rancho Agua Caliente by midday then."

Again Morengo nodded. This time, he rose and cleaned up the morning tins. Clint smiled, wishing he had gotten off to a better start with this man. The big Mexican would have been good company, could he have talked. *And as big as he is and as strong,* Clint thought, *I hope he is the forgiving sort. He won't be crowing like a rooster with his jaw hanging open if he decides to come after me again.*

But, hell, I'm going to be long gone before he heals, and he doesn't seem the type to ride two or three hundred miles to settle a grudge.

Clint went to saddle the horses.

* * *

After two hundred years of having been a Californio, the alcalde of Los Angeles—the old California equivalent of a combination mayor and head judge—was now a gringo, and had been since the revolution.

Don Juan Diego stood before the man, his own Mexican *abogado,* lawyer, at his side.

"He probably just rode off and maybe had a heart seizure or something . . . he was an old man," George Willington said, scratching his head.

"There were two sets of tracks. A goatherd said he was abducted against his will, and by a gringo. But that is neither here nor there. We did not come here looking for your help in finding my father, Señor Willington," Don Juan replied, trying his best to keep a civil tone. He disliked the new alcalde of Los Angeles, the man who was responsible for all management, including that of legal matters in the pueblo. The mayor was a large man, but gone to suet. His stomach bulged over his trousers, and his neck pushed out over his collar. A bulbous nose rose from his face like a pile of dirt clods, lined with blood veins. Watery eyes stared out over bags that were deep enough to hold one of the oak file cabinets in his messy office. Even his cuffs were too tight on his fat wrists.

"Then why did you come, Don Juan?" he asked, seemingly already bored with the whole matter.

"I understand Don Carlos was here to see you the day he was abducted, Señor Willington," Antonio Alverez, the lawyer, said with quiet dignity. A tall, hawk-nosed man, he had penetrating black eyes that seemed to bore into his fellowman as he spoke. "Since Don Carlos is missing, Don Juan and his sister only wish to be reassured that he had no problems here in Pueblo de Los Angeles that could have precipitated this abduction."

Don Juan had come to town to see his old friend and lawyer about the problems of the old man's absence, and what would happen under gringo law if he disappeared and was never found again. He discovered, however, that the lawyer had seen Don Carlos coming out of the alcalde's office the same day he had disappeared.

George Willington's watery eyes narrowed to the size of a pig's, and he would have arisen to confront this questioning of his integrity, but it required a little too much effort to do so. He did manage to lurch forward over his desk and shake a fat finger at the lawyer.

"Are you inferring this office might have had something to do with this abduction? Don't you doubt the honesty of this office, señor, or the next time you're in a courtroom with one of my judges, I'll make damn sure they find good reason to hold you in contempt. You'll spend a week in my jail."

Alverez stood even straighter—a ramrod of a man, with him straight meant just that. "I don't fear the *juzgado,* Alcalde. I only want what is right for my clients."

"Besides, you should know of Don Carlos's affairs."

"I did not represent Don Carlos."

"Did not? You've got the old man dead already. I thought you said he was just missin'?"

"And that is all," Don Juan said quickly. "Missing. Still, my sister and I are concerned."

"Was he represented by counsel when he came to see you?" Alverez asked.

"No! Don Carlos was here on his personal business. Now I have other things to do."

Don Juan knew he would throw the man through the window, if he stayed a moment longer. He spun on his heel, heading for the door, and his lawyer followed him out. By the time he reached the street, he had calmed down some.

"He is a pig," Don Juan said without emotion.

"And one I have to deal with weekly," Alverez said with a tone of disgust.

Don Juan, not carrying his own timepiece, reached over and pulled his lawyer's watch from his waistcoat pocket and checked the time, stretching it as far as the gold fob would reach. "Come on, Antonio, it is almost noon, not too soon to buy you a glass of *aguardiente*. We need to find out what Don Carlos did during his visit to Los Angeles, and why he was here."

"I normally drink only after six, old amigo, but I will make an exception today. It is so seldom you come to town." They moved away toward the Perico Callado, the nearest cantina. Antonio placed a hand on his old friend's shoulder as they walked. "I pray old Don Carlos is all right."

"I think we will hear something soon. Who would take an old man, unless it was for money? And the gringos think we have far more gold than we do. Either the muchachos will find him and be back with him, or we will get a demand of some kind."

Antonio laughed quietly. "Gold is the province of northern California, and beef is the coin of the south. Beef you have."

"But if this gringo who took the old man wants gold, what then?"

"Sell your beef?" Antonio questioned.

"There are no buyers for beef, Antonio, you know that. I would have to ship my beef north to San Francisco or Sacramento. The buyers who come here want to steal from us. I was going to send Emilio with a shipment in the fall. . . ."

"There are buyers for land," the attorney said quietly, knowing the Diego family had fought long and hard to hold on to their land. He also knew he might receive a fat fee if he brought the San Francisco buyers one or more prime southern California ranchos. Many people right in Los Angeles would love to own Rancho Del Robles Viejo, for it had water, and water would one day rule this growing basin. His dark eyes narrowed as he waited for Juan's response to his suggestion they sell their land.

"If the old man is not dead, then selling the land would *kill* him. It is out of the question."

"And if it comes to selling the land, or losing your father?"

Don Juan stopped in the middle of the rutted dirt street and studied his friend for a moment, then strode on toward the cantina without answering.

Finally as they reached the cantina door, he turned back. "The best thing is to find this gringo and kill him, and return Don Carlos to his rightful place at Rancho Del Robles Viejo; then the problem is resolved."

He pushed through the bat-wing doors, needing a drink. Maybe the problems would be solved if his sons found the gringo, but if they found old Don Carlos dead—which he did not doubt they might—maybe the problems would just be beginning.

He would have to deal with the gringo law, for to the best of his knowledge, his father had no will.

The Perico Callado, the Silent Parrot, crouched on Main Street just two short blocks from the public buildings. In the last five years, since the arrival of the gringo and statehood, the Pueblo de Los Angeles had changed with old adobes giving way to wood-frame and even a pair of granite buildings—but the Parrot was a holdout of more relaxed times. Unlike its newer neighbors, the Parrot's worn adobe walls had neither iron shutters nor fancy painted signs. Pedro Moreno slept behind its plank bar, shotgun at hand, when the final customer had left. And the old dons, the *hijo del país,* native sons, still gathered there to drink and gamble, and to argue whose horses were fastest.

The five not-so-square blocks of the former pueblo were now almost twenty, and the new blocks to the east and west lay square with New England preciseness, where free-form orchards and vineyards once had been. The pueblo now wrapped around the intruding Cahuenga Hills. *Zanjas,* irrigation ditches, had been rerouted to serve the remaining fields that separated the city and the Cahuenga Lomarias, or low Cahuenga Hills, to the north and west, from the Rio de Los Angeles to the east and south. South of the river the many vineyards, orchards, and bean and corn fields were only occasionally spotted with a tiny tile-roofed adobe, now housing mostly farmhand employees of the land owners who resided in the city.

In the old town were three imposing residences. The Bell palace extended a full block from Aliso to Commercial Street,

on the east side of Los Angeles street—still the finest house
in all southern California. Commodore Stockton had occupied
it for a time as military governor, as had General Fremont.
The old Pio Pico house was almost as imposing, as was Don
Abel Stearns's, which extended from Main Street all the way
back to Los Angeles Street.

Now nine cantinas peppered the town, but the Perico Callado was a favorite of the *gente de razón*, the gentlemen of
reason, or upper crust of the Californios, and the gringos.

A three-foot-high wooden carving of a parrot, always silent,
sat at the end of a plank bar in the cantina and surveyed
entering customers. Actually, it didn't sit, but was carved from
the upper three feet of an oak whose lower trunk now served
to support the end of the rough planks that served as bar and
wrapped around it, giving it the appearance of sitting on the
bar. Kegs of beer and one of *aguardiente*, the Californio form
of brandy, sat under the bar and the crude back bar, and whis-
keys, gins, and liquors lined its shelves.

The cantina's bar and its dozen tables sported an assortment
of Californios, gringos, and a handful of Chinese. Faro and
poker predominated, but another half-dozen games went on to
the shouts and groans of the participants. Smoke roiled up
from cigars and cigarettes and layered in haze under the low
ceiling, and sawdust covered the hard-packed dirt floor—the
number of plank floors in the pueblo could be counted on
one hand, but the packed dirt floors of the fine houses were
hidden with ornate Chinese carpets. A half-dozen dogs reclined about the cantina at the feet of their masters, judging
each other in silent contempt or a low growl while trying to
avoid being trampled on by the occasional staggering drunk.

Two mestizo girls, dressed in soft, full skirts and colorful
low-cut blouses stretched over ample bosoms, carried trays of
mugs to the tables, dodging the pats and grasps of already
drunken patrons.

In the very back corner, near the door that led out to the

privy, three Californios strummed a guitar and mandolin and bowed a violin, adding melody to the constant din.

The few white women in Los Angeles crossed the dusty and oftentimes muddy street rather than pass in front of the Parrot, new doors or not.

The largest of the tables, a round one that would hold eight players comfortably, resided in the front corner away from the bar, separated by the Parrot's carved bat-wing doors, and near the cantina's only window—also a recent addition. Only in the last year had Pedro Moreno given up the cowhides that had covered both the doorway and window in favor of improvements that would bring his establishment in closer continuity with the taste of his new neighbors.

In the front corner opposite the bar, where every nook and cranny of the cantina could be surveyed, rested the most grand of the chairs in the place, with carved arms and a high, straight back. Its red velvet upholstery seemed out of place in the rough surroundings, but then, so did its occupant.

Don Juan and his *abogado* knew the man in the large chair well, but he was not among their favorites. They did move away from the plank bar and closer to the table to watch the game, for one of the area's most respected *hijo del país* seemed deeply involved.

Across from the old don, Thomas Salathiel MacKendrick filled the large chair with a confident ease, and its red velvet appeared drab compared to his tailored black swallow-tail coat, purple brocaded waistcoat, and gray trousers. Every so often he ran a thick-fingered hand through a shock of salt-and-pepper hair, then popped and stretched his knuckles by entwining his thick fingers and bending them backward. His thick mane of hair sported one thin solid-gray stripe, almost the same color as his eyes, which sat deeply under thick black brows. His hair glowed with a sheen, but the eyes lay cold and flat. T.S., as he was known, was square headed and lantern-jawed enough to be a Dutchman, but claimed Scotch-Irish heritage. Occasionally he would pull a heavy gold chain, which freed a garish but finely carved gold watch, inset with large pearls and colored stones, from the waistcoat pocket. He liked to have the repeater out—the finest made Swiss watch—so he could push its stem and impress the table's players and spectators with three bars of the tune "Green Sleeves" and then the striking of the time, down to the minute, that the watch performed on cue. Perched on the chair's arm was the intricately carved gold handle of a heavy walking stick, which only T.S.'s most intimate friends knew concealed both a short rapier and a single-shot cap-and-ball pistol.

But most knew T.S. carried at least two other pocket guns, one a two-barreled .36 caliber, and the other a four-barreled .31-caliber pepperbox.

While intimate friends called him T.S., the Californios knew him as Don Tomas, or more commonly as El Boticario, the druggist. Each day, when El Boticario closed his apothecary shop, he retired two doors away to the Parrot to continue the most profitable of his many enterprises, playing poker and lending money to the losers—if, and only if, they had the proper collateral.

Fortunately, many of the old dons did: land, horses, and cattle.

And, equally important to El Boticario, few of them had cash money to repay loans carrying ten percent per day interest, a rate that would double the original face amount every ten days. Loans of $1,000 would require a repayment of $8,000 by the end of a month—El Boticario already owned five prime ranchos between the Tujungas and the old mission San Juan Capistrano in the south. And he owned them legally, endorsed and title transferred by legal action—foreclosure—in the newly established courts.

T.S. dealt the cards with surprising deftness for a man with large hands and thick fingers. The night was slow; only three players joined him, but one was Don Embustero de Guzman, whose Rancho Potrero had long been coveted by T.S. El Boticario played his cards very close to his brocaded vest.

"Sam, are you going to open, or wait till those cardboards change their spots?" T.S. impatiently asked the man to his left.

"Hold yer horses, MacKendrick," the man growled. A burly first mate off a coastal schooner docked in San Pedro, he continued to study his cards.

Don Embustero anxiously drummed his fingers on the table. He was into the game for over $100, and with uncommon ardor, wanted to win his money back.

"He's right, they won't change spots," the man to the don's right said. He was a drummer, or traveling salesman, whose leather sample case sat at his feet. No one had bothered to ask his name, since he hadn't offered it.

Sam Olglethorpe eyed the drummer over his cards and snarled, "If you got a stage to catch, neighbor, then go on an' catch it, or go peddle yer wares. . . . I'm gonna study these cards in my own good time."

The drummer looked a little sheepish, and had nothing else to say to the thick-necked sailor. Finally T.S. spoke again, "Open or fold?"

"Four bits," the first mate said, flipping the coins into the center of the table.

Don Juan Diego stepped closer, hoping to catch the eye of his old friend and discourage him from continuing this foolish gringo pastime, but Don Embustero was far too involved to look up.

Don Embustero studied his cards for only a second, then flipped a tiny $2 gold coin to join those of the sailor's. "And a dollar and a half more."

"Damn the flies, you boys are proud," the drummer said, and quickly folded his cards.

"You've got to pay to play, sir," T.S. said to the drummer, but eyed Sam and Embustero while he spoke; then he called, also adding a small $2 gold coin to the pile.

Sam's eye began to twitch and he pulled at his chin with a rawboned hand, but made no move to fold or add the $1.50 he owed the pot if he wanted to stay in the hand.

"It ain't gonna get any less expensive with time," T.S. said quietly, his mouth curled in a wry grin.

"Hell, this ol' Mexican is bluffin'," Sam said, then hesitantly shoved a $5 gold piece to the growing pile, "an three-fifty more." Then he grinned like he'd just been made captain of the brig he served aboard.

"I am not a Mexican, sir, I am a Californio, and I call," the old don said, nervously adding $3.50 to the pile.

The drummer sat with his arms folded, disgusted at his bad luck for the half hour he had been sitting in.

"Well, well," T.S. said, eyeing the others, then he fingered the pile of gold coins in front of him. "Yes, sir, Don Embustero de Guzman is from a fine old family here in California, and for your information, Mr. Olglethorpe, our proud citizens are Californios, not Mexicans . . . at least those who founded this fine land. T.S. flipped a solid $20 dollar gold piece into the pile. "A Mexican is and always has been a foreigner here in California. . . . Now let me see, I guess that's your three-fifty, and sixteen-fifty more."

"You called the last bet," Don Embustero complained.

"An' now I raised Mr. Olglethorpe's raise, Señor de Guzman." T.S. eyed Oglethorpe, then smiled at Don Embustero. "Put up your money, or fold your cards, boys."

Sam held his cards tightly together, tapping them nervously on the tabletop. He fanned them carefully in front of his eyes, studying them again as if they might have changed for the better since he had last looked at them. They hadn't.

"Damn the luck, and all confidence men," he muttered, and flung his cards into the center of the table with the money.

"I am short adequate funds," Don Embustero said, carefully studying his diminished pile.

"You're good for it," T.S. said, his smile sincere. "If you want to bet, bet. Your credit is good with me, Señor de Guzman."

For the first time Don Juan Diego spoke up. "Don Embustero, would you care to join us at the bar?"

"Don Juan." The older Californio glanced up. "Thank you,

Juan, but I am involved at the moment." Don Embustero reached into his *charro* pocket and pulled a short cigarillo out and lit it, then exhaled a billow of smoke. "I am in," Don Embustero said with a nod, acknowledging El Boticario's kind offer to extend him credit.

"Fine. Draw?"

"Three," Don Embustero said, and a satisfied look crossed T.S.'s face as he dealt the cards. Then he looked even more satisfied as he mumbled, "I'll take two."

Four

An obviously disappointed look crossed El Boticario's face as he studied his draw, then he looked up, and apprehensively challenged, "Another five dollars," flipping the coin to the table's center.

"I call," Don Embustero said quickly, not having a coin to offer.

T.S. fanned his cards on the tabletop. "Three kings . . . and a propitious draw . . . two little ducks," T.S. said and smiled tightly at the old don.

Don Embustero noticeably winced, then slowly smiled, but only with his mouth. His eyes were flat and dead. He stretched his arms and yawned in feigned relaxation. "Ah, the gods have smiled on you again." He relaxed back in his chair, then turned and snapped his fingers at the girl who leaned against the bar. She reached for a pitcher, then crossed the dirt floor and poured his mug of *aguardiente* full.

"I owe you twenty-one-fifty," the don said to T.S. He downed the drink in a series of gulps, then rose.

"Hell, Embustero. If you leave, the game is over. I don't want to play three handed. Sit awhile." T.S. pushed another $100 in five $20 gold pieces across the table. "This will hold you. . . . Your luck's bound to change. Now you owe me one hundred twenty-one dollars and fifty . . ."

Don Embustero studied the money for a long moment, then

slowly retook his seat. He clamped the cigarillo tightly in his teeth. "Deal," he said quietly.

"Yeah, deal," the drummer repeated.

T.S. nodded, then deftly shuffled and dealt the cards. He greeted two other well-dressed men who approached the table, "George, have a seat and join in?" He invited the mayor of Los Angeles to sit. The other man, he also knew well, and knew he would never play cards. Oscar Bonny was a close compatriot of T.S. MacKendrick's, being one of Los Angeles's two doctors. "El Medico," he teased his old friend, "grab a chair and try your luck."

"No, T.S., I'll leave the games of chance to you."

"Deal," Don Embustero chastised T.S. MacKendrick.

Anxious to lose that beautiful rancho, are you? T.S. thought, but merely smiled and began the deal.

At the bar, where he had returned to join Antonio, Don Juan downed his mug. "Let us go to Maria's Cantina. I cannot watch this old fool hand his life to that snake, El Boticario."

The two left, but the game continued.

Emilio and Enrique Diego, backed by their vaqueros, sat their stallions atop the vista of Condor Canyon.

At the edge of the drop-off, the digger pines quit, not attempting to gain a foothold on the rugged sandstone cliffs of the south canyon wall. Below, in the canyon bottom, a few river willows and a string of cottonwoods promised a creek or seep, but other than that, what they could see of the canyon bottom was desolate. On the far side of the narrow cut, the slope was slightly more gentle and covered with buck brush, and higher with digger pine.

"This gringo is a madman," Emilio said quietly, and his younger brother shook his head in agreement.

"Let's get down there and make him a *dead* madman."

"I don't like this . . . this trail is narrow and offers no cover. This man shot at Lazo."

"Or so he said. I still have no trust for that man from the north. He has the green eyes of a *gato.*"

"His eyes are not those of a cat, brother. I saw them as blue."

"Green, blue, I still don't trust him, Emilio."

"The tracks of grandfather's horse and the gringo's were up the canyon side, just as he said. You trust no one, Enrique."

"I trust this trail, so let's get down it."

Without glancing at his older brother, Enrique gigged the stallion, and the big animal leaped forward and began the descent dangerously fast.

The others fell in behind, trying to keep pace with the hot-blooded younger Diego.

The trail clung to the side of the precipice, then began a switchback down the crown of a steep ridge, so serpentine that the horse behind would be facing the opposite direction of the one in front, and the third the same. Switchback after switchback on the gravel-strewn, slippery sandstone, until they had descended half of the six hundred feet. The cliff was barren above and below for three hundred feet, when the deer-brush-covered slope on the far side of the deep canyon, a hundred yards away, exploded in gunfire.

A dozen guns barked at the seven riders, kicking up chunks of sandstone from the cliff side, and the more accurate shots slammed with deadly bone-shattering thuds into horseflesh and men.

The two riders at the rear of the seven managed to spin their animals and start back up, only to have their horses shot out from under them. Kicking free, they tried to cling to the slope, but it was just too steep. They began to slip, then career, spinning on the slick slope until they were airborne, hitting only every ten or a dozen feet. They landed in heaps at the bottom of the wall in a rampart of rubble—and if they were not dead already, musket balls slammed into each of them. One of the horses managed to crawl to his feet at the bottom of the slope, then fell to his knees and over on his side, still.

Enrique watched in disbelief as his brother's stallion reared.

Trying to get the big horse moving back up the trail, Emilio jerked its head around hard. The horse lost its footing, his eyes rimmed white, and neighing in shrill panic careened over backward.

Emilio cried to his younger brother, "Run, run, Enrique, tell the rancho . . ." As he and his horse tumbled away, the big stallion rolled on top of Emilio. The boy tried to kick free, and when he did, he managed to kick himself out away from the cliff side. He spiraled down and struck the hard sandstone fifty feet below, bounced, and continued in the air another fifty before he landed in a crumpled unmoving heap.

Tears blinded Enrique, but he knew he must live. He must tell his father, Don Juan, of this treachery. He must tell him of the whereabouts of Don Carlos.

Enrique's horse made the turn, and with powerful legs began the ascent. Another of the vaqueros pounded in front of him, and was blown out of the saddle by a musket ball. The riderless horse charged on, slipping and sliding, but making headway.

Enrique's piebald had always been a sure-footed animal, and he proved it now as never before, racing up the steep slope as if he were an antelope, carrying his rider crouching low in the saddle.

None of the other vaqueros reached the canyon's top; all were left behind as Enrique peaked the trail. He spun the horse back, the shooting had stopped a hundred yards behind him, and no one followed. The last of the shots' echoes were long gone when he dismounted and walked to the edge and stared back at the canyon side across from where his brother and their vaqueros had been slaughtered.

A dozen men, each carrying at least one long arm, began to appear out of the deer brush and made their way carefully down the far canyon side. They were five hundred yards from where Enrique stood. Still, he jerked his musket from its saddle scabbard, and shaking in anger, he fired at them, then pulled his *pistola* and fired its single shot.

He could make out the men hesitating; then they casually continued down the canyon side—as unconcerned about his presence as if he were a songbird on the cliff top.

His mouth tasting of bile, shaking with an anger and frustration he had never felt before, he gathered up another horse that had led him up the trail so he would have two mounts, and began a pounding lope home—back to Rancho Del Robles Viejo.

Back to tell his father, Don Juan, of their failure.

Back to tell his father that they had not been able to help his grandfather.

Back to tell his father about the death of his eldest son.

Enrique hunkered low in the saddle, dedicating himself to not stopping until he reached his father's hacienda.

But it was many miles before the tears stopped. And the anger nestled in his gut like a hot stone.

He knew it would burn there forever—at least until he returned and avenged his brother and his friends.

And he knew in his heart that the man, Lazo, had something to do with, maybe was at the heart of, this treachery.

The trail down San Fernando Pass out of the Tujungas had of late become a wagon road; the secondary route from Los Angeles north, it turned west at the Santa Clara River and followed it to Santa Paula and San Buenaventura, where it joined the coast road and met the sea, then north again, along the coast. Just north of the spot where it joined the Santa Clara River and turned west, only a trail continued north up and over the mountains, passing through Grapevine Canyon, dropping down to the San Joaquin Valley. North of the river, the road rose awhile, then dropped south out of the Tujungas into the San Fernando Valley, winding past the ruins of an old San Fernando mission, then two miles later joining the east-west valley road.

Don Juan Diego, heading east and returning to the rancho, reached the intersection of the more narrow Tujunga Road and the Valley Road and glanced up to see two riders and two pack animals approaching. He reined up and waited. Possibly these riders, coming down out of the Tujungas, had seen his sons and vaqueros and would have some word of them.

By the time the men were within one hundred yards, Don Juan realized the trailing rider was his vaquero Morengo. He spurred his horse and galloped to them, sliding to a stop in front of the little string.

"Morengo, what is the news . . ." He stopped and stared at his big vaquero, ignoring the other man, realizing his vaquero was beaten and bruised. "What has happened to you? Where are Emilio and Enrique?"

"He's not talking so good, señor. Broke his jaw," Clint said, without further explanation.

"And your name, señor?" Don Juan asked.

They exchanged handshakes, and Clint introduced himself by his Anglo name, John Clinton Ryan.

"Have you seen my sons and their vaqueros?" the don asked with concern.

"If Don Enrique and Don Emilio are your sons, I have. We met on the trail, just at the top of Grapevine Canyon, almost into the San Joaquin."

"And they did not have my father with them?"

"They told me of Don Carlos and the Anglo . . . but they had not caught up with them."

"So they went on?"

"They went on," Clint said. "I agreed to bring this man back with me. Emilio requested it."

"He did right. You will follow me to Rancho Del Robles Viejo and partake of our hospitality."

"I appreciate that," Clint said, trying to beg off, for he knew Californio hospitality could stretch into days, "but I'm going to an Andalusian sale at Rancho Agua Caliente. And I'm afraid I must press on."

"It is only a few miles from my hacienda. You can stay with us. I insist. The sale is not for two days, if at all."

"If at all?"

"There are some legal problems with the Vasquez property, and if they are settled, the sale will go ahead, if not. . . ."

Clint sighed deeply. It had been a long ride, and he had visions of adding some strong new bloodlines to his herd. "I'm sorry to hear that," he said. "I'd hoped. . . ." He dropped it.

"The Vasquez horses are a sorry lot," Don Juan offered without being asked.

"Sorry?" Clint asked, surprised, for he had been told they were a fine-blooded bunch. Then he smiled inwardly, knowing that every Californio don felt he owned the finest horse stock in the land.

"Chicken-chested, bandy-legged," Don Juan said, and laughed. "Nowhere near the quality of Rancho Del Robles Viejo stock. You have ridden far?"

The conversation continued for the better part of two hours until they reined up in front of Don Juan's hacienda, a sprawling tile-roofed adobe that could easily have housed a half-dozen families. A stand of sycamore shaded the grounds. Beyond stood an *establo,* barn, also adobe, that could shelter a hundred horses. Other whitewashed mud-bricked outbuildings separated the house from a garden—green with peppers, beans, squash, and other vegetables—almost two acres in size, and beyond, several acres of corrals. A hill climbed away to the south of the house and rose, covered with orange, fig, plum, and other fruit trees, as well as a vineyard that could have kept southern California in wine and brandy.

A *zanja,* irrigation ditch, encircled the hill and dumped into a rock-lined cistern, maybe fifty feet above the level of the house. Again below the house, Clint could see where the *zanja* took up again and served the garden, barns, and corrals beyond.

The rancho showed generations of hard work and pride.

Clint started to dismount as a stable boy ran up to take his reins. He pulled up short, though, as two of the most beautiful young women he had ever laid eyes on stepped from the front door.

In full lace gowns and mantillas, they crossed the two dozen steps to the hitching rail. Clint sat his horse and enjoyed the fluid movements of the women. Both centered emerald-green eyes on him, even as they spoke to Don Juan.

"Tio, you have brought us a stranger—" One of them had begun, flashing a smile, but then she noticed Morengo, and his black-and-blue face.

Both girls ignored the man they had called uncle, and his guest, and hurried to Morengo's side.

"You have been hurt, old friend. Get down and let us tend to you."

"What happened?" the other girl asked.

"Oken jaa . . . ," he attempted through narrowly opened lips, and both girls giggled. They looked sorry for their laughter when the huge Morengo appeared as if his feelings had been hurt.

Only then, after the second of the women had spoken, did Clint realize they were twins, although one stood slightly taller.

Morengo dismounted dutifully, and flanked by the girls, allowed them to lead him toward the door.

"This is Mr. Ryan," Don Juan said, seemingly a little miffed that all the girls' attention had been given to the injured Morengo.

Both of the girls gave Clint a glance. "Come inside, Señor Ryan," one of them said, flashing him a smile that would melt an iceberg, "and we will give you something cool to drink . . . but first"—she pouted her lip—"we must attend to this poor hurt man."

"Thank you," Clint mumbled. He dismounted, and the boy led his stock away. The girls brushed by him, one on either side of the big vaquero.

Both he and Don Juan bent and removed their spurs and hung them on a rack provided for that purpose near the huge carved front door.

"Conchita is the pretty one," Don Juan said, and Clint wondered which one he thought wasn't pretty. "Friends and family call her Chita. The other, slightly taller, is Consuela . . . and she is called Conce. They are the daughters of my sister and her husband." Clint noticed his eyes flashed darker and his voice dropped an octave when he said "husband." Clint sensed a problem. "Their last name is LaTour."

"French?" Clint inquired.

"Half French," Don Juan answered, almost spitting the words. "Luckily, they inherited their grace and fair hearts from their mother."

Then that explains the green eyes and very fair complexion, Clint thought, but said nothing. The subject was obviously a thorn in old Don Juan's side, though he appeared to love the girls and be very proud of them.

"My sister has done a fine job with them, Señor Ryan," he said, confirming Clint's belief. "A fine job."

"I can see that," Clint responded, trying not to sound as convinced, nor enthused, as he was.

"We will gather at six, Señor Ryan. Maybe the girls will play for us for a while before we dine. Supper is at nine." An Indian woman appeared as if out of nowhere. "Maria will show you to your rooms."

"Thank you," Clint said, then followed the old woman away down a wide hallway. *Rooms?* he wondered. *Hell, my whole house on Rancho Kaweah is only one room—albeit a large one. Here Don Juan is offering more than that to a guest, and a stranger at that.*

He wondered what the twins would offer a weary traveler.

Even the simple smiles had already warmed his heart. He had not laid eyes on a beautiful woman since his last trip to San Francisco.

Don Carlos Diego stood in a camp deep in Condor Canyon, rubbing his thin wrists. Rings of blue bruises testified to the roughness with which he had been tied for almost four days. But his wrists didn't pain him nearly so much as his heart. He had been left hog-tied in the camp while the dozen rough-looking gringos had hurried out to set up the ambush against his family and vaqueros. When they returned, they were laughing and bragging about their shooting, carrying extra weapons taken from their victims, and leading horses carrying the brand of Rancho Del Robles Viejo.

And the worst of it was, one of the horses was the prized mount of his eldest grandson, Emilio.

Emilio had been only twenty. That was much too young to have your life ended. And Carlos was sure his treasured grandson had ended his life in the rain of gunfire he heard, and on that terrible cliff side.

Where was Don Juan, his son? Where was Don Jacques, his son-in-law? How could they have let this happen?

Jory, his captor, had cut him loose from his bonds, and he had ignored his questions about what had happened, but Don Carlos had heard the shots—many, many shots. And the riffraff had returned with the tack and belongings of his vaqueros.

A seep pooled water at the base of a cliff, the beginning of a small trickle of a creek, and Don Carlos limped over to it and sat and washed himself, but his thoughts were with his grandson.

He wished *he* were dead, and his beautiful, strong grandson alive. But he had business he must take care of in Los Angeles, business that would not wait, business that loomed over him like a specter, that every day became more and more expensive, more dangerous to the very existence of his family—at least existence as they had known it.

He must get free of these gringos. Financially, he was in the grips of others—and that could only be resolved if he returned.

He glanced down the canyon and his stomach turned.

A dozen condors and a hundred turkey vultures circled in the late-afternoon sky, a sky speckled with scavengers.

"Mi Dios," Don Carlos said aloud. Then he turned to the band of men, who had gathered around a fire twenty paces away, and began to yell at them. "Are you not going to bury them? You

are the scum of the earth! You will let them be ravaged by scavengers? You are no better than the crows and skunks!"

Jory stood and glowered at Don Carlos. "Shut up, old man!" Then he turned back to the men who sat around, passing a jug of whiskey between them. "Belay that. Get some ropes and yer horses and drag those greasers on down the canyon."

"Bury them!" Don Carlos shouted. The bile rose in his throat at the thought of his proud vaqueros and grandson rotting in the sun.

"Drag them down the canyon and dump them. Horses too."

A burly, red-bearded man rose and faced Jory Mortenson. "To hell with what that old man wants!" he snarled.

"You want to smell them ol' boys when they begin to swell up an' pop?"

The man's expression turned to puzzlement, then the rationale of what Jory had said dawned on him. This camp would not be fit for anything but a buzzard in a day if they did not move the bodies far down the canyon. He turned to the others, his tone disgusted but convinced. "Get the horses and some lines. We gotta drag all them ol' boys on down the mountain, or change camps."

"Then let's change camps," another of the men, still perched on rock, said, grumbling. The red-bearded man stepped over and brought his clinched fist down on top the speaker's head, flattening his hat, knocking him from his rock to the ground. "I said get the horses."

The man struggled to his knees, bleary eyed, then managed to stand. He focused his eyes on the red-bearded assailant and mumbled as he reset his stained hat.

"No reason to do that, Striker."

"Do as yer told, McGillicutty," snapped the red-bearded Striker. All the others rose obediently and headed for their horses. "Not you, Howard." A gaunt man, whose neck, arms, and ankles protruded from his clothes like sticks, stopped and looked back apprehensively. "You stay and get some grub going. These boys will come back with a vacant spot in their guts."

Striker walked over to Jory Mortenson. "That suit you, Capt'n Mortenson?"

"Suits me fine, mate. Suits me fine."

Don Carlos watched the men with wonder. He had never seen such animals as these. What had become of his fine country? What would it come to, now that these gringos were everywhere? He shook his head sadly, then his chest heaved and the burning returned to his throat as he thought of his grandson.

Then his great cauldron of grief turned to simmering anger. Better he remain angry . . . he would work on remaining angry. For the last days it had been troubling him, where did he know this man Mortenson from? The man had refused to answer any of his questions on the matter, but Don Carlos knew that he did know the man, had known him in the past, *but when?*

And his family would come again, he knew they would, and more would die.

Everyone would be better off if he were dead, he decided, then crossed himself and asked God to forgive him for thinking about committing the ultimate sin—and the problems he had left behind in Pueblo de Los Angeles would go on, even if he were dead.

No, he must escape.

And he saw his answer, only a few steps away, a musket leaning against a rock.

If only he could get to it—before they got to him.

Don Juan, Don Jacques, and Doña Angelina, the twins, and Aleandro Dominguez gathered at the supper table at 10 P.M.

Clint had washed and combed, shaved, and brushed his rough clothes as best he could. In deference to his surroundings and the company, he had buttoned the collar of the linsey-woolsey shirt he wore and tied his bandanna in the best semblance of a four-in-hand tie he could muster.

Even then he felt a bit self-conscious. Even Aleandro Dominguez, the *segundo,* foreman, of Rancho Del Robles Viejo, had on a tie, although he wore it under a short *charro* jacket. He was a barrel of a man who stood a half head shorter than his boss, his thick neck strained at the collar of the buttoned shirt. The other men wore striped trousers, city coats, white shirts and ties, and both sported a brocaded waistcoat even in the heat.

The women were resplendent, and Clint could readily see where the twins got their looks as he gazed at Angelina and Jacques LaTour.

Clint took a seat at the end of the table, with Don Juan facing him. The chairs had been evenly spaced for the guests, and seven only half filled its length.

After listening to Don Juan and Aleandro talk business for the first half of the meal—Don Jacques was obviously not included in rancho conversation—and receiving the coquettish glances of both the twins, who bracketed him on either side of the table, Clint was surprised when Doña Angelina interrupted her brother.

"Juan, you are being rude. We have a guest and all you can talk of is rancho business."

The heavy, jowled don reached over and covered his sister's hand with his. "You are right, Angel, I have been rude." Then he turned his attention to Clint, and the hard manner in which he had been talking to his foreman softened. "So you are also a landowner?"

"I have taken a rancho far up the Ton Tache, on the banks of a river called Kaweah."

"This must be far, for I don't know of it."

"We have a small cattle herd—nothing like yours, of course—and swine and sheep, but the Andalusians are the reason for Rancho Kaweah's being."

"It is good. With all the new stock being introduced to California, it is good you continue the true strain. Why is it, if you don't mind my asking, that a gringo has chosen the Andalusian?"

"Never have I seen a horse so gallant—yet so docile—as that breed. No other breed of stallion will stand side by side without bowing their necks and laying back their ears. Only when there's a . . . pardon me, ladies . . . when there's a mare on the wind"—the girls giggled and covered their faces with turtle-shell fans, but Clint ignored them and continued—"do they bare their teeth at each other. I have ridden one for many years and have never been disappointed."

"My father," Angelina began, then her eyes saddened and she glanced at her brother. "My father breeds the finest Andalusians in all of California." But she almost choked with the words.

"He will be found soon," Don Juan reassured her. The topic of the old don had been conspicuously absent from the supper table.

As if summoned by Angelina's tears, Maria, the Indian servant woman, appeared in the outer doorway that led to the *cocina*. "Pardon," she said, her look almost fearful.

"What is it?" Don Juan replied.

"An old *paisano* is here, claiming he must see you."

"Bring him in," Don Juan instructed.

Before Clint could bring his mug to his lips for a sip of the rich red wine served with the supper, an old man shuffled into the room. He held his hat in his hand, with gray hair splaying out from the sides of a liver-spot-mottled face. Through a toothless mouth, he gummed, "He said you would give me a coin of gold if I brought you this message. . . . You are the *patrón?*"

The old man attempted a glower with watery eyes, as if he doubted what he had been told.

Don Juan snapped his fingers at the Indian woman, who walked to a cabinet, swung open its door, and fished into a blue-and-white china bowl sitting on a high shelf. She brought a coin to Don Juan, who extended it in a flat palm to the old *paisano*—but he snapped it back when the old man reached out with a feeble hand.

"What do you bring that is worth a gold coin?" Don Juan questioned.

"A message regarding Don Carlos."

Don Juan, Aleandro, and Angelina arose as if one. Don Juan took a step and shoved the coin into the man's palm. "Where is this message?"

From the inside of the crown of his hat, the old man fumbled with a paper. Don Juan snapped it out of his hands, unfolded and studied it.

Finally, with an exasperated and slightly embarrassed look, he lifted his eyes to Clint. "It must be in English. Do you read English?"

"I do, and I would be proud to be of service."

Clint rose and walked to Don Juan's end of the table. He could not help but notice Doña Angelina's hopeful look as he approached, nor the fact that her husband continued eating as if nothing of consequence was happening.

Clint studied the note for a short moment, then read aloud. "I have your old man, and his release will cost ten thousand dollars in gold. Coins only, point ninety-nine fine, at the generous value of sixteen dollars per ounce. You will receive another note in a fortnight telling you where to bring the money. If you follow or search for us, or if the law is contacted, many will die, including the old"—Clint hesitated before he continued, then decided he must read—"old greaser."

Don Juan collapsed back into his chair.

"How are we to come by ten thousand dollars in gold?" he mumbled.

"Sell the herd, sell a rancho," Don Jacques said without looking up. Finally he did so, dabbing at his mouth with a linen. Don Juan stared at him, the hate in his gaze apparent to Clint.

"At four dollars a head, we could only gather a thousand or so. . . ." Don Carlos shook his head, speaking through clinched teeth. "We could not begin to get so much."

"Then a rancho. I know a man—"

"Silencio!" Juan roared. "We will not sell land. Don Carlos would die before he saw the land sold."

"But, Juan—"

Angelina tried to speak, but was overwhelmed by Jacques's booming voice. "He will die if it is not sold! That much seems certain!"

Don Juan's eyes narrowed, and both his ham-size hands lay flat on the thick oak tabletop as if he was about to spring to his feet. "You seem to know too much about our missing father, Jacques."

"What do you insinuate?" Jacques leaped to his feet, followed in a heartbeat by Juan.

Clint, still near Don Juan, restrained himself from interfering, but the hate in these two men's eyes would soon lead to blows, or worse. As the tension grew, Clint stepped around them, then sidled in between. Both men were of equal height to him, and he looked from one to the other.

"I would be happy to go in search of Don Carlos. I know some of the country, and I have a hunch that if your sons were on his trail, I know where he might have been heading."

"Where were my nephews?" Angelina wrung her hands nervously staring at her husband. Then she turned her attention to her brother.

But before she could speak, Juan's voice rang out with derision. "Jacques knows nothing of Papa's kidnapping, *Hermana,* or anything else that happens on this rancho. Please take your seat and we will eat; then over brandy we will talk of Señor Ryan's helping.

"I will pay handsomely," Jacques offered, then cast a hard look at his brother-in-law.

"Humph," Juan said, but he sank back to his chair and retrieved his utensils and began eating. "Enrique and Emilio will bring him back," he mumbled.

"I hope so," Angelina said, equally low in tone, "I pray so."

Supper was finished with little additional comment. Only an occasional glance from the girls lightened Clint's heart.

Finally the women retired to a sitting room, and brandy was poured for the men.

"You said you wanted to buy horses?" Don Juan inquired after a sip of the strong brandy.

"I do, but this is a problem for your family, and I must repay your hospitality."

"The boys will find him," Don Juan assured no one in particular.

"Those sons of yours can find their way to the saloon, but little else," Jacques snapped, and Clint thought Juan was going to rise again, but Aleandro had taken a seat next to him, and placed a hand on his forearm. Don Juan seemed willing to accept his *segundo's* silent advice.

Jacques turned to Clint. "We would not ask you to help us without payment. I will pay five hundred dollars in gold, and"— he turned to his brother-in-law—"Don Juan will match it."

"Or in horses or cattle," Don Juan put in quickly, casting a puzzled look at Jacques.

"It is not necessary. I have to return that way—"

"It is done. The sale is scheduled for tomorrow, if you wish the poor stock of our neighbors. Then, if the boys have not returned with Don Carlos, you will ride. . . . But Aleandro here will ride with you."

"Bueno," the *segundo* spoke for the first time since he had concluded talking business with his *jefe.* "I should have been allowed to go with Emilio and Enrique."

Don Juan frowned at him, but said nothing.

"Then after the sale tomorrow?" Clint said and raised his crystal decanter to the others.

"But of course, Señor Ryan," Jacques put in before he lifted his glass. "You will return with Don Carlos, safe and well, or you will not be paid."

Clint was beginning to get a little irritated with the man's manner. He took a long breath before answering. "The money was your idea, Don Jacques. I will hunt for your *patrón* because he needs help. If I'm paid, so be it; if not, I'll lose no sleep."

Don Jacques and all the men drank to that, but now it was Jacques's turn to look puzzled.

The shorter and prettier of the twins, Chita, swished into the room and paused by Clint's chair. "You men must surely be finished with business by now."

"Finished, little Chitalito," her uncle, Juan, said, a warm look returning to his eyes.

"Good, then Señor Ryan can walk with me in the garden. I am bored with stitching and sewing, sewing and stitching."

Clint gazed up at the girl, a little surprised at her brazen approach, but pleased. She stepped back and eyed him. "A gentleman would give me his arm," she said, a mischievous look in her pretty green eyes. And she took Clint's arm as soon as he arose and directed him toward the garden.

As they passed through the portal leading to an inner court, Clint heard Doña Angelina's voice ring out from behind. "Do not get out of sight, *muchachos.*"

Neither answered. They began a walk that would circle the forty-foot square patio.

Finally Clint responded to Doña Angelina's admonition, and her calling them children, but he did so quietly to the girl. "Children? Are you a child, Señorita LaTour?"

The girl flashed her eyes up at him. "Call me Chita. Everyone does . . . at least everyone who knows me well, or wishes to."

"Chita, then," Clint said, agreeable to that pleasant choice.

"Do I look the child to you, Señor Ryan?"

"Clint, please, if I am privileged to call you Chita. No, you certainly do not look the child."

"Good, then tomorrow night, you may accompany me . . . Conce and I, because I have to take her, to the fiesta following the auction. You will be my escort, though."

"Is that so?" Clint responded with a quiet laugh.

"That is so."

"And if I cannot?" Clint asked, the amusement showing in his voice.

"Then you would be a foolish man." She reached over and took his hand as they walked, and squeezed it with the insinuation of promise. "A very foolish man."

"Then I guess I'm a foolish man," he said, stopping as far from the portico, where they had entered the patio, as they could. It was the darkest part of the poorly lit area.

She looked surprised, then pouted.

"I have to ride out tomorrow in search of your grandfather."

"You would do that!" she said, the light back in her eyes.

"I'm going to do that."

"That is wonderful, thank you," she said, but before he could reply, she was on her toes with a hand around the back of his neck, and her lips pressed to his.

Her taste was as sweet as the aroma of the honeysuckle that grew on the patio's walls.

"Chita!" a voice rang out from the portico. Clint stepped back and focused on the taller of the two twins, who strode across the patio. "Mama said I have to join you," she groused, then began to walk the same path they had been following. She stopped and looked back, seemingly exasperated. "Are we walking?"

"We're walking," Clint managed. "Walking and talking."

Chita laughed gaily and covered her mouth with a fan that she pulled and unfolded from its spot neatly tucked into her *rebozo*. The handy shawl was tied around her waist.

"Talking and walking," Chita muttered through her fan.

"And kissing. I saw you." Conce's voice rang with accusation, and some resentment.

"Jealous!" Chita snapped, dropping the fan to her side. Conce, who was a step or two ahead of them, spun on her heel and came face-to-face with her sister.

"Vixen," she said.

"Swine," her sister retorted.

Clint wanted no part of this growing confrontation. He would much rather be caught between their big French father and Californio uncle.

"Señoritas!" he said, his tone ringing with authority. He stepped between them and gave each an arm. "It's time to go inside."

But just as they reached the door, they again traded quiet barbs.

"Puerca," Chita whispered.

Clint winced at one sister calling the other a pig, a slatternly slut.

"Puerca gorda," Conce replied.

As much as he had enjoyed the short interlude outside, he was happy to be back under the influence of Señora LaTour. But as the girls returned to the sitting room, and he watched the pleasant sway of Chita's taut backside, he wondered how her sister could call her a fat pig.

She was anything but, but being called a pig by her sister demanded a response of some kind, he guessed. And his response had only been surprise. He had never heard a "decent" woman call another by such an insulting term, particularly a sister.

These girls were not such good friends as they had at first appeared.

But their animosity was nowhere near that of their father and uncle, Clint decided as he made his way to the front door, determined to find the sleeping quarters and share a little strong *aguardiente* with the vaqueros. And maybe watch a nice quiet knife fight . . . between men.

Half-breed French-Californio cats moved a little quickly for his taste.

Five

Don Carlos lay bound, hog-tied, and bleeding from a gash in his head. He'd not reached the rifle leaning against the rock before the gruff redheaded man called Striker had brought his long-barreled plains rifle across his pate.

He awoke, trussed tightly. But in the darkness of night and the deep canyon, Striker and Jory Mortenson did not know he was awake, and they sat near him, out of earshot of the others, talking quietly.

"Shootin' up all those greasers is likely to bring half of Los Angeles a'huntin' us, Capt'n," Striker said in a low tone.

"The deal I made was to keep the old man here for two months . . . and keep him I will," Jory Mortenson said, then spat a gob of tobacco onto the hard sandstone canyon floor.

"You think those *paisanos can* raise ten thousand in gold?"

"You'd better hope so, Striker. Your double share of a thousand will get you back to Boston in high style. Me, I'm starting to like this California."

"But can they do it?"

"Stop bellyaching, mate. They'll bring the money along, when and where I tell them. Five hundred apiece for all these soggers, and a thousand for you . . . and four thousand for the brains of this outfit . . . me." Jory Mortenson offered Striker a chaw off a twist of tobacco, studying the man's reaction. He had been surprised to receive no argument to his proposed division of the $10,000 ransom he had requested in the note he had given the old Mexican to take to the Diego rancho.

"I hope it's not a line with thirteen turns for all of us," Striker said, his tone ominous.

"What is it about the land that puts that yellow stripe down your back, mate?" Mortenson said, but his tone was light, and he guffawed quietly. "Ye'r a brave man, at sea."

"I wish I was back at sea."

"You will be, mate, as soon as those Mexe's pay up . . if that's what you want. But remember, when we pull this off yer locker will be stuffed full of shiny gold."

Striker nodded, then wandered away to join a group of men who sat around the fire, some playing cribbage, some quietly talking.

Jory Mortenson did not mention to Striker that he already had $500 in gold in his saddlebags, nor that he was promised another $500 if he kept the old man out of the San Fernando Valley and away from his family and Los Angeles for two months. That, and all of the ransom he could get from the Diegos, would be his, less of course the amount he paid this lice-eaten band that had gathered around him.

All men of the sea, they had been less than successful as miners and had drifted back to California's cities and towns after trying their hand at grubbing for gold. Now all of them, for one reason or another, were outside the law.

And Jory Mortenson knew he was among the worst of them. He had killed a man in Santa Barbara over a bottle of whiskey, and another who tried to stop him when he fled the cantina. Striker had cut a whore's throat in San Pedro, leaving her to bleed to death after she insisted on being paid in advance, wisely recognizing that Striker probably did not have the money, which he did not.

And Jory knew he was the toughest of the lot, having whipped the larger and stronger Striker long ago in Valliparisc in an argument over who owed for the next round of drinks. And to Striker's surprise, Jory had kept him on as first mate—

Jory figured it was better having a man working for you who knew that in every way you were his better.

The rest were a motley sort, all off the many brigs and ships that lay tied and waiting in California ports while their crews sought gold in the hills.

Jory and Striker had separated in California when the whole crew headed out of San Francisco to the diggings, only to tie up again in Los Angeles at the Parrot. After one more try in the local hills, the Tujungas, seeking the illusive gold, they had returned to the pueblo and decided on a life of relieving others of their hard-earned gold. They had used the Parrot as their base of operations, holding up stages and travelers on the road to Santa Monica, San Pedro, or San Bernardino.

But things had gotten a little hot for them, so Jory Mortenson decided to retire to a remote stronghold, a place impregnable to any who tried to find them and bring them to trial.

They had come upon Condor Canyon on that first gold-hunting trip together, a barren and inhospitable place with the exception of its clean cottonwood-lined creek, which only ran for two hundred yards before it disappeared into the canyon's bottom. It would take a battalion of dragoons to flush a dozen men out of that sparse, deep hole. From high in the mountains above the Indian village of San Emigdio, the canyon fell away to the floor of the Ton Tache as the Indians called California's great central valley, or the San Joaquin—named for Mother Mary's father—as the Californios called it. A branch led both east and west, in addition to the canyon's main entrance to the north, and if pushed out by an invading army, there were three means of escape. East to Grapevine Canyon, west to Santa Barbara with some of California's most rugged mountains in between, or north to the Ton Tache with hundreds of thousands of acres of tules and swamp in which to get lost.

It was a good base from which to raid Los Angeles and San Fernando, far enough away to be remote and unknown (even to most of the Mexicans), near enough to be reachable by a hard three-day ride or an easy four-day one. And game was plentiful and the water adequate.

They had learned on that first trip that even the Indians stayed out of Condor Canyon, so named by Striker because of the predominance of the huge birds. The Indians considered it a holy place, or haunted, the two gold seekers could not determine which when they had visited and made friends with the big village of Yocuts at San Emigdio village, where Condor Canyon opened onto the Ton Tache Valley. But the Indians did stay out of it, which suited Jory Mortenson just fine.

Striker had left Los Angeles ahead of an indictment, leading ten other ex-sailors and as many pack animals, while Jory Mortenson remained behind. He had told Striker he had other business to attend to before coming on, while his real reason was an unwillingness to be sighted riding with Striker and the others. The pueblo was not wise to Jory Mortenson yet, and he intended to keep it that way—at least not all the pueblo. He had been surprised when one of the area's leading citizens, and a major landowner, had approached him with the thousand-dollar offer to abduct old Don Carlos Diego.

Particularly considering who the man was—a man Jory would have never thought would resort to such an act.

That man knew of his alliance with Striker and what had been dubbed the Blue Stripe gang—for many of the sailors still wore the blue striped shirts of the *marinero*.

Striker had been surprised when Jory had shown up with Don Carlos in tow, but when convinced of the value of the old man and the coming ransom, he had fallen right in with the plan.

Jory Mortenson spat another gob of tobacco juice on the ground near where Don Carlos feigned being unconscious, then stretched and yawned.

He walked near where Striker sat with two of the sailors-turned-highwaymen. "Are the guards out?"

"Yes, Capt'n," Striker answered without looking up. "All

three stations are covered, and men are assigned the next watch. Everything is shipshape."

"Good. I'm turning in," he said, wandering away to his private tent. He admired the camp as he did so.

One large wall tent housed all the others, and the little creek separated his smaller, but adequate, tent from theirs. A wide-branched cottonwood sheltered his tent from the sun, and the creek babbled not a dozen steps from his front flap. Privies had been dug fifty feet up the hillside, and down the canyon were drying racks for making jerky from the many deer that were taken from the nearby hillsides.

All in all, it was a good camp, and he ran it like he ran his brig—shipshape, everything attended to and in its place.

Again he stretched, then turned and entered his tent.

Maybe, someday, he would build a real house here, and run a few cattle on farther down the canyon where the grass was better.

Truthfully, since he had been relieved of command by the ship's Boston owners after leaving his ship and following his crew to the gold fields, California had been good to him.

And soon, it would be even better.

Let Striker and the others go back to Boston and New York and Mystic. He would stay right here, and take up ranching in northern California, once he got a real stake.

Clint awoke in the spacious guest rooms of Rancho Del Robles Viejo with the sun just beginning to lighten the curtained windowsill. A rooster crowed his welcome to the warmth. Clint arose quickly and walked to a bureau where a bone-white pitcher and bowl awaited. He washed the sleep from his eyes, and with the provided turtle-shell comb, he slicked his hair back.

In moments, feeling somewhat remiss at not being in the *cocina* well before dawn, as was his practice, he gratefully accepted a cup of hot coffee from one of the two Indian women who worked there. Before he could wander back outside to watch the rancho begin to come to life, they had shoved two tortillas filled with chocolate in his hands.

He made his way out of the spacious kitchen building, with its walls lined with bins of beans, wheat, lentils, and vegetables, its walls hung with strings of red peppers and onions. One wall of adobe ovens emanated the luscious smells of baking bread, and its stove with pots steaming odors made Clint promise himself he would be back for the midday meal at eleven o'clock.

Shoving the cowhide door-covering aside, he had to stop short, then balance the coffee mug carefully to avoid spilling it, as Aleandro Dominguez, the *segundo* of the rancho, entered.

"Lazo, you have risen," the man said in a pleasant manner.

"Late, but I slept well . . . and I'm even better now that I have this *cafe negro* and tortillas."

"Good, then you will ride with me this morning. Then I will take you over to Rancho Agua Caliente after the midday meal?"

"That is well, Aleandro," Clint said with a smile.

"But first I must have another mug of coffee, and we must visit with Don Juan regarding the day's business for a few minutes."

"Good," Clint said again, then wandered outside while Aleandro sought another mug.

The sun was just beginning to line the mountains far to the east. The Tujungas to the north rose high, almost two miles above the valley floor, the most majestic of the mountains surrounding the basin called the San Fernando. At their foot the mission that gave the valley its name was falling into ruin. Rancho Del Robles Viejo sat at the valley's south rim, with the Cahuenga hills at the hacienda's back and the valley spread out before it. To the east a few miles, the Cahuengas died out and the Los Angeles River became the hill's eastern border, and there the little, but rapidly growing, pueblo of Los Angeles lay.

It was a beautiful spot, Clint decided for the tenth time since he had arrived. But then he got a twinge of homesickness, for it was not as beautiful as his own Rancho Kaweah on the banks of the river of the same name.

He hoped he would be heading back over the Tujungas for home in a very few days, and away from the troubles of civilization. He hoped that Don Emilio and Don Enrique would ride in safely with the *patrón* of Rancho Del Robles Viejo before this day was out. Clint couldn't help but feel a twinge of guilt at not riding on with them in search of the old man; then his feeling was somewhat assuaged as Morengo walked up beside him—the main reason he had not ridden on with the Diegos.

"Amigo," Clint said, nodding to the big, still swollen vaquero.

The man merely nodded, but there was no indication of anger or vindictiveness in his manner.

"Coffee's on," Clint suggested, and Morengo nodded again, passing Aleandro who was leaving the *cocina*.

"Come to the hacienda *grande* with me, Lazo," he called to Clint, who hurried over to join him. Just before they reached the large carved front doors, Aleandro stopped short, and staring into the rising sun, he shaded his eyes with a hand.

Clint, too, looked into the distance.

A mile away a rider approached at a dead gallop.

Aleandro shoved open the massive door and called out, "Don Juan!" He waited a moment, getting no answer. "A rider approaches. Don Juan!"

Well before the rider reached the adobe wall that separated the hacienda grounds from the rest of the rancho, Don Juan had joined them.

The rider came on in earnest, flinging aside the lead rope

of a second horse. He hunkered low in the saddle, whipping the horse from side to side.

"It is Enrique," Don Juan said, a worried look furrowing his brow. "Alone."

The horse pounded through the wide gates of the inner yard, and the young vaquero jerked his rein. To everyone's surprise, as the horse set his feet and slid to a stop, he tumbled forward out of the saddle and rolled on the hard-packed earth in front of them. Both Aleandro and Don Juan were immediately at his side. The horse staggered away, sweat caked and heaving, obviously spent. A stable boy ran to the animal's side and dropped the saddle away, leaving it where it fell as he quickly set to rubbing the quivering horse's legs. He had to jump aside as the horse fell to its forelimbs, then with a mighty effort, struggled and regained its feet. Staggering behind, the animal followed the boy, who led him to the *establo*.

"Señoras!" Don Juan shouted into the wide open doors of the hacienda. Then he returned his attention to his fallen son. The boy looked exhausted, but other than that, he showed no sign of injury.

Clint stood aside, not wanting to interfere in this family matter. Angelina and the twins joined Clint; then realizing who the man on the ground was, they hurried to his side.

"Let me be . . . I'm all right," Enrique managed, but his voice echoed hollow with exhaustion. Aleandro took one of his arms, and Don Juan the other, then dragged him to his feet. The boy's eyes were closed; when he opened them, they were wet with new tears.

"They are dead, all dead." He shook his head as he spoke in a low tone.

"What," Don Juan snapped.

"All dead!" Enrique repeated.

"Emilio . . . and the others?"

Enrique's hollow eyes went from one person to the next; then his gaze fell on Clint.

His face suddenly hardened as he shook Don Juan and Aleandro's grasp away.

Enrique stared at the man who had struck Morengo down, who had been on the trail of his grandfather, who had watched as they rode away to find villainous death in a deep canyon. This man was a gringo, like those who had shot down his brother and so many of his friends. Enrique's exhausted mind reeled in confusion, then all seemed to focus in anger.

"Madre de Dios," he said, and grasped for the pistol at his belt.

Clint gave a step forward, almost reaching the young cold-eyed vaquero, as the gun came up.

Don Juan shouted and also lunged forward, but too late.

The pistol bucked, blowing flame and smoke.

The ball slammed into Clint's side, knocking him off his feet. His head struck a hitching post, and all faded black.

While the others looked on in shocked silence, Conce hurried forward. Using Clint's hat, she slapped out the flames where Clint's shirt had caught fire from the muzzle blast. With surprising agility, she ripped a swatch of the shirt away and applied a compress to the gushing wound.

"This is bad," she said, casting a hard look at her cousin.

Don Enrique let the spent pistol fall from his grasp, then sank to his knees, utterly exhausted.

"Let us get them both inside; then maybe we can find out what this is all about. Get Morengo," Don Juan commanded as he and Aleandro lifted Enrique into their arms and hurried inside while all the women attended to Clint.

Don Juan and Aleandro returned after a few minutes to carry Clint inside.

"Will he live?" he asked Angelina, who bent over Clint as Conce worked on him.

"I don't know. He is bleeding badly, and the ball did not exit," she said, then looked up at her brother. "Maybe he is not what we thought."

"Let's get him inside . . . then to the bottom of this."

"We cannot treat this wound," Angelina said. "He will need the medico."

"Maybe it is better if he is not here at the hacienda," Don Juan thought aloud, then turned and yelled to his stable boy. "Raphel, get the buckboard and hitch up the team. Pronto!" Then he turned back to his sister. "This was an accident, Angelina—"

"Enrique was not himself, but this was no—"

"If what Enrique says is true, Emilio . . . my son . . . and the others are dead. All dead at the hands of the gringos. Do you want your remaining nephew to face a gringo court?"

"Of course not."

"Then this *was* an accident. Call a meeting of all those who witnessed this. We must speak as one, no matter what this *forastero,* this stranger, El Lazo, says. An *accidente.*"

"*Accidente,*" Angelina repeated, then hurried inside to call the others together.

El Boticario, the druggist, fumbled with the lock on the iron shutters of his drugstore, finally working the large brass lock on the pair that covered the entry door, then each of the two pairs that covered windows. He entered, his hands burdened with the three brass locks, and went straight to the stove. He rested the locks on a display of ladies' tonics—featuring Lydia E. Pinkham's Her Medicine for Female Complaints—and stoked up a small fire. It was far too warm to need a fire, except for the coffee that was the morning ritual for T.S., Oscar Bonny, and George Willington—druggist, doctor, and mayor. Three of the town's most stalwart citizens.

T.S. had barely gotten the pot boiling when his two friends entered.

They sat around a small, round table next to the stove, surrounded by jars and bins and baskets of packaged liquids and herbs and pills.

T.S. propped his booted foot up on a barrel that contained

the most revolting of the druggist's tricks—leeches, used by the medicos for bleeding their patients—and leaned back, two-legging his ladder-backed chairs. His friends followed suit, propping shined brogans on the same water- and leech-filled footrest. "You fellas will be getting an invite to the *bendición* of my new house. The redoin' of Hacienda MacKendrick should be finished by the end of the week."

Oscar Bonny held out his mug and inhaled deeply as T.S. poured. "That looks like gully wash."

T.S. paused in the pouring. "I can let'er boil awhile?"

"No. I'll have a sitting room fulla patients as it is. Pour."

George Willington also held his mug out, his belly bulging as he leaned forward to do so. "When's this housewarming? You've been working on that old hacienda for a month of Sundays."

"In two weeks, and at over ten thousand square feet of house, a month of Sundays is what it takes. Old man Menti-roso picked a fine spot for his home. Too bad he wasn't a better poker player."

All of the men chuckled quietly. Then Oscar Bonny turned serious, his heavy gray brows furrowing. "Who would have ever thought the old man would shoot himself over a little land and a house. . . ."

"The old fool," T.S. said, in quiet reflection. "But then, twenty thousand acres is hardly a little land." He shook his head and changed the subject. "George, if we keep on growing here in ol' Los Angeles, this town is gonna need a hell of a lot more water. An' what's the city council gonna do about it, Mr. Mayor?"

"Might be already solved . . . and by the mayor, T.S., not the council." He guffawed, and T.S. leaned over and tapped mugs with him in a toast.

"And just how did you do that, and how are *we* gonna make some money at it?"

"Just sit back and wait awhile. You and Oscar will get your pound of flesh out of this deal, if it happens. . . . And, of course, you'll give the old Mayor Magician his cut of the action."

"Of course, Mr. Mayor," T.S. agreed, again touching mugs with Mayor George Willington.

"The Diego place?" T.S. asked, his curiosity niggling at him.

"In good time, T.S.," George said, winking at Oscar. It wasn't often they had the upper hand on their friend T.S., and George would ride it for all it was worth. All of them knew that if a land deal was going to be made, then T.S. would get his pound of flesh, or more.

After all, these good old boys all propped their boots on the same leech barrel.

Before their second cups of coffee were finished, a local Californio youth stuck his head in the door.

"Señor Bonny, come quick. Don Juan Diego has brought in a wounded man . . . a gunshot."

"See you boys at the Parrot," Oscar said, striding for the door.

"Hurry, El Medico, he is very bad!"

Six

The boy did not lead Oscar Bonny to his two-story home-over-office, but rather next door to the rooming house that lay between it and the Parrot. Bonny glanced into the buckboard as he walked past, noticing its floor was stained with blood, and hurried inside the rooming house.

Mrs. Davylou Pearl Boxworth, a buxom woman dressed in a white high-collar blouse and long black skirt, stood in her parlor, wringing her hands and furrowing her brows. Clint, having regained consciousness, lay quietly on the dining-room table, his hand pressing a linen napkin to the wound in his side. His head rested on a wadded-up linen tablecloth. His eyes moved from Conchita LaTour to her uncle, Don Juan, to the doctor, who hurried to the table's edge.

"I don't know why you had to bring him here," Mrs. Boxworth said, approaching them from the adjoining parlor.

"He will need a place to rest," Juan Diego said, giving her a quick, hard glance. Behind her, a willowy Californio girl watched over her shoulder.

"Esperanza," Don Juan said, recognizing the girl, as Dr. Bonny tore away Clint's shirt.

"*Sí*," the girl answered, stepping around her employer.

"You will need hot water?" Don Juan asked the doctor.

"Yes, and send someone next door to fetch my bag."

"I'll get the water," Mrs. Boxworth offered, "and some lye soap to scrub my table . . . ," she groused in a low tone, then directed Esperanza to fetch the doctor's bag as she hurried into the kitchen. "Good thing breakfast was done," she said more to herself than any of those watching as Dr. Bonny studied the wound.

He glanced up at Don Juan. "What happened here?"

"Accident," Juan said, but did not meet Dr. Bonny's eyes.

Oscar Bonny glanced at Conchita, then down at Clint. "That right?"

Clint said nothing, but Conchita spoke quickly. "The pistol just went off. My cousin was exhausted, trying to remove his belt. . . ."

"And the pistol just cocked itself, aimed itself at this man, and went off?" the doctor added, studying the wound.

"Just went off," Conchita repeated, with more confidence this time.

"You've got an old wound here," Bonny said, inspecting the scabbed grove cut in Clint's side, just above the newer entrance wound, now puckered and seeping blood.

"Someone took a shot at me a few days ago," Clint said, seeming to select his words carefully, his face pale from the loss of blood, his voice low.

"Seems you attract lead like flies to a dung heap," Bonny said, glancing up at Clint, who didn't dignify the remark with an answer. "Have you been spitting up any blood?"

"No, sir."

"Looks like you may have a busted rib, and a ball I can probe for, but probably not find . . . and the trauma might kill you."

"More than one man totes a lead pill around. Guess I can do the same."

"Then rest and hope this doesn't go green, or didn't bust a bowel. I guess this is the best I can do. Time will tell, and with God's will . . ."

Esperanza arrived, slightly out of breath, with the doctor's bag in hand. Mrs. Bonny, who served as her husband's nurse, followed behind, wearing a simple gray dress, a white apron, and a dust cap over her graying hair.

Dr. Bonny removed a small stoppered bottle and dipped in a cotton-tipped stick. "This'll burn a little," he cautioned, then cleaned the wound as best he could while Clint clenched his teeth. Bonny dug another bottle out of the bag. "Raise his head," he instructed the slender girl who had fetched his bag, and Esperanza quickly lifted Clint slightly so the doctor could put the second larger bottle to his lips. "Take a good swig of this," he said, and Clint complied.

He gagged and shook his head as the doctor removed and closed up the bottle. "What was that?" Clint asked, his expression that of a man who'd just been skunk sprayed.

"Laudanum. Happy juice . . . opium based. It'll help you rest." Bonny bound the wound with a clean cloth, having to make a sash all the way around Clint's waist in order to do so, then turned to Mrs. Boxworth. "You do have a room?"

"This is no hospital," she said, again wringing her hands.

"Can you pay?" Bonny asked Clint, who nodded his head. "Do you have a room?" Bonny asked again.

"Number four is empty," Mrs. Boxworth conceded. "But we're not nursemaids around here. . . . This is a place of business."

"Did you bring my things in?" Clint asked Juan Diego.

"I'll see it's done this afternoon," Don Juan answered, unable to meet Clint's steady gaze.

"Tack and horses too, please," Clint said, wanting all of his things away from Rancho Del Robles Viejo.

"Everything," Don Juan said. "I'll deliver them to Hackman's Livery."

"And my bedroll here, please." Clint's pouch of gold was rolled in the bedroll, and from what he'd seen of Mrs. Boxworth, he'd need it at hand.

"As you wish."

"Give me a hand," Bonny instructed Don Juan. They carefully spun Clint around and helped him upright, sat him on the edge of the table, then entwined their arms to make a seat. With Esperanza reaching across the table and pushing from behind, and Conchita pulling Clint's legs, they got him into position. Clint's brow was deeply furrowed and beaded with sweat, but he made no sound. Esperanza and Mrs. Bonny followed close behind as they struggled up the Boxworth Boardinghouse's stairway, then deposited Clint in a small but spotlessly clean room.

Clint suddenly felt very tired, and the last thing he remembered was Don Juan, Conchita, and Mrs. Bonny hurriedly leaving the room as Dr. Bonny and the girl, whom they had called Esperanza, stripped away his clothes and tucked him into clean sheets. Then Conchita's voice rang out from the hall. "I am sorry, Clint Ryan . . . so sorry."

As she did so, he flushed slightly at the thought of the girl Esperanza undressing him, then even that faded as he heard Bonny's voice. "Call me when he wakes up . . . or if he breaks a fever sweat."

"Sí, señor," the girl said, and again Clint faded into blackness.

Striker had shaved his red beard, giving in to the heat. He stroked the red stubble on his narrow jaw, absentmindedly fingering the ragged scar across his cheek—the reason he usually wore a beard—and eyed Jory Mortenson. "You know the stage now runs up from Los Angeles and turns west at Soledad Pass to San Buenaventura?"

Jory said nothing, knowing what Striker was driving at. But Jory was satisfied with the gold he already had and the prospect of the gold he expected to get. The risk of robbing a stage was not on his agenda.

"It slows to a crawl at San Francisquito Creek, just after the road turns west. Wouldn't be nothing to stop it there."

"I'm staying right here, watchin' this old greaser, and waitin' for the time to tell his kin where to bring the money."

"The boys are restless, and so am I, Capt'n."

"Then go roust the damn stage, but don't expect me to go along, and don't take more'n four men. I want the others here in case those Diegos try and hit our camp again."

Normally, Jory would have chastised Striker soundly for even suggesting a course of action not initiated by himself . . . but the thought had occurred to him: If a few of these boys take a bullet or a load of buckshot, then that's just fewer he had to split with.

"Yeah, Striker, that's a good idea. We'd hate to have the Blue Stripe gang not heard of for a while. Hell, we probably haven't made the *Los Angeles Call* for a week or more."

"It'll take a hard day's ride to get there, so we'll hit it day after tomorrow, then be back the next—"

"Don't come straight back, fool," Jory chastised. "Take a roundabout route so they don't trail you back here. Hell, there's enough scum know we're here as it is."

"Then the next day."

"Good, see you in four days . . . and you know I'll still expect a cut of the take."

George Willington sat behind his broad desk in the alcalde's office, drumming his fat fingers rhythmically.

"You have told no one of the note?" the man who stood before George's desk asked, his manner slightly superior, his accented English almost perfect.

"I told you I wouldn't say nothing to nobody about the old man's note. You bought and paid good money for it, and it's nobody's business but yours and mine."

"Not even El Boticario's?" the man asked, his eyes narrowing.

"Not even his. Though he got his money."

"And no one has been here asking about the note?"

"Look here now. I told you that it was just your business and my business, and that's how it is. . . . 'Sides, why the hell are you so concerned? You got somethin' on your mind that I oughtta know about?" He got no answer, so he continued. "As I told you before, you oughtta be cuttin' me in on this deal. You couldn't of made it without me, and you said you didn't want no one to know." Willington kept fishing, not knowing what the deal was all about, but sensing a bigger profit than he had already made. "That oughtta be worth a piece of the deal; besides, I can help, being alcalde and all. . . ."

"What's going on across the street there?" the man asked, staring over Willington's shoulder.

The alcalde spun in his chair and stared out the tall, thin window. "What?"

"There," the man said, and rounded the desk to point with a long, thin finger.

"I don't see noth—"

The dagger drove to the hilt low in the alcalde's back, the pain so intense in his kidney he couldn't have cried out even if the man's hand had not been across his mouth. The blade was twisted and jerked free, then driven into his throat, then ripped outward, severing his voice box so a cry was impossible.

The alcalde managed to kick away from the window and slam against his desk, dropping to his knees.

The man stepped aside as Willington grasped at his throat, blood gushing between his fat fingers. One hand found the desktop, and slowly and with utmost effort he struggled to his feet, only to receive another blow from the knife. This time it ripped upward to just below his rib cage. The angled blade cut his aorta, and he stumbled backward, only to crash against and through the window, cartwheeling among flying shards of glass to the boardwalk four feet below.

The man calmly wiped the knife blade on the drapes, then moved toward the office door.

"Mr. Willington?" a male voice rang from the outer office. The alcalde's secretary had not been there when the man had entered. The intruder stood aside so he would be behind the inward opening door if the man pursued his inquiry.

With the blade held low, perfect for another numbing kidney shot, he waited.

"Mr. Willington?" the secretary's voice inquired again, this time from just outside the door.

Poised, the man waited in absolute silence as the door opened.

"My God," the secretary said, seeing the remaining razor-edged remnants of glass in the window opening, and hurried through to carefully check the cause. "Help!" he yelled half-heartedly when he saw his employer's prostrate form on the boardwalk below, blood pooling and dripping through the cracks in the boards, but already townspeople were running toward the scene.

The fat bastard tripped over his own feet, the secretary thought. Now what will I do for a job?

The man inside slipped quietly through the inner office door, then out the rear door of the courthouse, while the secretary stared in horror at his fallen boss.

The crowd who had gathered around the fallen alcalde was joined by the man who had murdered him. With the skill of a Shakespearean thespian, his face appeared as shocked as any of the others when George Willington was pronounced dead at the scene of the "accident" by Dr. Oscar Bonny.

Don Juan Diego deposited his niece at a friend's house, then returned to Main Street. There, he found a crowd gathered and the undertaker removing the body of the alcalde.

He had no love lost for George Willington, but still stared shocked at the man's bloody death. Willington had been among those Juan wanted to talk with while in town. But that was not to be.

When Juan had ridden out from the rancho with the man

known as El Lazo lying in the back of the buckboard, there had been some argument over who would accompany him. Chita insisted that she go along, as she had always been the one with the greatest gift for nursing, and she had ridden in the back trying to stem the bleeding of her charge. Her father, Jacques, suggested he come, too, but Juan—as usual wanting Jacques to have no involvement in rancho affairs—had insisted that Jacques not accompany them. So he was surprised to see the tall, imposing Frenchman among those watching Willington's body being loaded onto a dray for transportation to the undertaker's.

Juan said nothing to his brother-in-law, irritated that Jacques had followed them into town. Juan had other business, so he caught Jacques's haughty glance and left the crowd, heading for El Boticario's clapboard store.

Don Juan entered El Boticario's well-stocked emporium and remained near the front door, removing his hat and holding it in front of him. He waited while a gringo woman purchased a variety of woman's paints and scents. Finally she left.

The tall, broad-shouldered man turned to Don Juan Diego and smiled tightly. "What brings you here, Don Juan?"

"I need to have a talk with you . . . privately."

"Is this business?" Thomas MacKendrick, the druggist, asked, a rather self-satisfied look on his face. The Diegos had always treated him with some contempt, as if they were California's royalty and he was an interloper. So Don Juan's coming to him, hat in hand, gave him a feeling of great satisfaction.

"It is business, señor."

"Then let me close up and we will walk, if that suits you."

Juan nodded and stepped outside, happy to be away from the strange smells of the store, while the large druggist fetched his hat, coat, and walking stick and a padlock. He closed the iron shutters over the entry with a bang, locked them, then led the way across the street to the courtyard.

"What's on your mind, Don Juan?" he asked, falling into step with the shorter but more stout Californio.

It was obvious Don Juan was having a hard time with his request. Finally he stopped and faced the druggist.

"The Diego family needs a loan."

"Oh . . . ," MacKendrick said, folding his hands behind his back and shaking his head. "No buyers for cattle these days?"

"It's not that. It's an emergency."

"Everyone has heard of Don Carlos's being missing. Does this have anything to do with that?"

Carlos lied, for the note had told them not to get the authorities involved—or there would be dire consequences. "No. We just need a little money for a while, until we can round up and sell some cattle."

"How much?" El Boticario asked.

"Ten thousand dollars in gold."

Again the druggist began to walk, his hands still folded behind his back.

"That's a *great deal* of money, Juan."

"It is nothing, compared to what we have . . . the ranchos, the cattle," he said defensively.

"I don't keep that kind of money at hand." Now it was El Boticario's turn to lie. "But if I could get it, what would Don Carlos offer as collateral?"

"Don Carlos is not available," Juan said, irritated, knowing the druggist knew Don Carlos was missing.

"Then who would sign the note? Perhaps you should discuss this with the alcalde and see if the Diegos' property can be offered as collateral without Don Carlos signing—"

"I am his direct heir . . . besides, the alcalde is dead. You didn't know?"

"What!" Again the druggist stopped his stroll and turned to Juan.

"He fell from his office window, not a half hour ago."

"A waist-high fall wouldn't kill him," MacKendrick said, an astonished look on his face.

"He fell through those fancy glass windows he insisted on having installed . . . he was badly cut."

MacKendrick reversed direction and headed toward Dr. Bonny's office. Now his pace was hurried. "Look, Juan, your Rancho Del Robles Viejo has already been borrowed against, so that leaves only the other three ranchos—"

"What do you mean?"

"I mean your father borrowed from me and offered Rancho Del Robles Viejo as collateral—"

"He would not!"

"But he did."

"How much," Don Juan asked, his tone suddenly indignant.

"Only two thousand dollars," the druggist said offhandedly, still striding toward Oscar Bonny's office.

"Then if we borrowed more, we could pay you off and still have money remaining."

"That would be fine, but I no longer hold the note. Besides, it's bad business to lend someone money only so they can repay what they already owe you," he said, and the thought continued: *That's like feeding cracked corn to the hog that's already fit to butcher.*

Don Juan grabbed the taller man by the shoulder and spun him to face him, forcing him to stop.

"Then who does?" Juan demand. Noting the druggist's confusion, he continued adamantly, "Who holds the note?"

"I don't know. The alcalde handled the transaction. I handed the note to him as a holder in due course; he handed me the money I was owed. I was sure your father could repay the note, so I took a fast profit. A good one, I might add."

"Then to whom do we pay the two thousand?" Juan snarled, beginning to become truly irritated and frustrated.

"It's no longer two thousand, Juan," MacKendrick said, trying to hold his temper. He wanted to get to Oscar's to see just what had happened to their friend.

"Then . . . what . . . is . . . it?" Juan asked, beginning to tremble, his face reddening.

"The note bears interest at ten percent per day. . . . It's a hell of a lot more than two thousand already," MacKendrick said, resuming his stride toward the doctor's, now just across the dirt road called Main Street by the gringos. "Had I thought you folks would let it go this long, I'd have hung on to it."

"I want that note!" Juan shouted, again spinning MacKendrick to face him.

This time, the druggist lost his temper and shoved Don Juan back roughly. He shook the walking stick at him and cautioned, "Keep your bloody hands to yourself."

Don Juan stared, his jaw clamped tightly and his jowls quivering. His hand rested on the small Allen's pepperbox shoved into the sash around his waist.

"You pull that and I'll shove it down your throat," MacKendrick growled in a low tone. But he really didn't mean that. What he would have said, had he wanted it commonly known, was that he would cock and fire the concealed pistol built into the handle of his walking stick, and if that one shot was not enough, he would reach for either of the two concealed guns he carried.

"I want that note," Juan said, his tone equally quiet, and equally determined, and his hand still resting on the butt of the little gun. El Boticario stood back, his walking stick pointed at Don Juan's chest as if to fend him off.

"And I don't have it. You'll have to ask George Willington who the new owner is . . . and he's dead, or so you say."

MacKendrick shook his head, disgusted, and spun on his heel, giving Don Juan his back. With disdain to a man who rested his hand on the butt of a pistol, the druggist strode across the street to Oscar Bonny's office-residence. "And you even think about pulling a gun on me," MacKendrick said over his shoulder, "and you'll see him in hell, so you *can* ask him."

Don Juan stood, his thick jowls shaking in anger as the druggist strode away.

But he did not know what to do.

His father had already borrowed against the main rancho,

and even if he could borrow to repay that note, there seemed to be a legal question—a gringo law question—about his ability to borrow on the family's property with Don Carlos missing. He had no idea who now owned the first note; he had no idea why Don Carlos would borrow money, particularly without saying anything to his family about it. His father seldom gambled, with the exception of an occasional horse race. Don Juan was sure he had not lost money in a card game to El Boticario, or he would have heard about it, if not from Don Carlos, then from bystanders.

He thought about following the druggist to Oscar Bonny's place, then decided he must have help. He spun on his heel, confused and frustrated, and hurried toward Ann Street, where Antonio Alverez maintained his office. He needed his *abogado,* his own lawyer—a Californio lawyer.

He had to find this note his father had signed.

He had to get someone to find Don Carlos.

He had to find his son's body, and get him and the Rancho Del Robles Viejo vaqueros buried properly, with the priest at hand.

Everything around him was falling apart.

He glanced up to see Jacques LaTour standing in the doorway of the Parrot, a strangely smug look on his face, but Juan did not cross the street. He had other business.

Thomas MacKendrick arrived at Oscar Bonny's front door, only to meet Mrs. Bonny on her way out.

"Where's Oscar?" he asked without polite preliminary.

"He's at Jorgenson's," she replied, equally perfunctory.

MacKendrick spun on his heel and headed for the undertaker's office, two blocks away on Magdalena.

He arrived at the same time as Sheriff Sam Stoddard.

The tall, gaunt-faced, ruddy-complected sheriff touched his hat brim and with deference allowed the druggist to enter in front of him.

"A terrible accident," MacKendrick said, shaking his head.

"Nope, a murder . . . Oscar sent for me. He's inside."

MacKendrick stopped short, staring at the sheriff.

Stoddard shook his head. "I was on my way to Boxworth's Boardinghouse . . . regarding a shooting . . . when a boy who Oscar sent told me the alcalde's been murdered. What a day."

MacKendrick took a deep breath. "Let's see what happened."

Clint had no idea how long he had slept, but he awoke with a dull ache in his side, his throat dry as ashes, and a beautiful woman busying herself at the foot of his bed.

"Water," he said, but his voice came in a whisper. Then he remembered the girl's name as his voice strengthened. *"Por favor,* Esperanza."

She flashed him a smile. "We have the juice of oranges," she offered.

"Water first," he rasped, and she quickly moved to a bone-white pitcher and poured some into a glass. She came to him, placing a cool hand at the back of his neck, and helped him up to drink.

Clint winced in pain.

"I know it must hurt terribly, but you have no fever, and that is a good sign," she said as he sipped the water.

"Are my things here?" Clint asked.

Esperanza gently lowered him back to the pillow, then bent to reach under the bed. She hefted his bedroll so he could see it. "Your guns are there also. Would you like me to hang these and beat them out? This smells of dirt and many days on the trail."

A little embarrassed, Clint found a small smile. "It has been strapped to the back of a hardworking horse for many days. A good beating would not hurt it. But first, there is a pouch rolled up inside. Could you get it for me?"

"And then I will bring you a little soup. You have slept for more than a day. You must be hungry."

She loosened the leather thongs binding the bedroll, one

end of which was stuffed into a nose bag, and fished out the rawhide pouch and handed it to Clint.

"Ask the lady . . ." Clint trailed off, not remembering the proprietress's name.

"Mrs. Boxworth?" Esperanza offered.

"Yes. Mrs. Boxworth. Ask her to come see me."

"When I bring back the soup."

In a few moments she returned with a tray, and with Mrs. Davylou Pearl Boxworth in tow.

The ramrod, straight woman eyed him without compassion. "Are you well enough to leave?" she asked with a cold tone.

"No, he's not," Esperanza quickly said before he could answer.

"You have a pile of pots and pans to attend to!" Mrs. Boxworth snapped at the girl.

"I should help him with the soup."

"Pots and pans. I'll see he takes his soup," the landlady said with finality, and Esperanza left the room with a swirl of skirts.

"These Mexicans . . . ," she said, shaking her head in disgust, then picked up the tray from the bureau to position it on his lap.

"To answer your question, I'm not ready to leave, Mrs. Boxworth, and won't be for a few days. How much do you charge per day for the room?"

She stood with tray in hand, studying him. "With the extra service since you'll be needing it, seventy-five cents. If you have a horse . . . say a dollar a day, plus laundry, of course."

Clint pulled the pouch out from under his sheet, opened it, and shook out flakes of gold onto his palm. "You'll need something to put this in."

With deftness belying her ramrod demeanor, she snatched a small china knickknack bowl from the bureau and held it out to him.

"This is twenty or so dollars in gold. And there's more where this came from." For the first time since he had seen her from flat on his back on her dining-room table, she smiled. Clint was surprised at what a handsome woman, if a middle-aged one, lurked beneath the sour expression she normally wore. "My horse and tack are supposed to be at Hackman's Livery. Can you send your husband for them?"

"There is no husband, Mr. Ryan, but there's a boy who works for me. I'll send him. Now sit up and let me give you some soup."

With a great deal of effort, Clint worked himself into a sitting position, but the sheet fell away and his chest was bared for a moment. To his surprise, she had no qualms in viewing it. She even sat and reached over and helped him reposition the sheet. Teasingly Mrs. Boxworth ran her fingers through the mass of sandy hair, combing it with her fingers for only an instant.

"You men are hairy creatures," she said.

Clint had no comment, but he felt the heat flood his loins. He must not have been hurt as badly as he supposed—he laughed silently to himself.

She sat on the edge of the bed, with the bowl in one hand and spoon in the other. She carefully offered him a spoonful of the broth. "This is a little hot."

"I can do that, Mrs. Boxworth."

"Davylou, if you don't mind."

"Davylou, then . . . I'm Clint . . . Clint Ryan."

"Eat your soup, Clint; then when you finish, we'll see about changing that bandage."

"You'll need Esperanza's help."

Her eyes flickered with humor. "Esperanza seemed to enjoy undressing you just a little too much, Clint. I'll change it myself. She's too young to be exposed to such things."

"And you're not? You look barely older than the girl."

"Thank you for the compliment . . . if that is what it was meant to be."

"It was sincere," Clint said, eyeing this woman who had

changed so completely when she realized he was not a penniless saddle tramp.

"Then thank you. But no, I'm not too young to see a man a'natural . . . I've nursed many. . . . Nor, for your information, Mr. Ryan, am I too old to enjoy it. There was a Mr. Boxworth, and before him, two other husbands."

Clint smiled. "Worked themselves to death, I presume."

"You could say that, Clint. It has never been an easy life for me."

Again she offered him a spoonful of soup. As he savored it, she reached up and unfastened the top two buttons on the stiff white blouse she wore, then smiled at him.

"It's getting warm already."

"Yes, it is," he managed after he had swallowed.

"You eat, and get your strength back, Clint Ryan."

"Yes, ma'am," he said, and she leaned forward to spoon another his way, brushing his forearm with the feather touch of a weighty breast as she did so. That and the scent of lilac made the heat flow again.

She seemed not to notice, and he made no comment, even though it had sent a blast of tingling fire up his arm.

Only two days in Los Angeles and he was surrounded by lovely girls and equally beautiful women.

Maybe the city wasn't so bad, after all.

Then his side cramped and spasmed, and he closed his eyes and furrowed his brows, which broke out in a sudden cold sweat.

"Damn," he muttered.

"No," she offered with a brilliant smile, "you won't be ready to go for a good while." Before she left the room, she turned to him and her look grew serious. "You tell the law what happened out there at Rancho Del Robles Viejo. Those Mexicans have been getting away with things too long around this country. Think they still own it. It's time those Diegos were taken down a notch."

Clint managed a nod, then closed his eyes.

* * *

As Don Juan Diego plodded slowly home, he pondered his situation. Soon, he knew, the sheriff would come calling. If the gringo filed charges, what then?

What had possessed Enrique to shoot Clint Ryan?

Did Enrique know something beyond what Morengo had told him regarding their meeting Ryan on the trail? Maybe Ryan was involved with Don Carlos's abduction?

And why had Don Carlos been abducted? Was it really for the money? Surely, the gringos thought all the dons had much more money than they really had. Selling beef had been good to them since the gold rush began, but none of them saved any money. Old debts had been paid. Improvements had been made to the ranchos. Wardrobes had been improved, and the women had all wanted the new fashions worn by the few *gringas* in Los Angeles. The church had been a factor, too, and money had been donated to bring the priests to a new cathedral in the city, now that the missions were in ruin. Children who had gone wanting for an education had been sent to Europe, to Mexico, or to the Sandwich Islands to be educated—partly because of academics, but partly to get them away from the rash of violent men who now roamed California.

And there was always the gambling. The dons had always gambled, particularly on their horses. More than one rancho had been lost over a horse race. And now, with newfound money, they gambled even more.

And the gringos had brought a rash of new taxes. The ranchos had been heavily taxed by the new divisions of the state called counties. And the counties had used the money for improvements, but mostly in the cities. The roads were still bad, and neither San Pedro nor Santa Monica had decent port facilities.

No, the old dons had little money, no matter what the gringos thought.

Antonio Alverez, his lawyer, had suggested Juan sell cattle

or even one of the ranchos. Antonio, who had been his friend since childhood. Antonio, who had brought himself up by his own initiative, and who had studied hard to become a qualified *abogado,* then studied hard again under a gringo lawyer. But he knew little of the land. He had been a peon when he started out and had been befriended by Juan, but never by Don Carlos. The old man never trusted the peon who became an *abogado*—and would never use him for family business, no matter how good a friend he was of Juan's. Don Carlos always referred to Antonio as that *mestizo* who became a gentleman, who claimed to be a *hijo del país*—then laughed as if he knew that it could not be, could never be.

No, selling a rancho was not in the stars for a Diego. Land was all they had—the basis of everything—and they would keep it, and Antonio would never understand that, for he had never been a landowner.

But he had been Juan's good friend, no matter what Don Carlos thought. And even though considerably older, he had always had an eye for Conchita. He had even come to Juan to discuss the matter, but Juan knew that Don Carlos would never hear of his granddaughter becoming betrothed to a common mestizo, a man of mixed blood, a man of Indian extraction, even if it had only been his maternal grandmother. Even if that man was now a respected *abogado*—in fact, one of the most respected lawyers in all of southern California—Juan was forced to tell his friend to bury his passions, for he would never be accepted into the Diego family. Never would Don Carlos hear of anyone other than a man of pure Spanish blood marrying one of his precious granddaughters—even though they were half French. He had never really accepted Jacques, though his son-in-law was of pure French blood and claimed to be the second son of a marquis—but his only daughter, Angelina, had always gotten her way with Don Carlos. Besides, Juan thought that the old don had feared she had already been compromised by the handsome French scoundrel.

Still, Carlos did not accept the Frenchman, and never would, though he did love his granddaughters. Juan, likewise, not only did *not* accept him, but had grown to hate the man his vaqueros called El Coyote behind his back, for Jacques did have many of the characteristics of that sly beast, always conniving and working to get his own way. And too often he did.

Maybe, just maybe, it was Don Jacques behind all of this. The thought made Don Juan's blood boil. He would tack Jacques's hide to the *establo* wall, if he even truly suspected such a thing. Nothing was worse than a man who feigned friendship to do evil. Nothing.

He would be home soon, he knew, and perhaps Enrique would be rested enough so he could tell him why he had shot the gringo.

Almost without thinking, Don Juan reined in the big gray Andalusian stallion he rode as he heard the stagecoach approaching from the rear. It passed, its six-horse team at a brisk canter, the coach swaying on the rough road. It was the stage from Los Angeles to San Buenaventura, then on to Santa Barbara. It was a new thing, this stagecoach, Juan thought as the stage rocked and rumbled by, sending up a plume of dust behind. And a fine stage it was, an Abbott, Downing & Co. Concord.

Only the very best for the gringos.

But he, and the Diego family, had the best land, the best water, and with a resolve that steeled his backbone, he swore no one would ever wrest it away.

And even now, every day was more expensive, for there was a note of $2,000 at ten percent interest, *per day.*

Tomorrow, after he set his vaqueros into motion, he would return to Los Angeles and find out what he could do about the note.

Seven

Don Carlos had sworn by all the saints who protected him that he would not again try to escape.

Taking him partly at his word, Jory Mortenson had had the old man bound by a single ankle with a ten-foot leather thong, which allowed him to reach the creek and far enough up the hill so he could relieve himself without messing his own nest. Jory had personally pulled the knot in the leather thong tight, straining his powerful arms and broad shoulders to do so. Then he wet the knot so that when it dried it would be impossible to untie.

As the old man began to heal from his wounds—gouges in both ankles and wrists from being bound, a cut on the head from Striker's rifle, and abrasions and bruises from being beaten—he resolved more adamantly to escape, or at least escape from this torture. And worse, they kept him on short rations of only half a plate of frijoles a day.

The saints would forgive him, under the circumstances.

He sat by the stream, boots removed, washing his old bony feet and studying the camp, always studying the camp.

He had watched the four riders leave the day before and hoped they would be gone for a while. With them out of camp, and three guards on duty in the canyons beyond, only five men remained in camp. The fewer the better, if he was to escape. Even limping badly from the old break, and exhausted and bruised as he was, he decided he could get far enough into one of the side canyons to hide himself, and maybe, just maybe, escape.

To aid his effort, he had watched the cook Howard rebuild his fire, since he had let the coals go dead on the old one. And the fool rebuilt it within reach of the leather leash that bound Carlos. Rebuilt it using a piece of sharp flint and steel to strike sparks, and had left the sharp-edged flint within reach. Even if it was moved away, the fire itself would sever the thong, and he could slip away into the night. Howard was a methodical man, Don Carlos noted, or maybe just a little slow of mind. He had a hulking way, with thin neck and heavy hooded dark brows. Don Carlos hoped his plodding manner reflected a slow, not methodical, mind. For a methodical man would remember the flint.

Don Carlos was careful not to move to the side of the tree where the fire was. He wanted no one to notice that it was within his reach. And he was careful to appear almost like an invalid. He wanted them to think he could not escape, even if set free.

Jory Mortenson had left him. Left him to watch the continual circling of the condors, vultures, and crows far down the canyon. Left him to imagine the tearing and ripping of the flesh of his vaqueros and his grandson by the huge birds.

If only he could set himself free.

Maybe, just maybe, he could make a quiet stop in the dark tent of Jory Mortenson before he slipped away into the night.

He stretched his tired and bruised bones and winced at the pain, but casually eyed the flint that was still within his reach, and the cook busily beginning the evening meal.

He lay back and closed his eyes, ignored his aching bones and the circling predators far down the canyon, and dreamed of slitting Jory Mortenson's throat.

Immediately upon his return to the rancho, Juan sent riders out to the outlying Diego ranchos to bring in his other *segundos* and their vaqueros. Soon, over thirty men would arrive.

This time the Diegos would ride in overwhelming force.

If El Boticario would not lend him the necessary money to ransom Don Carlos, the most swift and sure alternative was to try to save Don Carlos.

And Enrique knew where they had taken him.

But before Juan had left Los Angeles, he had played another card. He had empowered Antonio Alverez to employ ten vaqueros to begin rounding up the cattle on the home ranch, Rancho Del Robles Viejo, and to sell them for the best possible price. He hoped to raise at least $5,000 in the next week in that way.

Antonio had suggested again that he be allowed to obtain offers on the rancho itself, but Juan had adamantly refused. Antonio had insisted Juan sign a power of attorney, empowering the *abogado* to sell the cattle, and he had done so.

Abogados were all alike—paper, always paper.

Enrique did not join them at the dinner table, and Juan, Angelina, and the girls ate in silence. As soon as they were finished, Juan poured himself a goblet of *aguardiente* and went to Enrique's room.

He knocked and received no reply. He entered quietly and found Enrique sleeping soundly, with deep even breathing. Dishes, from where the servants had brought him dinner, were cradled in a thrown-back down comforter at the foot of his bed.

Juan shook him gently.

He awoke and sat up.

"We need to talk." Juan addressed his son with quiet authority.

"In the morning, while I lead us back to that terrible place." Enrique seemed purposefully evasive, wanting to avoid any conversation—confrontation—with his father.

"No, now."

Enrique rubbed his eyes and shook his head to clear it.

Juan continued. "What possessed you to shoot the gringo?"

"I know he was part of it—"

"How do you know, Enrique?"

"He was there, so near—"

"He was on his way here. On his way to buy horses."

"He broke Morengo's jaw—"

"Clint Ryan did that? Morengo said nothing."

"When we came upon him in his camp, we restrained him so he could not reach his weapons."

"So when accosted in his camp, he defended himself?"

Enrique began to look sheepish.

"So again, why did you shoot him?"

"I . . . I was exhausted from riding for two days straight. He was a gringo, and it was gringos who killed Emilio and our vaqueros, and tried to kill me. I . . . I was seeing demons by the time I got home, *Padre*."

"So you drew your weapon and fired at a man who was under the protection of our home?"

"All I saw was evil. Gringo evil, and Emilio dying as he tumbled into that terrible canyon. Evil, *Padre*, all of them."

Juan sighed deeply. "Maybe he was part of it. Maybe you are right. But a gringo court is another matter. . . ."Juan arose from sitting on the bed. "Sleep well, Enrique, for tomorrow you and the vaqueros return to find your grandfather, and end this."

"I-I'm sorry, *mi padre*," Enrique said, and his eyes were almost immediately closed.

Juan stood for a moment and eyed his son, his son who had grown into a man, but who now reminded him of a time long ago when he was a small child, playing with his brother. Juan's throat constricted and burned, and his eyes glazed over with water as he thought of his dead son.

This was far from over. Even if they returned with Don Carlos, the gringo law would have their say in the matter of Enrique's shooting of Clint Ryan.

As Juan left, he said a silent prayer that the gringo Ryan was tough and would heal.

If he died, there would be hell to pay—and Juan had seen

more than one man wake up well one moment, and then turn green, bloated, and dead almost the next.

Please, God, Juan silently prayed, *let the gringo live, and let him be merciful when he speaks to the law—the gringo law.*

Clint had slept the day away, and he had been asleep the first time Sheriff Sam Stoddard had come to talk with him. But the sheriff told Davylou Boxworth that he would be back after dinner, and if Clint was able, would talk with him then.

Clint was awake and sitting up when Stoddard arrived. The sheriff formally introduced himself and gave Clint a tight smile. "Looks like you're gonna shake this off."

"I've got things to do, Sheriff Stoddard. Horses to buy. I've got no time to lay about."

Stoddard pulled up a ladder-back chair and straddled it. "What happened to get you shot, Mr. Ryan?"

Esperanza entered the room before he could answer, a tray in hand, offering them coffee. Stoddard took time to stir two spoonfuls of sugar into his.

She gave Clint a look that seemed to be pleading, then quickly left the room.

"Now, what happened to get you shot?"

Clint eyed him for a moment. *What had happened?* It was clear to him that the boy had shot him intentionally, had drawn and fired in cold blood with every intention of leaving him cold meat. But Enrique had the wild look of a crazed man in his eye, the look of an animal driven and cornered. But the Diego family had welcomed Clint into their house with open arms—and knowing the way the gringo law had treated the Californios, he knew that this would cause trouble for all of them. And the last thing Clint wanted was to be tied up here in Los Angeles for weeks, maybe months, while a trial went on. And he would heal.

Besides, he was used to settling his own grudges.

Clint cleared his throat before he began. "The boy . . . Don Juan's son Enrique. . . . He rode in dead tired, more than two days of straight riding, day and night. He stumbled off his horse . . . a damn near dead horse. He tried to get shed of his belt and gun, and the damn thing went off."

"Guns don't just go off, Mr. Ryan." Stoddard shot him a doubting look.

"He was trying to shed himself of it and dropped it. Must have lit on the hammer."

"So the pistol was dropped?" Sheriff Stoddard looked unconvinced, and a little irritated that this was Clint's story. "Don Juan and his daughter, Conchita, said it just went off. Nobody said anything about it being dropped."

"I guess I was just the unlucky one. Several of us were standing around."

Stoddard rose. "Doc Bonny said you had another wound, healing but fresh."

"Some bushwhacker up in the Tujungas . . . actually almost all the way over to the San Joaquin Valley. Guess he was after my poke. When he didn't drop me, he lit a shuck out of there."

Stoddard studied him in silence for a moment. When he finally spoke, he changed the subject again. "What about old Don Carlos? Is he still missing?"

Clint chose his words carefully, for he had been cautioned not to say anything about the Diegos' problem. "Yes, he's still missing . . . at least the last I heard of it."

"So what's being done about it?"

"The Diegos are handling it in their own way. They've had parties out hunting for signs of the old man."

"I'm surprised they haven't asked for help."

Again Clint chose his words. "They are an independent lot, seems like."

"True." Stoddard touched the brim of his hat, then strode to the door. He paused at the doorway. "You try and get your business done and ride on out, Mr. Ryan. We have a peaceful little town here, and I mean to keep it that way."

"I've had enough excitement, Sheriff Stoddard. I came to buy horses at the Rancho Agua Caliente auction, but I guess I missed that. No reason for me to stay around here now. I've got a ranch to tend to up the San Joaquin."

"Actually, the auction was set back a week. The lawyers are still haggling it out. It'll be a week before you're ready to ride anyway. . . . But right after next weekend, you ride on out, auction or not."

"Sounds right to me."

"If you think it's right or not, Mr. Ryan, ride out." The sheriff gave him another tight smile, but his eyes were hard. With a touch of his hat brim, he was gone.

Esperanza entered the room, almost as soon as Stoddard had left. She walked to his bedside and took his hand in hers. "I heard. You have been a good friend to the Californios. The law here, all the gringo citizens of Los Angeles are looking for any excuse to attack the Diegos."

"Why?" Clint said, a little surprised at her statement and at her eavesdropping.

Before she could answer, Davylou Boxworth's voice rang up from the lower floor. "Esperanza! Where are you?"

"Agua . . . water," she said quietly, then spun and left the room in a swirl of skirt and raven-black hair, closing the door behind her.

Water? The Diegos had plenty of water on their rancho, and Los Angeles was growing. Water did rule this dry country.

It was only a moment before Davylou Boxworth knocked on the door and called his name.

"Come on in," Clint said.

"You're looking chipper this afternoon," she said, a bright smile on her face. She crossed the room and fluffed up his pillows and straightened the bedclothes, with him still prone in it. "We have guests for dinner tonight. Dr. Bonny said you could get up as soon as you felt like it. . . . Maybe you'd like to try dinner downstairs, then sitting out on the porch in the fresh air for a while?"

"I was going to suggest that myself," Clint said.

"Good. Esperanza laundered your clothes. I'll have her bring them up, and some hot water so you can freshen up. Do you need any help? If so, I'll come back and help you. It wouldn't do to have Esperanza—"

"No. Thank you. I can handle the washing and combing, but there is something you can do. I don't imagine you have any newspapers around? Even old ones?"

"She'll bring what we have. Dinner is an hour later tonight. Seven . . . so you'll have time to read awhile."

"Who's coming to dinner?"

"We've got a house full of paying guests, plus a friend of mine. Thomas MacKendrick, the local druggist."

"Mac with an A, or just Mc?"

"He's a Scotsman by blood, Mr. Ryan," she said with a laugh, "but Scotch-Irish from a family long in Northern Ireland, so you should get on fine. Actually, he's Irish as Paddy's pig."

"Just asking," Clint said, a little sheepishly. It wasn't his nature to prejudge, and he was only curious about what kind of friends Mrs. Davylou Boxworth might have. He really didn't give a damn if her dinner guest was a bloody Englishman or a mangy hound.

But she was a fascinating woman—unlike any Clint had ever known. Independent, operating the boardinghouse with an iron hand. Beautiful, Clint had decided, after seeing her smile a few times, which softened the lines in her face. Well endowed, he knew, for more than once she had brushed against him while adjusting his bedclothes, yet still with a girlishly small waist.

A fascinating woman.

He was looking forward to being up and joining a room full of folks at dinner. As soon as he sat up, though, he broke into a cold sweat. It wasn't going to be as easy as he had thought.

* * *

San Francisquito creek was little more than a trickle this late in the summer, but the crossing on the Los Angeles/San Buenaventura road was a fairly deep ravine, and the Concord had to slow to a walk to traverse it.

Striker, his thin face framed by unruly red hair, along with four of the Blue Stripers, waited patiently in the stand of thick river willows that lined the creek. Downstream one hundred yards south, the creek entered the Santa Clara River, which flowed almost due west all the way to the ocean. Its broad banks lay lined with towering cottonwoods for a mile, but its wide bed was mostly sand, glistening white in the late-afternoon sun where the long shadows of the trees did not shade it.

Striker could not remember if it was an even or odd day, for on the even days the stage passed in the morning, westbound, and on the odd in the evening, eastbound. Well, at least eastbound for another mile before it swung due south leaving the river and heading over the San Fernando Pass into the valley of the same name, past the old dilapidated mission, to where the road joined the valley road. Then it swung east and followed the Los Angeles River until it wound around Cahunga Peak and turned south to the pueblo.

The steep mountains flanking the Santa Clara River lay deep golden in the late-afternoon simmering summer heat, except where the ravines lay shaded by deep-green oaks.

Striker checked the elevation of the sinking sun, then yelled to his men to get in their prearranged positions on each side of the road, flanking the steep drop into the creek bed.

If the stage was coming from the west, it wouldn't be long now.

Clint paused at the door to his room, already out of breath. It would be a long trip down the stairs to the dining room. Before he reached the head of the stairs, Esperanza was at his side. She took his arm and put it over her shoulder, and to Clint's surprise, the lithe girl seemed very strong. More slightly built than Davylou Boxworth, Esperanza was still shapely—and her curves were certainly all her own. Unlike Mrs. Boxworth, she wore little under her *jerga* garments.

He could feel the heat of her skin through her blouse as his arm wrapped her shoulders.

"You are still very weak," she said as they had to stop after only four stairs.

"Like a baby bird on short rations. Sorry to be so much trouble."

"I am proud to help. I want to talk to you later," she said quietly, almost under her breath.

"Of course. My door is always unlocked." Clint wished he were in better health, for the girl's firm body continued to push up against his, helping him down the stairs. Firm breasts strained against the cloth of her blouse, and she smelled of fresh-baked bread and spring flowers.

"I will come later."

But Clint's mind had turned to the stairs. Only two-thirds of the way down, and he felt unsure if he would make it. A number of people in the living room were watching him with somewhat furtive glances like they thought he was going to roll the rest of the way down the stairs. Finally, they reached the bottom. Instead of walking to a waiting chair, he sat on the last step.

"Give me just a moment." He sat, embarrassed at his weak condition.

Davylou Boxworth hurried out of the dining room and came to face him. With irritation, she snapped at Esperanza, "You shouldn't have hurried him."

"She didn't, Mrs. Boxworth—"

"Davylou, Clint. You let me help you into the dining room."

Clint knew he should remain sitting, but he didn't. He rose slowly and let Davylou Boxworth take his elbow, and Esperanza supported him with an arm over her shoulder. He nodded at the others in the room as they passed, then gratefully took a chair next to the left of the head of one of the two long tables in the dining room. Each would sit a dozen, and almost that many followed them in and took seats.

Esperanza hurried away to the kitchen while Davylou went from guest to guest and poured wine from a large pitcher.

The conversation centered on the fine funeral that the town had given George Willington that day.

For the first time Clint noticed the large man directly across the table from him to the right of the head of the table. The man studied him intently. Clint nodded, and the man extended his hand across the table.

"I'm Thomas MacKendrick."

Clint took his large hand and shook while he introduced himself.

Davylou Boxworth took the seat at the head of the table and offered a toast, then the conversation continued.

"You're the fella that got shot out at the Diegos'?"

"That's right," Clint said, not offering any more.

"I heard tell it was an accident," MacKendrick said, and Clint replied with a nod. "I also heard tell, from another source, that the Diego kid shot you down like a dog."

Clint could feel the heat rush up his backbone, but he collected himself before he replied. "Where did you hear that?"

"Talk. Just talk."

"And that's all it is, Mr. MacKendrick, just talk. Pistol fell and lit on the hammer. Not the first time it's happened, and it won't be the last."

Esperanza served the meal and was helped by a young Californio boy, who Clint presumed was the boy who had gone after Diablo and his tack. He made a mental note to ask for the boy to come up so he could tip him, and so he could give him instructions regarding the big horse's care.

"I understand you're the local druggist," Clint said, trying to get the conversation back to a better subject.

"That and other things," MacKendrick offered.

"Such as?" Clint asked with uncharacteristic curiosity.

And MacKendrick was more than pleased to talk of his accomplishments in front of Davylou Boxworth, who acknowledged them with a smile as MacKendrick spoke. "I've got a few ranchos between here and San Juan Capistrano, and I'm involved in a little banking on my own."

"Banking?"

"Yes, Mr. Ryan. I understand you're a landowner. If you ever want to borrow a little money, come see me."

"Neither a borrower nor a lender be," Clint said, not remembering where he had heard the line, but thinking it appropriate at the moment.

"But, Clint," Davylou offered, "every community needs a way to finance itself. And I think it's a great community service Thomas performs here in Los Angeles. We're a growing town, and money is scarce."

"To each his own," Clint said, turning his attention to his food and what the others at the table were talking about.

MacKendrick seemed unconcerned about Clint's attitude toward his lending endeavors. His attention turned to Davylou, only occasionally offering a comment to the others at the table.

The chief topic of conversation focused on the death of George Willington. Many of those in attendance thought the alcalde had died of cuts received when he fell through the window, and that Dr. Bonny had misdiagnosed the cause of death. After all, who would want to kill George Willington?

Clint said nothing about the subject, and MacKendrick only offered the opinion that Dr. Bonny was competent and capable and if he said the alcalde was murdered, then the alcalde was murdered. And that he, for one, was going to make damn sure the killer was caught.

Clint ate sparingly and accepted reluctantly when invited out onto the porch to take a little brandy and watch the sun set.

Before that happened, though, he excused himself. He was surprised when Thomas MacKendrick stood and warmly shook his hand, and was even more surprised when the large man invited him to attend the *bendición* of his new home the following Sunday.

"I would be pleased," Clint said, meaning it. He was beginning to like the man, in spite of the fact he didn't approve of his avocation, lending money.

Clint excused himself and was helped upstairs by both Esperanza and the boy, who was named Pablo.

He gave the boy instructions regarding Diablo's care and tipped him before he left.

Esperanza paused at the door, "I'll be back after the house is quiet."

"Great," Clint said, wondering what the girl expected of him as he settled into the sheets, suddenly feeling dead tired.

In moments he slept.

The Concord, with a six-horse team of two leaders, two swingers, and two wheelers, rolled out of the west at a hard gallop, but reined up to take the steep drop into San Francisquito Creek at a trot.

The stripers in wait were a mangy crew: Striker; a ruddy-faced Dutchman known only as Adolph; a thin Welshman called Dick; a swarthy Italian called Aldo the gimp, because of a bad limp; and an Englishman who went by Courtney. Striker rose out of the willows, an apparition in the failing light, with red hair askew and green eyes glowing in the red sunset—and a sawed-off scattergun leveled on the driver and guard.

"Pull 'em up, or die!" he shouted.

The driver drew the twelve traces up hard, but the guard on his right swung his own shotgun at the bandit.

The double barrels in Striker's hands bucked and spat flame, and the guard was blown clean out of his seat. He landed flat on his back in the road at the feet of two of Striker's men, Courtney and Aldo, who were approaching the coach from the far side.

"You son of a bitch!" the driver yelled, his eyes flared wide.

Striker would have shot him, too, but he had to reload the scattergun. He threw it aside and pulled his sidearm, a stubby eight-shot pepperbox, and fired at the driver, missing.

The man jumped from the high seat of the Concord, and with arms and legs churning, he fled back along it, away from the crazy redheaded bandit—much to the consternation of a passenger who stuck his narrow-brim-hatted head out of the door and shouted, "Where the hell are you going?"

But the shots from Striker's pepperbox whizzed by the man's head, and he jerked it back inside.

Striker fired three more of the remaining seven shots at the fleeing driver, without effect. Then he yelled at the remaining Blue Striper, the square-jawed Dutchman, who sat his horse back in the willows. "Adolph, ride that bastard down and kill him." Then he helped himself to the Navy Colt of the Blue Striper who stood beside him, the diminutive Welshman, Dick.

With the look on Striker's face, Dick made no complaint.

Striker's mouth flung spittle and his brows furrowed. His face reddened to match his hair. He ran around the nervous horses and charged to the Concord's door and flung it open. The drummer met him coming out the door, a single-shot belly gun in hand, a frightened but determined look on his face. The drummer fired, and the ball creased Striker's cheek, near the scar it already bore—blood filled the furrow.

Striker's newfound Colt bucked and blew flame, and the drummer was blown back inside. Striker followed with both hands filled with guns, standing at the door, firing at everything that moved inside the coach. Screams reverberated as he began his indiscriminate slaughter.

When the six-shot Navy Colt he'd grabbed from Dick was finally empty, and before the acrid smoke from its muzzle had drifted away, the screams had stopped. Striker stepped back as the drummer stumbled out, holding his stomach with both hands, moaning quietly, blood oozing between his fingers. Striker let him pass.

"You've kilt me," he managed, stumbling off the road and into the shade of the willows. He collapsed there and began to pray under his breath, awaiting the darkness he knew was coming.

A shot rang out from down the road, and soon the Dutchman, who had pounded away in pursuit of the driver, returned—his grim look, silent testimony to his success. Only then did the fifth Blue Striper, Courtney, the Englishman, step out of the brush, his cold sidearm hanging at his side.

Striker climbed up into the driver's seat and fished the strongbox from the floor and flung it off to the roadbed. It landed with a heavy thump and kicked up a cloud of dust.

Striker and the other three men began studying the problem of opening it while Adolph reined up and dismounted. He studied the drummer, still mumbling in the shade of the willows, then walked to the door of the Concord.

He stared in perplexed silence, then spun on his heels and walked to the side of the road, put his hands on his knees, and vomited his lunch into the low grass.

Striker looked up from the strongbox, and his angular face broke into a snarling grin. "What's the matter, square head? You ain't got the stomach for it?"

Adolph raised his face to Striker. "You shot a woman . . . shot her right in the face. And a little girl. We're all gonna hang, sure as cholera kills."

"I don't hold with killin' no women and children," Courtney mumbled.

"Get over here and help with this here box . . . and quit your whining," Striker snapped.

But the other four Stripers glared at him, then looked at each other and shook their heads.

"Let's get out of here," one of them said. "That's cursed money, sure as hell's hot . . . and we're all gonna find out just how hot it is!"

Aldo, Courtney, and Dick turned and headed into the brush.

In a moment, Adolph, who had become sick at the sight, spat; then he, too, went for his horse.

"Damn fools," Striker said, then walked into the shade and sat to reload his pepperbox, thinking he would shoot the lock away. He was not unhappy that the others were leaving—all the take would be his. Dick and Aldo rode out toward Los Angeles to the South; Adolph to the east, up the Santa Clara River, then to the desert; and Courtney north, back the way they had come.

Striker stood staring after Courtney; he was heading back to tell Jory Mortenson what had happened, and Jory would be fighting mad at the killing of the woman and kid. Then he stared at the strongbox. If it was enough, he had no intention of returning to Condor Canyon. It was all his. Captain Jory Mortenson and the Blue Stripers could go to hell.

The drummer, on his back in the grass, hands clamped across his belly, his face gone gray, managed to turn his head to face the reclining redheaded man. "You're gonna rot in hell," he whispered.

"Maybe, but not as soon as you," Striker said, tamping the last of the loads home into the eight-shot cylinder of the pepperbox and carefully replacing the caps.

Striker rose and started back toward the box. Then he paused and turned back, raising the pepperbox toward the drummer, centering its eight eyes on his forehead.

"Boom!" he said, feigning a shot. Then he laughed a ringing cackle that echoed up and down the quiet road in the still sunset while he slapped his thigh with his free hand.

"Bastard," the drummer whispered, then his eyes went flat and his mouth fell open with a gasp. And, as sure as if he had been actually shot in the head, he moved no more.

Old Don Carlos Diego feigned sleeping.
The cook, Howard, had brought him his half plate of fri-

joles, which he had picked at but managed to finish. He would need his strength before this night was over.

The guard was changed, and the men stationed in the three branches of Condor Canyon came in and ate, and three others took their place.

Only five men remained in camp, while three were on guard in distant places—one up the canyon trail coming in from Grapevine Canyon, one down the main canyon closer to where the vaqueros had been dragged after their killing, and one up a smaller west branch of the canyon.

Mortenson didn't bother to place a guard up the main branch of the canyon, for no man could come at them from that direction, from the south. The canyon narrowed and ended less than a half mile away in sheer cliffs of broken, shattered rock that proved to be great, insurmountable escarpments—at least for horses.

Don Carlos had decided to escape that way.

No guards, and it was the last place they would expect a feeble old man to attempt.

He had hoped to steal a horse, but decided it was out of the question. The remuda was near the creek, almost between the two tents, and by the time he saddled up and tried to mount with his bad leg? It was too great a risk.

It took a long time for the camp to quiet. A card game went on for two hours after the sun fell below the high canyon wall to the west. And an argument ensued, which resulted in a short decisive fistfight, then a stern chastisement by Jory Mortenson.

The men broke up the game and wandered away to their tent. The man who had been knocked down in the short fight stayed by the fire, rubbing his jaw and murmuring quietly to himself for another half hour; then he, too, made his way to the large tent—where the lamp had already been long out.

Don Carlos sat up and stayed sitting, unmoving, for a long while, his old watery eyes searching each shadow. His ears, dulled by age, strained to hear any sound that would indicate the wakefulness of anyone in the camp.

Nothing.

Quietly, moving an inch at a time, he made his way closer to the fire, now burned to coals.

The flint and steel still rested on the rock where Howard had left them. Don Carlos gathered up the flint and inched his way back out of the dull glow of the coals.

He began to saw at the thick thong with the sharp-edged flint, and with each stroke, wished it was the throat of each of the gringos he was cutting.

Finally the leather thong gave way, and he was free. Free of the physical restraints of the strips of hide that had bound him, but not free of the physical restraints of age and of being dragged and denied, bound and beaten, for days.

But overcome that he must.

With the greatest care, he managed to pull his boots on, then climb to his feet. He pocketed the flint and steel and moving a creaking step at a time—carefully placing each foot for the sake of silence—he moved away and up into the darkness of the hillside.

He stopped and caught his breath and studied the dark camp below. If he circled, he could cross the creek and approach Jory Mortenson's tent from the side opposite the main tent, out of sight of anyone who might happen to get up in the darkness to relieve himself. With luck, he could find a blade to cut the gringo's throat with the man's own knife while he slept.

No, he decided. Escape was all important. Escape—so he could find his family and the rest of his vaqueros; then he could return and take his revenge on all of these gringos. And so he could solve his financial problem.

He worked his way toward the west branch of the canyon, limping along on the soft canyon floor, deliberately dragging his feet—having to stop every dozen steps to catch his breath and rest his bad leg. He picked up a dead branch to use as a walking stick and made sure his trail was so well marked even a gringo *marinero* could follow it. Finally he moved up out of the canyon bottom to a rock face, then abruptly reversed his direction and returned to the main canyon, careful not to leave a trail. He was even more careful not to fall and injure himself again, fearful that a fall would end his escape attempt as surely as waking the camp would.

When he reached the main canyon, he began working his way up it, again passing the camp, but keeping above it to the rock ledges where he would leave no track.

Now, with his bad leg beginning to ache in earnest, he wondered if he could get far enough away by dawn.

He heard shouts in the camp behind him and hurried his pace, risking all in the darkness.

If he fell, he was finished.

Eight

Clint dreamed he was at sea, but the rolling of the ship became someone shaking him awake, gently but firmly.

His eyes focused and saw Esperanza. In the faint light of the moon coming through the open window, she was perched on the edge of his bed.

"I told you I would come," she said quietly.

"Yes, you did."

"I hope you don't mind me bothering you, Lazo, but Mrs. Boxworth interrupts each time I try to speak with you."

"I've noticed. Pour me a little water, please."

Esperanza crossed the room and poured Clint a mug from a bone-white pitcher. Clint could see the free-flowing form of her nightgown in the moonlight, and for the first time realized she must sleep in the house, as well as work there.

She returned and put a hand behind his neck to help him into position to drink the water. He started to complain that he could do it himself, but the nearness of her and her soft touch quelled his pride, and he remained silent.

She stayed quite near, perched on the bedside, leaning across him, her face little more than a foot from his when she began speaking.

"Don Juan Diego is my family's good friend and my godfather. He asked me to speak to you before the sheriff had a chance to, but I failed."

"Did I say something to upset the Diego family?" Clint

asked, taking a little umbrage. He thought he had been very careful to protect the Diegos.

"No, no, I don't mean to suggest that you did. I came here because you did quite the opposite. You lied to the sheriff—Don Juan told me the truth—and for that the Diegos and I are very grateful . . . all the Californios are grateful. We need no more trouble with the gringo law, Lazo."

"Enrique and I will settle this between us. . . ."

"He has always been *muy peligroso* . . . and was very distraught."

"He may be wild, but I am very shot, and lucky to be alive. But that's neither here nor there at the moment . . . it is for another place and time. You mentioned trouble before. You also mentioned water. What does water have to do with Los Angeles and the Diegos?"

"Water was very short last year. Los Angeles and the landowners to the south, where all the crops and orchards are, used every drop that trickled in from the river last summer, and it was not enough, while Rancho Del Robles Viejo, upriver, had all the water they could use. The gringos say the Diegos squander it. The gringos covet the rancho of the Diegos, but Don Carlos would not talk of selling either water rights or the rancho itself. I have overheard El Boticario, El Medico, and the *gordo* alcalde"—then as if sorry she had called him fat, added—"God rest his soul. . . . They talked of it many times, and with many other gringos, right here in the parlor of the boardinghouse while sipping Mrs. Boxworth's brandy. They say the city must have the Diegos' water rights if it is to grow."

"Esperanza, do you think that has anything to do with Don Carlos being missing, abducted, so Don Juan believes?"

"Yes. I think it does, but Don Carlos thinks it is only *banditos,* bad gringos who will do anything for a few pieces of gold. He cannot bring himself to believe that the *good* men of Los Angeles, the *gente de razón,* would be behind such a thing."

"And what do you think?" Clint asked, then waited as she seemed to search for words.

"I think there are evil men of all races and colors, as well as good."

As Clint considered her last comment, a board squeaked just outside his bedroom door, and he lowered his voice to a whisper.

"Someone's there."

Esperanza stood and silently moved around the narrow bed, between it and the wall, just as the doorknob rattled. Quickly she dropped to the floor between bed and wall.

The door opened slowly and Davylou Boxworth stood, candle in hand, searching the dark room with her gaze.

"Clint," she said softly.

"Yes," he answered in an equally low voice.

She set the candle holder on the bureau and crossed the room, taking Esperanza's place on the bedside. Clint almost held his breath as he heard Esperanza slide out prone on the floor. At the same time, he shifted in the bed to cover the rustle of her movement.

"I thought I heard talking," she said, but the tone of her voice was husky, not suspicious.

"I had a bad dream. Maybe I spoke out in my sleep. It awoke me."

"I'm sorry," she said, and her hand reached out and caressed his cheek. "Is there anything I can do?"

This time she was not trussed in whipcord and whalebone, and even as modest as the silk wrap was that she wore over her nightgown, her full body moved voluptuously under the cloth.

"Possibly, but I doubt if I'm up to it," Clint said, smiling mischievously, then felt the heat rise in his cheeks. It was probably the most forward thing he'd ever said to a woman with whom he had not been intimate.

She laughed, a quiet husky sound that made him begin to realize that he might *just be* up to it. She picked up his hand in both of hers and took it up to her own cheek, purposefully—or so Clint thought—brushing her full breast as she did so.

"Maybe you could be convinced to rise to the occasion," she said, then brushed her lips over his palm.

"Give me a few days and I'll thank you properly for all the wonderful care I've received here," he said, pulling his hand back with a little too much energy.

Davylou smoothed the gown with her hands, a little taken aback at his seeming rebuff.

"This damn side is killing me. I don't imagine you have some ice left over from what was brought in for dinner?" He tried to repair any damage he'd done to her ego. Hell, he was normally tongue-tied enough around women, much less trying to talk to one with another hiding under the bed.

She reached out and felt his cheek, this time more as a true nurse without an ulterior motive, and her tone altered slightly. "You may have a little fever, but not much. I don't have even a tiny chunk of ice left, I'm sorry. Perhaps a cold, damp towel."

"No . . . I'll be fine. Thanks for worrying about me." Then he let his own voice go husky. "But save a little of that attention for when I'm capable of returning it."

She rose and studied him for a moment, then spun on her heel and made for the doorway, but she paused before exiting. "Esperanza hasn't been too much bother, has she, Clint?"

"She's been a godsend . . . doing everything you instructed, Davylou. Hell, I bet if I yelled out now she'd be next to me in a flash." It was all he could do not to laugh out loud when a fine-boned hand slipped under the covers—and he got a sharp pinch on the arm for his effort.

"Ow," he said, flinching. "Sorry, but the side is killing me."

"About Esperanza . . . just what I instruct . . . no more?" Her tone hinted at sarcasm, but Clint didn't answer. "Just so she's not pestering you," Davylou said.

"Everything here at Boxworth House has been wonderful."

She was quiet for a moment; then, even in the glow of the

flickering candle, Clint could see her smile. "And it will get even better, if you want it to."

"I can't wait. . . . I *can* wait," he added quickly. "I mean, until I'm up to it . . . then I can't wait."

She retrieved the narrow taper in its holder from the bureau top. "Good night, Clint."

" 'Night, Davylou."

The door closed quietly, and it was a long moment before Esperanza's head appeared over the edge of the bed.

Her face was very near Clint's, and he could feel her warm breath on his cheek.

"You are a terrible tease, Señor Lazo," she said, her voice pouting. "A little of the *diablo* is in you, I think. A man who likes to live dangerously."

He started to answer, to tell her he thought there was a little of the devil in her, too, but she proved it before he could speak. Her lips covered his as she kissed him deeply, covering his upper body with hers. He found the fullness of her *jerga* blouse with his hand, but she was gone almost as soon as he did.

"I don't think you are 'up to it,' señor," she said, her voice a teasing caress.

"Come back here and find out," Clint said, his manhood beginning to overcome his good sense.

"I think if I do something that will cause me to have to say a hundred Hail Marys after my next confession, I want you in full strength. Otherwise, I might have to pay penance for less sin than I desire—'

"Come here and find out, *mujer diabla*," he said, calling her the devil woman she was acting like, his pride a little hurt.

"You should sleep," she said in a loud whisper, escaping to the door. Before Clint could answer, the door opened and closed, and she was gone—they were gone.

It was a long time before he could sleep.

* * *

They had not pursued him. It must have been something else in the camp that caused the uproar. Maybe they were fighting among themselves again?

Don Carlos moved with increasing difficulty as the terrain grew steeper and more heavily wooded. The almost barren canyon floor gave way to oak, an occasional buckeye, and chaparral-covered canyon walls, then to even steeper escarpments with only brush and the occasional Lord's Candle, with its spiked bottom and tall stem topped by the huge white blossom that gave it its name. Even in the disappearing moonlight, Don Carlos could make out the flower. He had always loved the oversize blossoms and took seeing them as a good omen.

But his enthusiasm was quickly fading to utter exhaustion.

His bad leg was failing him, and he had almost decided he must find a spot under the brush, on the far-too-revealing hillside, when he found the cave opening. He was maybe fifty paces above the narrow canyon bottom, on a rock outcropping, his hand following the face of the rock rising above, when the rock face turned inward. He studied the opening for a moment, hoping against hope that it would be deep enough to shield him from the eyes of his searchers, and was elated to find it widened to a true cave. He entered only far enough to assure himself he was out of sight of anyone on the opposite hillside, then let himself sink to his knees.

He brushed away the small bones of rodents and the regurgitated fur balls of owls and bobcats. Knowing that the cave must house predators, he hoped that none of them were predators of man. The last thing he needed was an encounter with a cougar protecting her cubs, or a bear—but he allowed himself only a moment of hesitation, then continued to clear himself a spot.

On the walls of the cave, he made out the drawings of Indians and wondered how many years ago other men sought the safety of the cave. Antelope and bear adorned the walls, as well as shapes he could not identify.

The drawings gave him solace. Others had been here, others

had survived, maybe for thousands of years, maybe for time immortal. He, too, would survive.

In less than a heartbeat after he had stretched out on the rocky floor, he was asleep.

The meeting at the Diego rancho went on well into the late evening. It was a gathering of many, but this night, there would be no *música,* no fandango.

Don Juan paced the floor, three dozen of his assembled vaqueros stood and sat in the great room of the hacienda—a place most of them had never been granted admission.

First the women, including Doña Angelina and the twins, Conchita and Consuela—also an unheard of accommodation to the men—served them a hearty meal and more wine than normal, then Enrique arose and described what the gringos in Condor Canyon had done to their fellow vaqueros, and to his brother Emilio.

They had all heard it secondhand, but Enrique's broken-voiced recollection—and the wetness in his eyes—made them want to ride out right then, not even awaiting dawn.

Don Jacques, in uncharacteristic fervor, spoke of the kindness Don Carlos had shown them all, and even Don Juan was touched by his brother-in-law's seeming sincerity. But not so touched that he stopped suspecting the Frenchman's duplicity, somehow, in the old don's abduction.

Then their acting *patrón,* Don Juan Diego, arose, and with the most entreating speech he had ever given, aroused the Diego vaqueros to an almost fever pitch.

With rousing voices, and a great resounding *"Viva Don Carlos"* they toasted the coming recovery of their old *patrón* with a mug of brandy each, then headed out to the *establo,* the barn, to get as much sleep as possible before Don Juan would awaken them to ride out.

Within two days' time, Condor Canyon would ring like thunder with the clap of dozens of Diego guns, Don Carlos would be returned to his rightful place, and Emilio and the others would be avenged.

It would be gringo bodies feeding the condors and the crows.

Doña Angelina, with Jacques by her side, waited as her brother saw the last of the vaqueros out the great front doors of the hacienda. As he closed them and turned, his shoulders seemed to sink.

"Don't tire now, Juan," she said. "Your job has only begun. We will finally find Don Carlos and get him home where he belongs."

"And kill many gringos doing so, Angelina." He downed the last of his mug of brandy and handed it to her. "We may win the battle and lose the war."

"They killed your son, Juan. That is important. The only thing more important now is getting Don Carlos home."

"That is true, they killed my son. Now I must make sure my remaining son has a bequest. And Don Carlos will not want to come home, if he does not have a home to come to."

"They cannot take our rancho if we are only defending our father. . . . Can they?"

"No, they cannot," Juan said, then started on down the hall, only to be stopped by another question from his sister.

"Then, is there something else, Juan? Something you have not spoken of?"

"No, Angelina, there is nothing else." He had decided it would do no good to trouble her about the note Don Carlos had signed before he was abducted. There was nothing she could do about it, and he had Antonio Alverez working on the problem.

"I will keep the rancho in good stead while you are gone, Juan," Jacques said, and both Angelina and Juan turned to him.

With hard derision in his voice, Juan questioned, "Jacques, you are not going to accompany the men in search of Don Carlos?"

"Why, no. Someone has to keep things going here . . ." Angelina gave him a look so hateful that he spun on his heel and stomped away down the hall to their private quarters.

"I am not surprised," Juan yelled after him, his tone exhausted. He had thought to stay himself, and resolve the matter of the note—a matter almost as important as the return of Don Carlos—but decided suddenly that he must ride with the men. He turned to his sister. "Antonio Alverez is arranging to round up and sell cattle off the rancho. He will be directing that operation while I am away." He swung his lantern-jawed face back to his retreating brother-in-law. "Just don't get in his way, Jacques!"

Jacques had paused at the door to their quarters, but slammed it with a boom that echoed through the hacienda after Juan finished his chastisement.

Angelina watched Juan shuffle down the hallway. It was not like her brother to give up, not like him to be defeated before the fight was fought. A chill ran down her spine, and she didn't know why.

She put it off to the fact that her husband, Jacques, was not riding to avenge his nephew, or to seek the return of her father. With that thought, another chill racked her backbone.

It was a bad omen.

The Diegos were not the only ones keeping late hours.

Striker had not been able to believe it when the other four Blue Stripers took off in three different directions from the stage robbery—leaving him with the unopened strongbox.

He had cut the strongest-looking of the Concord's team from its traces and fashioned a pack saddle by cutting up the coach's leather boot, which covered the luggage at its rear. It was a makeshift affair, and he had to load the hundred-pound-plus strongbox on one side of the packsaddle and offset its weight with provisions, and even a few rocks to balance it.

The horse was strong, but heavily laden. Finally, in the deep darkness of the canyon, Striker set out to the west, retracing the track of the Concord.

He wanted to get as far from the coach as possible before he found a spot where he could concentrate on opening the strongbox. He knew it was full of gold, for it was terribly heavy.

He would not return to Condor Canyon; he had found his stake. To hell with Jory Mortenson and his ransom; to hell with old Don Carlos Diego; to hell with the rest of the Blue Stripers—the four with him on the stagecoach robbery had proved to be spineless cowards.

He was on his own.

Like Striker, Thomas Salathiel MacKendrick, known as El Boticario to the Californios, was up late plying his trade, or at least one of his avocations if not his vocation—he was playing cards. As happened so often, Oscar Bonny, known as El Medico to the Californios, was sitting nearby, not participating in the game, but sipping a drink and enjoying his friend's success.

But the night was a slow one, and the game penny ante.

Finally even T.S. tired of it. He pushed away from the table and picked up his chips, making his excuses to the drover and whiskey drummer still playing. He slid his large chair around to the table where Oscar sat, sipping lemonade.

MacKendrick was never idle and immediately eased into a conversation wherein he would glean information. "I had dinner at Davylou's earlier . . . and met the man you treated . . . the one shot by the Diego boy."

"Ryan's his name," Bonny said.

"Ryan, that's it. He's a strange duck."

"I thought he was all right, T.S. He had a pretty bad wound, and didn't complain a lick while I treated it."

"I don't mean that, Oscar. He's lying about how it happened. About how he got shot. I've got a little bird out at the

Diego place who lets me know what goes on there. He lied to you, lied to Stoddard, and lied to me. He carries a greaser nickname. Why would a man lie about being shot by another man?"

"You just want to see more trouble made for the Diegos," Bonny said with a chuckle.

"I . . . this town is going to have to get their hands on the Diego water, if this town's ever going to amount to a hill of beans. I never should have sold that damn note of old Don Carlos's . . . then I never could turn down a sure profit."

Oscar Bonny chuckled, knowing that no truer words were ever spoken. "There's Alverez at the bar. Let's twist his tail about the Diego boy . . . maybe we can learn something."

MacKendrick turned to see the Californio attorney alone at the bar. He rose and walked over. "Come on over and join us, amigo," he said in a friendly manner.

Antonio looked up, a little in his cups from a night of drinking, and eyed MacKendrick a little suspiciously. "I am not about to get in a card game with you, MacKendrick."

"Doc and I want to buy you a friendly drink, Antonio. We're not playing cards."

Antonio focused his eyes on the table where Oscar Bonny, El Medico, sat, and saw what MacKendrick said was true—there were no cards on the table. "Okay, one drink, then I must find my hacienda. . . . I'm a little *borracho* already." He admitted with uncharacteristic candor to being a little drunk.

He followed MacKendrick back to the table and took a seat between doctor and druggist.

MacKendrick poured him a stiff jolt from the doctor's bottle. "What do you hear about ol' Don Carlos?" MacKendrick asked casually.

Antonio looked up from his mug, a little bleary eyed. "Why would I hear anything? I know nothing about his abduction—"

"Do you think it *was* an abduction? If so, why haven't the

Diegos filed a complaint with Stoddard? Why hasn't there been a demand for ransom?"

Antonio laughed sarcastically. "Do you really want to know, MacKendrick . . . or do you already know?"

"What are you driving at?" MacKendrick said defensively.

"You are a gringo. You know how much attention is paid to Californio problems. . . . Besides, you told me yourself, the whole town wants to get its hands on Rancho Del Robles Viejo."

"Legally, Alverez. The town wants to get its hands on the Diego property, but legally. You of all people, being an attorney, know that all the town wants is legal access to the Diegos' water."

"The town? You told me you would pay fifty dollars per acre for the flat lands, and the water. Is that not true . . . is that not still true?" Alverez began to raise his voice.

"Of course . . . but legally."

"Of course," Alverez said, his tone still sarcastic. "You had a Diego note, won in a poker game. Why didn't you keep it?"

MacKendrick's face turned blank. It was obvious he had wondered the same thing. Why hadn't he kept the note?

"It was a small note. I didn't think there was any odds in keeping it, so I sold it . . . at a rather handsome profit, I might add."

The men locked eyes for a moment, then MacKendrick had a second thought. "How did you know about that note?"

"I heard about it," Antonio said, now his tone turned defensive.

"Only the doc here, and me, and George Willington knew about Don Carlos borrowing that money. So how did you know about it?"

"I am the Diegos' attorney . . . I know everything they do."

"Horse crap. Old Don Carlos wouldn't use you for Diego business . . . everyone in town knows that." Antonio reddened at MacKendrick's barb, but MacKendrick continued unabated.

"There is one other man who would know about it. The man who bought the note from George, who handled its sale for me."

"Don Juan told me . . . of course. It was Don Juan."

"That makes sense," Oscar said.

MacKendrick sat back in his chair, his tone sarcastic. "Why don't you talk the Diegos into selling, if you're so close to them?"

"I have tried. I have tried and tried."

"But to no avail."

"I have to go to my hacienda," Alverez said suddenly through clamped teeth, then stood with red face, spun on his heel and left.

"You trying to be a detective?" Oscar asked.

"I just think that note might have had something to do with George's death. Hell, one of the Diegos might have killed him."

"If they had killed him for the note, you wouldn't have gotten your money for it. Why kill for something you've already paid for?"

"That's true," MacKendrick agreed quietly, "why kill him if you bought the note already?" Then he added, "Although, I wouldn't put it past that Jacques LaTour to kill a man just to watch him die. He's a bad one."

"You're seeing ghosts everywhere."

"Maybe," MacKendrick said, downing the rest of his drink. "Hell, maybe I'm just tired. I'm hitting the hay, too." He rose and turned from the table, then paused and studied his friend for a moment before he spoke. "Whoever bought that note didn't want anyone to know their identity. George wouldn't even tell me who the buyer was. I've got the feeling that whoever bought the note, killed old George." MacKendrick paused again, then smiled at Oscar Bonny. "You didn't buy that note, did you, Oscar? You knew about it."

"Why the hell would I want to overpay for a personal note? Hell, no, T.S., I didn't buy it, and why the hell would I care who knew it if I did, and besides, I would have made you an offer directly if I wanted it. You are tired. Go to bed."

MacKendrick left with a laugh.

Oscar Bonny watched him go. *I wonder if T.S. had some reason to kill George,* he thought as he watched him push aside the bat-wing doors. He had seen Thomas Salathiel MacKendrick lose his temper more than once. Maybe he and the alcalde had a falling-out, and old T.S. shoved him a little too hard—right through the window. No, Oscar knew damned well he was not wrong about the cause of death. George Willington had his throat cut, and not by a window shard, but by a blade. And blades weren't MacKendrick's style.

I wonder whose style it is, Oscar thought, then killed his lemonade and followed MacKendrick's lead.

It was bedtime—but still it gnawed at him. Who had killed old George?

Nine

It was with great trepidation, in the predawn light, that Don Juan Diego led his vaqueros out of the *establo* at Rancho Del Robles Viejo—not because of the possible fight ahead of them, but because of the note left behind. A note that grew at ten percent per day, a note that doubled every ten days. It hovered in the background like a swarm of locusts, growing, swelling, and waiting to devour all the Diego clan.

But he felt he had no choice. He had to ride to find his father; he owed the old man that much, he owed himself that much. And Jacques LaTour would not go, even if Juan would have trusted him to fulfill the mission.

Even Morengo had joined them, ignoring his still unhealed jaw.

Jacques, wrapped in a silk robe, coffee mug in hand, stood in the doorway of the main hacienda and watched them ride away, a cloud of dust billowing up behind the thirty horsemen. By the time the first rays of sunlight lit the inner court, his wife, Angelina, joined him at the big carved dining-room table.

"Will they find him this time?" she asked quietly, pouring herself a cup of coffee from the jug left there by the serving woman, then mixing a little chocolate and sugar into the black liquid.

"If he is alive, *ma chérie.* Let us pray they do."

Her eyes snapped up from the steaming coffee. "If you

pray for my father's safety, then why did you not ride with them?"

"I've told you a hundred times, *ma chérie,* I am a man of commerce, not a man of the *caballo.* Let the vaqueros and your brother ride to avenge Don Carlos. It is better . . . he would tell you it was better . . . better that I stay here and help continue what he has built."

She sighed deeply, rose and headed for the central patio, then paused and turned back. "Is it true that Antonio Alverez has been retained to hire a crew and begin rounding up cattle to sell?"

"That is Carlos's wish. Antonio and his hired men should be here this morning."

"Well, then it is well you are here to see we get a fair count and a fair price. You will do that much, won't you, Jacques?"

"I will watch and count every head, Angelina."

"Good," she said, shuffling out, her head hanging, even though the day had just begun.

Clint awoke, feeling refreshed and strong. He used the chamber pot, managed to pull on a shirt and his britches, then started the long trek down the stairs to find the kitchen and coffee. It was still too early for the house to be up. Winded and surprised at his continued weakness, he found only Esperanza at work.

She saw the pale look of him and made him sit at the kitchen table. In a moment he had what he had come for, a cup of hot, strong coffee. It fired his insides and brought back the strength he'd lost in the descent from his room.

"You should have let me bring it up," Esperanza scolded. "You could break that wound open."

"I have to get my strength back. I have a ranch to tend to—"

"You cannot tend it if you don't get well. Eat this."

She sat two rolled tortillas in front of him. As he suspected, they were filled with sweetened chocolate. He ate them slowly, watching her go about her morning chores, and enjoying the watching as much as he did the tortillas and coffee. He knew then he was healing fast.

Finally, with biscuits in the oven, she turned to him. "I'm through in here for a few minutes. Would you like me to help you up to your room?"

"No, thank you. And thank you for the coffee and tortillas, which were delicious. What I'd like to do is go out on the front porch and watch the town come alive."

"I'll help you—"

"No. You take care of your chores. I'll get out there alone."

She smiled, poured him another cup of coffee, and let him navigate his way alone.

He found a chair on the porch and sipped his coffee. He'd been in a thousand towns in fifty countries, and had always had a fondness for early morning, and for judging a town by the way it awakened—and found the same pleasure in watching Pueblo de Los Angeles.

The town was a contradiction. Half of it still the sleepy Californio pueblo, half of it a bustling town of commerce— commerce fueled by Americans and Frenchmen and Germans and Australians and of late, Chinese. Watching the town come awake was like watching an international roll call. First the Chinese bustled about, then the Anglos of many European origins, then finally, the Peruvians, Mexicans, Chileans, Indians, and old-line Californios.

Clint sat back, sipped his coffee, smiled at Esperanza when she brought him a plate of biscuits dripping in honey, and continued watching.

If the wound didn't go green and kill him, these women would with food and attention—but then there could be a worse death.

* * *

By the time Clint had made his way to the front porch of
Boxworth House, one group of Californios had been moving
at a trail-eating canter for well over an hour. By the time they
were well into the second hour, Don Juan Diego raised his
hand, and the band of riders following reined up. Enrique
nudged his stallion up alongside his father to ask him what
the trouble was, then saw the stagecoach up ahead. It sat quiet,
down in the creek-bed cut, and from where they observed,
only its top and top-railings could be seen. The horses should
have been visible, for a six-horse team would have reached
well up the bank in front of the coach.

"Something is very wrong here." Don Juan turned and
waved his *segundo,* Aleandro Dominguez, up alongside. "You
take some men and circle to the north," he instructed his foreman. "Enrique, you take a third of the men and circle to the
south." He knew he was being very cautious, but he would
have none of the ambushing his vaqueros had already expe-
rienced. As riders broke away to the north and south, he prodded his stallion forward, then reined up behind the abandoned
coach and dismounted. A dozen crows and a pair of vultures
flew out ahead of him as he moved forward, gun in hand, and
inspected the drummer, dead in the grass, then the coach
where a woman passenger and her young daughter also lay
grotesquely splayed across the seats amid their own gore after
a violent, bloodletting death.

Finally all the men reunited, investigated the scene themselves—and still no one spoke. In a violent land, it was the
most heinous crime any of them had ever seen.

No one killed women.

No one killed children.

Don Juan waved over one of the vaqueros.

"Chico, you ride into Pueblo de Los Angeles and inform
Sheriff Stoddard of what we have found here. I will leave a
man to watch over these poor dead souls, but the rest of us
will ride on. The men who did this are likely the same band
who abducted Don Carlos and killed our *compadres.* If we

find them, then maybe we will find Don Carlos. But find them and hang them, we will." He waved the man on, then galloped away.

"We should go straight to Condor Canyon, *Padre,*" Enrique pleaded.

"You don't think the gringos are fool enough to stay there? No, they left Condor Canyon shortly after they realized you had gotten away. We were only riding there in hopes of picking up their trail—and a very cold trail it would have been."

He remounted and looked down on his son and his vaqueros. "No, my belief is that this was done by the same men who have Don Carlos. They are a blight on our land. . . . Felipe," he called to a grizzled, old half-Indian vaquero, "you are the finest tracker. Tell us how many there were, and what trail to follow to find them."

"Sí, jefe."

For twenty minutes the rest of them cooled their heels, watered their animals, and smoked, careful not to disturb the sign while old Felipe pussyfooted the camp—pausing and studying. Finally he returned.

"Jefe, they were five and have ridden out in four directions."

This came as a surprise to Don Juan, who presumed they had ridden out together, and as such, could be easily trailed.

"They rode in together, from the north," Felipe continued. "Then two of them rode south, jefe. I'm surprised we didn't see them on the trail to Pueblo de Los Angeles this morning . . . but this could have happened last night. One of them, leading a packhorse—one of the wheelers from the wagon—rode west, toward Santa Buenaventura; another rode up the Santa Clara River, east; and another rode north, backtracking the way they came in. All of them, except the man with the pack, rode out in a hurry."

"How do you know it was a wheelhorse, *viejo* . . . and how do you know it wore a pack?"

"He carries a canted shoe . . . just a little off, but off.

Makes him appear duck-footed. He was unhitched from the wheelhorse position." The old man walked to the tongue of the wagon and pointed. "From here, jefe, off wheelhorse. A big animal, and loaded heavy with a big man or a heavy pack when he left. Probably a pack . . ." The old man walked to the rear of the wagon and picked up the scraps of the leather boot. "He made something with the boot leather, jefe. Probably contrived a packsaddle to carry whatever he stole from the wagon."

"Four directions," Juan pondered, accepting what the old man had told him as fact. Felipe had seldom been wrong in the forty years he had ridden for the Diegos. "They went in four directions, then so shall we—"

"But, *Padre*—" Enrique snapped angrily.

"Do not challenge me, muchacho," his father snapped almost as quickly. "We split up and ride in four directions. I want these men captured."

"You are wrong, *Padre*. We should ride after—"

"You are riding after Chico. Go into Los Angeles with him and tell Stoddard of our actions. And watch out for the two who rode that way."

"But I'll never catch up with you," Enrique complained.

"True, so return to the rancho and help your uncle watch over the place." *And maybe one of my sons will live,* he thought, but kept the thought to himself. Enrique would be safe at the rancho.

"But, *Padre*—"

"Don't question me, muchacho. Do as you are ordered."

"Sí, *Padre*," Enrique said, angrily quirting his horse, galloping off in pursuit of Chico.

As Enrique disappeared, Juan called the men together, then began splitting them up into mini-posses. Before Enrique was out of earshot, four groups rode out in different directions, tracking the Blue Stripers. Morengo and a group were sent tracking the pair that had headed back toward Pueblo de Los Angeles.

Don Juan Diego, his skilled tracker Felipe, and four of his other vaqueros rode west in pursuit of the man with the pack animal.

Don Carlos slept the sleep of the innocent in the deep cave. Its darkness kept him asleep, well after sunup. Long enough, fortunately, that the mounted men looking for him had ridden up the canyon and down, missing any sign of him or of the cave.

He awoke disoriented, wondering where he was until the odor of guano assuaged his nostrils and then he remembered . . . remembering also the loss of his grandson and vaqueros, and his circumstance.

Collecting himself, he arose, having to use the cave walls to brace himself. He stood, shook out the kinks in his old legs, then moved forward carefully into the light. His bad leg was particularly bothersome with the dampness of the dank cave. He was only a half mile from the gringo camp, and he could see the smoke from the fire, and men on horseback returning. At first he thought of moving on farther up the canyon, then thought better of it. What if he were caught out in the open? What if he could not find another place to hide as good as this one? He could stay right here. They had not found him. Odds were, they would not find him.

His first problem was water. The cave was damp and maybe there was a seep somewhere deeper. He could go deeper, but he could not get out of the sight of the light—it wouldn't do to escape the gringos only to become lost forever in the depth of this hellish place.

He sat in the morning sun, out of sight of the canyon floor, and decided he would wait and rest.

A rush of air awoke him. A massive shape filled the cave opening.

"*Aiee,*" he yelled, lurching back deeper into the darkness.

The condor was just beginning to fold its wings, secure on

its perch, but he, too, was startled. It flared them again, then turned in the tight space and ran and launched itself off the face of the cave. It disappeared for a few seconds, then its powerful wing beats caught and it rose, and the old man could see it escape, fighting to gain altitude.

Don Carlos caught his breath, then chuckled. "Not yet, old bird, not yet."

Then he climbed to his feet and worked his way back in the cave. He felt no water on the walls, but stepped in a spot that sucked at his boot as he pulled his foot away. He backed up, and used the wall to help him get down to his knees. Feeling around, he found the wet spot. His boot print had filled with water. He lowered himself until he could put his face down and sucked up a little of the brackish blend, happy that it was too dark to see what he was drinking. He found a loose rock and scraped at the spot until he had a hole the size of both fists. He smiled in the darkness as he felt the seep begin to fill with water. It would do. It would do just fine.

Again he moved forward to be near the opening, and shut his eyes and rested. Then he thought, *el que canta, su mal espanta,* he who sings, frightens away his ill fortune. He began to hum, and then sing in low tones. It, and the water, would get him through the day.

Jory Mortenson stomped around the camp a half mile away. "You bloody fools," he yelled at no one in particular. "How the hell you could let a feeble old man get away from you . . . you bunch of bloody soggers."

"Go out again. Up that west canyon where his tracks led. This old greaser's not smart enough or well enough to back-track. He's stumbling along up there somewhere and you soggers have missed him."

He yelled at two of the men who had returned to camp. "Saddle up again and go find him. He's money, you bastards, gold on the hoof. Now find him. Rope the old greaser and drag him back here."

One of the Blue Stripers turned back. "That'll kill the old man."

"I don't give a damn if it does. If it doesn't, at least he'll be stove up enough that he won't be able to wander off again." He stomped back to his tent. "Damn the flies, damn the bloody flies," he snarled and went inside out of the heat. He had to think.

Clint had dressed himself and was on the porch in the breaking dawn by the time the women began to rustle.

He was feeling much better. He could move without getting nauseous and dizzy, and the shooting pains that had troubled him were now only an ebbing ache.

The sun barely lay over the mountains to the east when Davylou brought him out a cup of coffee.

"I guess you missed the excitement last night," she said.

"Excitement?" he asked.

"Mr. Toy, the Chinaman who brings me the eggs, told me. Just after midnight a pair of riders came in at a full gallop . . . one of them you know a little too well . . . Enrique Diego. And one of the Rancho Del Robles Viejo vaqueros."

"Did they find Don Carlos?" Clint asked.

"No. Seems the stage was robbed and the driver, the guard, and three passengers killed. A drummer and—God save us if it's coming to this—a pair of women. One of them only a young girl, so the Diego riders said."

Clint sipped the hot brew, then asked, "Who found them?"

"Don Juan and the Diego vaqueros. Seems they were out looking for Don Carlos."

Maybe I'm out of a job, Clint thought, *if Don Juan decides to go after Don Carlos himself.* "Did Stoddard head out there?"

"He did with a posse of townsmen and a man from the stage stop leading a team to bring the coach in. They stole the team or ran them off. Enrique said his father and more than two dozen vaqueros were hunting the killers already. I'd hate to be those fellows, with three or four dozen angry men on my trail."

"Still no sign of Don Carlos?"

"He wasn't even mentioned."

"Did Enrique stay in town? I'd like to talk with him."

Davylou laughed. "I bet you would. But that's not wise. You wait until you're well and out of my place of business before you settle any grudges with Enrique Diego."

"No, Davylou. I really mean I'd like to talk with him."

She studied him for a moment. "I'll get the word out, if you're serious. Even if he went back to the rancho, he'll be at MacKendrick's housewarming day after tomorrow. I recall that you're invited, too, if you feel up to it by then."

"I feel a lot better."

As they talked, the stage rattled by, driven by the hostler who kept the stage-line horses at the stage stop on the edge of town.

He heard later that the two bodies—the woman and girl child—were taken to Jorgenson's and would be buried the next day. The driver and guard were taken back to Santa Barbara, where they had lived, and the drummer, unknown to anyone, had been buried where he had fallen.

Enrique sat at the table with his uncle Jacques and his aunt Angelina, a plate of fruit and chocolate-filled tortillas in front of him, hot coffee in a mug in his hand, glaring at his uncle who returned the look in kind.

"So," Jacques chastised, glaring down his long nose, "you've returned to the rancho because of finding this pilfered stage?"

"As I told you, Uncle, Father instructed me to return—"

"While he and the vaqueros are off on a wild-goose chase and while your grandfather is God knows where."

"I wanted to go—"

"You wanted to go chasing *banditos,* not looking for your grandfather."

Enrique's face began to redden. "You criticize me, while you linger here at a full table, with the women."

"Don't insult me, muchacho. You are not so old—"

"Stop this!" Angelina shouted. "Both of you." She arose and wrung her hands. The plate of food in front of her had not been touched. "If you two do not go in search of my father, then I will."

Her two daughters, Conce and Chita, entered the room to hear their mother's outburst. "We will go with you, Mama."

Jacques slammed a hand on the table. "You will do no such thing. None of you are going anywhere." Then he calmed and his voice lowered. "Tomorrow night, Friday night, is the MacKendrick housewarming. We will attend it. We will prepare to go on Saturday. If Don Juan and the vaqueros have not returned by Sunday, then after mass Enrique and I will go to the spot where the others were killed and see if we can pick up a trail."

"You swear?" Angelina asked, and sank back to her seat, while the two girls joined them at the table.

"I said I will, and I will," Jacques said quietly.

The girls looked from one to the other and spoke almost in unison. "We will go look for Grandpapa—"

"You will stay here," Jacques said with finality. "That's final."

Conce turned to her cousin. "Tell us about the stage."

He did so, relating the discovery of the bodies and his father and the vaqueros splitting up, and then his own trip into Pueblo de Los Angeles to report the news.

"And is Sheriff Stoddard doing anything?" Conce asked.

"He rode out with a posse just after sunup . . . after he spent half the night questioning me."

"What would you know about the stage that you could not tell him in a few minutes?" Chita asked.

"He did not question me about the stage so much, but about shooting . . . the gringo, El Lazo."

Conce looked up from her plate. "And Señor Ryan, how is he?"

"The sheriff said he was doing fine. He should be leaving soon."

Jacques rose to leave the table. "And Sheriff Stoddard obviously did not arrest you for assaulting Señor Ryan."

"Obviously," Enrique said, not lifting his eyes from his plate.

"Obviously, you continued the lie."

"Stop this," Angelina said, rising again. "That is the past—"

"Unless Señor Ryan takes a turn for the worse," Jacques said.

Enrique's gaze rose to meet his uncle's. "The sheriff said he was fine and would be leaving soon."

Jacques started for the door. "Let's hope so. You bring shame on this family."

"Please," Angelina cried, ready to bury her face in her hands. "Please, please, let's all stop this."

Morning brought Don Carlos out to the mouth of the cave and into the warming sun. The cave was a fine place to hide, but even with the stifling heat outside, its dank darkness chilled one to the bone.

He carefully peered out the mouth, wondering where the men from the camp might be. Smoke curled up from their campsite down the canyon. He put the thought of beans and bacon out of his mind. He had water, and so long as he had water, he could last for days—but each day, he knew, would weaken him if he had no food.

By tomorrow, he must find a way to get something to eat, or his refuge might become his mausoleum.

But that was for tomorrow, for a time when his pursuers

would think he was far away. When they would be unwary, even if he had to sneak back into camp to find something to eat.

He lay down and inched out onto the ledge, knowing he was invisible from the distance to the camp.

Across the canyon he heard the telltale low call of the quail, ending in a sharp note. Answering from near his cave, came another owllike cry and the same sharp-noted ending answer.

Quail. He loved quail. Now if only he could find a way to build a trap, and something to bait it with. He still had the flint and steel, and could make a fire and cook them if he dared—but the elusive quail, only steps away, might as well be miles from his fire if he had no way to trap them.

His old eyes searched the hillside while his memory searched what the Indians, the Fernandinos and Chumash, had used to build and bait traps.

His pursuers had youth and vigor, but he had stealth and cunning bred from years of knowing the land.

He would win this waiting battle with the gringo camp down the canyon—if he could trap the quail.

Then he heard the clump of horse's hooves—and they were very close.

He dare not try to move back into the cave.

He dare not move at all.

And they were coming closer.

Ten

By the fifth day from his shooting, Clint was up and about
and only favoring the wound slightly. It had not broken open,
and he had even gone out to Davylou's barn to curry Diablo
and do some work on his tack. As he curried the big horse,
he thought about how things had transpired.

His appetite was up, in more ways than one, but neither of
the women had sashayed into his room since two nights ago.

Tomorrow night was the *bendición,* the housewarming, at
T.S. MacKendrick's home. A home and rancho the man known
as El Boticario, the druggist, had won from an old Californio
who had killed himself not long afterward, or so Clint had
heard. And Clint had mixed feelings about going. About joining in the blessing of a home won in a poker game. A poker
game that had resulted in a proud old man's killing himself.
It didn't sit well with Clint.

But then, Clint knew it was not his place to judge. If a
man worried about all the injustice in California, he would
have time for little else.

And Don Carlos Diego . . . where was he? Davylou Boxworth's supper table was as good a place to learn the news
as the lobby of the *Los Angeles Call,* and Clint had certainly
been able to keep up with local happenings since he had fre-
quented the table. No one had any word about old Don Carlos.
His son, Don Juan, and thirty vaqueros had ridden out in

search of him and ended up riding after the murderers who robbed the stage.

Sheriff Stoddard and a dozen Los Angelinos deputies had ridden out after them. Four dozen men were on the trail of the murderers, and a dozen of the Diego vaqueros had ridden right back into Los Angeles yesterday, claiming they were trailing two of them—but they had not turned them up in the pueblo as of yet, and no one had seen any strange men leaving.

Enrique had not shown his face back in the pueblo, and Davylou had put the word out that Clint wanted to speak to him. Maybe that conversation would take place at MacKendrick's *bendición*.

Clint had also heard that the *abogado* Alverez had hired a bunch of vaqueros to begin rounding up cattle on Rancho Del Robles Viejo, and they were looking for buyers for as many as a thousand head.

The horse auction at Rancho Agua Caliente had been postponed again, since the lawyers could settle nothing as the main judge in Los Angeles had been killed—George Willington.

"And there was still no clue as to who had killed the fat alcalde, and probably would be none, as Sheriff Stoddard was busy chasing stage robbers.

"Señor Ryan," the lilting voice rang out behind him.

He turned to see Esperanza backlit in the barn doorway.

"Buenos días, señorita," he greeted her. "Why is it Señor Ryan again, and not Clint or Lazo?"

"Clint, then. Mrs. Boxworth said to come and tell you the noon meal is almost ready. We expect guests again today, and she thought you might like to freshen up."

"I would. Thank you, Esperanza."

"De nada."

Clint watched the pleasant swing of her hips as she headed back to the big house; then he turned back to the stallion.

"It's going to be a long, cold winter on the Kaweah, old

stud. For me anyway. Maybe I can still find a few new mares
for you."

The big horse shook his head and nickered as Clint led him
back into a stall and shut the gate.

At the dinner tables, with more than a dozen gathered
around, Clint was surprised to see two uniformed men. Fully
outfitted in dragoon uniforms, with shako hats removed but
perched on the sideboard behind them, they were already
seated when he got down from his room and his washbowl.
Davylou introduced him to Captain Alexander Tabor and Lieutenant Dudley Winchurch of the California Mounted Guard.
Sabers rattled as they stood, reminding Clint of a time when
he had ridden beside Kearny's similarly uniformed U.S. Dragoons at the battle of San Pasqual. The lieutenant was dark
haired but clean shaven and trim; the captain wore a full head
of wavy hair, bushy mustache, and the version of a goatee
known as an imperial, almost six inches and flowing in
smooth wavelets until it lay on his chest. He looked a bit
pompous to Clint.

They returned to their seats and Clint took one across from
them, with Davylou at his left at the head of the table nearest
the kitchen door. Esperanza was busily bringing in plates of
steaming food.

"So, gentlemen, what brings the California Guard to Los
Angeles?" Clint asked.

"A fort location in Southern California," the lieutenant answered.

"That brought us to San Pedro," the captain added, "but
this trouble with the so-called Blue Striper gang aroused my
curiosity. I understand you may have had a run-in with them."
The captain had a habit of stroking his long imperial as he
spoke, or was deep in thought.

"I doubt it," Clint said as he helped himself to chili con
carne, squash, tortillas, and a generous slice of beef haunch.
"I was shot at a fortnight ago, but I saw no one. It could

have been a lone Indian horse thief, a highwayman after my poke, or God knows who."

"Do you think the Stripers had anything to do with this missing ranchero, this Señor Diego?" the lieutenant asked.

The conversation continued until, on closing, the captain surprised Clint with, "I'm going to contact the governor and see if he'll authorize the guard to become involved in this search. This is just the kind of thing for which the guard was formed . . . in addition to the Indian problem, of course."

"Indian problem?" Clint asked. He had long believed that the so-called Indian problem in California was really a problem the whites had with the Indians just being there, not them causing any particular problems.

"You haven't heard? The Yocuts and Miwok are raising all kinds of billy-joe-hell—pardon me, Mrs. Boxworth—in the San Joaquin Valley. We got the report right before we sailed out of San Francisco."

"Where in the valley?" Clint asked, suddenly alarmed. He had long had a peaceful relationship with the Yocuts around Rancho Kaweah. If they were up in arms, he should be home.

"All the way down the valley," the captain put in. "Ranches and mines have been hit. Stock and food stores stolen, shots fired."

"But no one killed?" Clint asked, worried about Gideon and Ramon, whom he'd left behind.

"No reports, as of the time we left," the captain said. "But that could change in a hurry, with the whole country up in arms. We're ordered to ride on over the Tujungas and into the valley from the south as soon as we're finished with our business in San Pedro."

Clint finished his meal in sullen silence. He should saddle up and ride out, but he also knew he should give his side at least another two days to heal. He would do no one any good, bleeding to death on the trail.

Just as he sopped up the last of his plate with a tortilla, Davylou's young stable hand, Pedro, ran into the room. "Come quick," he said, almost out of breath. "Don Carlos Diego's vaqueros have hung two gringos."

"Gringos?" Captain Tabor snapped, rising and reaching for his cover. The tall hat was centered on his head and his sword hooked up before anyone could answer.

"Gringos," Pedro repeated. "Behind the stage station."

"By the gods," Tabor growled, "we'll see about this. There's gonna be hell to pay."

The riders, a pair from the camp, reined up almost directly below the ledge where Don Carlos lay—lay perfectly still, hardly daring to breathe. They were so close he could hear them as one dismounted and relieved himself in the brush.

"The old bastard has probably wandered into a ravine and fallen, or his old black heart gave out," one said.

The other answered, rather tentatively, "It's just as well. I been thinkin', Rosco. That Mex what got away will be leadin' half of Los Angeles back here. Mortenson is a crazy man if he thinks there's any money to be had out of his old hide when he's dead, or gone. Hell's fire, we ought to light out of here."

"You may be right, Norvel, but not without some grub. Let's pick our time. We been out long enough. Let's go back and tell him we rode all the way to the top of the canyon."

"Suits me. You lie and I'll swear to it."

He could hear them clomp away.

Don Carlos waited until they had time to ride all the way back to camp. He had spotted some greasewood and buck brush nearby, so he worked his way over on his hands and knees, using the sharp flint to cut away several branches of each. He thought it safe, as the gringos had just been there looking for him. The likelihood that others would return was slight, he hoped.

Don Carlos hobbled back into the cave and went to work. He carefully wove the fine branches of the greasewood around the frame of buck brush. He had no sinew as he had seen the old Indians use to tie off the intersections of branches in the cages they had so carefully constructed, but he did have the fine striplings from the greasewood bark, and he used it as best he could.

When the two-foot cage was complete, it was not pretty, nor did it have the box shape of the cages he had seen the Indians make; rather it was rounded, like half a ball. A crude basket. But it would do. He was getting gut-gnawing hungry and weak, but he could not risk going out as far as he knew he must to trap the quail.

He would have to set his cage up after dark, and hope for enough moonlight to find something to bait it with. He had noticed some light-green low plants down the hillside, and hoped it was dove weed. If so, he could gather some of its fine seed—he knew the dove loved it, and he hoped the quail would.

But it would have to wait until dark. It would mean another day without food, but that was as it must be. At least he had water.

He lay back and rested, pleased with his progress, and hummed a low tune to keep his mind off his growling stomach.

Clint arrived, still moving slowly, at the wide oak out behind the stage stop after a crowd had already gathered.

Swaying slowly, two men, heads awry, already blackening tongues distended, bulging eyes staring, swung from ropes thrown over a hefty branch. No one from the crowd of several dozen moved to lower them until Captain Tabor stepped forward with Lieutenant Winchurch in tow.

"Get under one of them, Winchurch," the captain commanded. "You there," he yelled at one of the bystanders. "Help him lower that man."

"General or no blamed general, I ain't touching no dead

man," the man said, and slunk back into the crowd. Tabor puffed up, but did not correct the man for the substantial promotion in rank. Another bystander stepped forward and steadied the hung man's legs as Winchurch took up a position opposite him. Tabor cut the rope's tail, tied to the trunk of the oak, and Winchurch caught the man's upper body. He and the volunteer lowered the corpse to the ground. They repeated the process with the other.

"That man's name is Adolph," someone in the crowd said. "I met him in the saloon a couple of weeks ago. And that other 'un was with him."

"Do you know who did this?" Tabor asked.

"A bunch of vaqueros," another offered. "They found them in the stage barn, hiding up in the loft. These here begged for mercy, but they just strung them right up. Said they was the stage killers and that Stoddard weren't here to do it."

"By G-God," Tabor stammered, "no matter what these men did, they deserve due process."

T.S. MacKendrick stepped out of the crowd and walked over and looked down at the two dead men. "They did that, Captain . . . deserve due process, I mean," he said, extending his hand. "I'm Thomas Salathiel MacKendrick. The druggist here in Los Angeles." The California dragoons introduced themselves, and MacKendrick continued. "We've got to stop these old Californios from thinking they still run this country. It's English law now." The captain nodded his head in agreement, then T.S. noticed another man in the crowd. "Baltazar, step over here," he commanded. A small Mexican stepped out of the crowd, his hat in hand, his head hanging.

"Who's this man?" Tabor insisted.

"He's the stable hand here at the stage stop. It was already said it was Diego riders. Who exactly?"

"I donno," the man said, without raising his eyes.

"You know every man that rides for Rancho Del Robles Viejo, Baltazar. Don't be lying to me. I'll have the stage company fire you before your hat can hit the ground if'n you throw it. Who was it?"

"I know them by sight, not name. I have to think, señor."

"By God, man, you'll speak up or I'll lock you in chains," Tabor snapped.

"By what authority?" Clint asked, stepping out of the crowd.

It became suddenly silent.

"Ryan, wasn't it?" Tabor finally asked.

"Still is," Clint said.

"By the authority of the governor of the state of California."

"Is this your business?" T.S. asked, stepping over to face Clint.

"It's any man's business when somebody talks about putting a man in irons because he can't remember something."

Antonio Alverez, the attorney, stepped out of the crowd. "Old Baltazar's done nothing wrong," he said.

T.S. ignored the attorney and addressed Clint. "It may be any man's business so long as he resides here, and votes here, and pays taxes here. It's not yours," T.S. said. "This is Los Angeles business, and as I hear it, Sheriff Stoddard has requested you leave Los Angeles, Mr. Ryan."

"That's true, MacKendrick," Clint said without apology. "Still, it's not right to talk about putting this man in irons. Hell, if you send a rider out, those vaqueros will probably come in on their own."

"Or have time to hightail it out of the country," T.S. said.

"I remember some of them, señor," Baltazar said, looking up for the first time.

"How many were there?" Tabor asked.

"A dozen, maybe more, maybe less," Baltazar said.

But Clint and T.S. MacKendrick still stared at each other, their eyes locked. Suddenly T.S. turned away and walked back to the small stable keeper. "Name them."

"Lopez, Candleria, Cuen, Morengo, and some others."

Morengo? Clint thought, *he must be feeling better, his jaw healing.*

"And where are they now?" T.S. asked.

"They rode out, señor. Before these two stopped kicking. They rode out, toward Rancho Del Robles Viejo."

"You give thought to who the others were," T.S. said. "I think the Diegos were with them."

"No, señor," Baltazar said quickly. "Don Juan or Don Carlos were not here. I know them well by sight."

"That is true," Antonio Alverez offered. "They are gone."

"How about the boy Enrique?" T.S. asked, and Tabor and Winchurch paid close attention to every word.

"No, sir . . . I know young Don Enrique. He was not among them."

"I say different," T.S. said, a hard look in his eye. "I saw Don Enrique here earlier. He was in town, and if his vaqueros were at this dirty business, then Don Enrique was leading them. And that Frog, Jacques, was probably with them."

"No, señor—"

"Don't lie, Baltazar," T.S. snapped.

"I do not lie, señor. *Es verdad.*"

"He tells the truth—" Antonio tried to support the diminutive stable hand, but T.S. cut him off.

"How the hell would you know, Alverez? You don't know everything that happens in Los Angeles."

Antonio's eyes flashed with anger, but he said no more and faded back into the crowd.

"My troop is back at San Pedro," Tabor said. "I'll ride back there this afternoon. Late tomorrow, we'll be back. In platoon strength, and we'll ride out to this Rancho Del Robles Viejo and bring these men in. They will stand trial for this." Several men in the crowd voiced their agreement.

"As long as it's by the book," Clint said, getting a hard look from the two dragoons and from T.S. MacKendrick.

"You well enough to ride yet, Ryan?" T.S. asked. "You must be . . . your mouth seems to be working just fine."

"By the book, gentlemen," Clint cautioned, as if he could back up his words—he didn't feel well enough to whip a small boy, much less stand up to three rugged men, and the three or more dozen who backed them up.

"We always abide by the law, Mr. Ryan," Tabor said, "you see, we are the law with Sheriff Stoddard out of town." Then he turned to T.S. "You townsfolk make sure Mr. Baltazar stays close by while I go after my troop; then we'll all take a ride out to this rancho. And I don't want any man going out to try and bring them in. With Stoddard gone, this is the guard's job."

"Suits us," T.S. said, speaking for several townsmen in the growing crowd, all of whom voiced agreement; then he pulled Tabor aside and spoke quietly. "But you may not have to ride on out to the rancho. The Diego family and half the territory is due to join me at my house tomorrow night. I'm having a *bendición*, a housewarming, for my new home. You gentlemen can join us all there. Your platoon can camp nearby." Then he turned his attention to Baltazar again and raised his voice. "You're not planning any trips between now and tomorrow, are you, Baltazar?"

The man shook his head.

"You could end up just like those two," T.S. said, then cut his eyes to Clint, his look challenging.

Tabor and Winchurch stalked off toward the boarding-house, where their horses were tied, and the crowd began breaking up.

T.S. again walked over and stood in front of Clint. "This is not your affair, Mr. Ryan. I don't understand—"

"I just want what's right, Mr. MacKendrick."

"As do all of us. A safe, God-fearing town is what we're after. For us, for our womenfolk and children."

"And the Diego water?" Clint asked.

MacKendrick hesitated a long time before answering. "Why would you say a thing like that, Ryan?"

"Just popped in my mind. Trouble for the Diegos may give them reason to sell."

"That's the Diegos' business, not yours, nor mine. All we want is a safe town."

"Everybody wants that," Clint said, and MacKendrick spun on his heel and left as the crowd dispersed. Meanwhile, four of them loaded the two dead men across a pair of horses' backs for the trip to Jorgenson's Barber Salon and Undertaking Parlor, where they would be properly cared for.

Clint waited until the crowd dispersed, then made his way back to Davylou's.

He had a bad taste in his mouth, and it sure as hell wasn't from Esperanza's biscuits and honey.

Antonio Alverez left the scene behind the stage stop before Clint did. He hated T.S. MacKendrick, hated everything he represented; still, he decided he would not ride out to Rancho Del Robles Viejo and warn the Diegos. They surely knew that the gringos would come calling, that their vaqueros hanging two gringos—even thieving, murdering gringos—would not be ignored by the law.

Had the *zapato* been on the other foot, Antonio wondered if the gringos would be so anxious to let law rule. But it was not. Diego vaqueros had hung two gringos, hung them right at the edge of town. Hung them before onlookers. It was long from over.

He wondered if the Diegos would come to town after what had happened.

Either way, he would win. If Don Carlos did not return, Don Juan would hire him to represent his vaqueros. If the Diegos came to town and protested the arrest of their men, and a fight ensued, he would still win.

As it stood, he figured he had the best of both worlds.

* * *

On his return to Rancho Del Robles Viejo, Morengo went straight to the hacienda, removed his spurs and hung them on one of the pegs provided for that use, then rapped on the big door. Conce answered, inviting him inside.

"Don Enrique," he requested. It was still difficult for him to speak, as he could not open his mouth as he once did.

"Wait in the great room, Morengo, and I will fetch him for you. I think he reclines in his quarters." The girl hurried away. It was not like Morengo to come to the big house for anything, and she knew something must be awry.

Don Jacques heard her rap on the door across the hall from his and Angelina's suite of two rooms, and he came to his door to hear her call to his nephew when he answered. "Morengo is here to see you, Enrique. Something is amiss."

"What is the matter, Jacques?" Angelina asked from her chair near the window, where she sat reading. Jacques was proud of her for learning, and proud of himself for teaching her, for none of the Californio women knew how to read. She was exceptional, in so many ways.

"It is nothing, *ma chérie,* just one of the vaqueros with a rancho problem. I will tend to it."

He pulled off his velvet robe and pulled on a loose shirt, then hurried out to see what was so important that Enrique had to be summoned by one of the men.

When he arrived at the main room, Don Enrique was already deep into conversation with Morengo.

"No, jefe, they denied knowing anything about Don Carlos, denied it to the end, and the sheriff did not come. He has not returned from his search," the big, heavy-jowled man was saying as Jacques walked up.

"What is the problem?" he asked.

Enrique turned to him, obviously worried. "A few of our men tracked a pair of the murderers from the stage into Los Angeles. They hung them where they found them."

"What!" Jacques snapped. "Hung them?"

"Right at the edge of town," Enrique said, looking at Morengo for assurance that this thing actually happened.

The big vaquero merely nodded.

"My God," Jacques said. "Why did you not hold them for the law, Morengo? Why . . . why?"

"They were hiding in the loft of the stage stop. They fought, and one drew his weapon and fired at Paco. He has a slight wound in his upper arm. He was very angry, all the men were. And when it was learned from Baltazar, the stableman at the stage stop, that the sheriff was not there . . . it just happened. It seemed the thing to do."

"My God," Jacques said again. "All may be lost with this. This is not how things are done."

"They were dogs, Don Jacques," Morengo said defensively.

"No matter, hombre," Jacques said, "they were gringos, were they not?"

"Si, jefe, gringos."

"Then there will be hell to pay . . . hell to pay."

"Will they come here looking for us? Will we go to the gringo *juzgado?*" Morengo asked, as if it had just dawned on him what he and the others had done.

"They will come," Jacques said. "They will come. I must think." He spun on his heel and headed back to his quarters.

Enrique let him get inside his door before he pulled Morengo near. "You and the men involved must ride out to Rancho Alimitos, and stay there until I send for you."

"I will send the others, jefe, but I must stay with you. Don Juan would want it so."

"Que sera," Enrique said. Morengo had always looked after him and his brother, and he was not surprised he would refuse to leave him now.

"Si, jefe. *Bueno.*" Morengo spun on his heel and left.

I wish Papa and Don Carlos were here, Enrique thought. *They would know what to do.* But they were not there, and he and the family were expected to ride to El Boticario's *bendición* tomorrow, then leave the rancho on Sunday to go in search of Don Carlos. It would mean leaving the rancho with only the women, and with the men of Antonio Alverez gathering cattle. It was an act he did not approve of, but his father had ordered it. He did not trust Alverez, and never had. He did not like the prospects of this new turn of events, did not like them at all.

I, too, must think, Enrique thought, heading back to his quarters.

Later, at the evening meal, the table only occupied by Jacques, his *tia* Angelina, and himself, Enrique broached the problem. "Jacques, we are expected to ride into the MacKendrick *bendición* tomorrow. Should we go, or stay and watch the rancho?" It was hard for Enrique to ask his uncle for advice; he knew what his father thought of the man—everyone on the rancho did—and he had been given no reason to form his own independent opinion. Still, they were the only ones there.

"Of course, muchacho. The ladies would be very disappointed. In fact, I will insist that all of our vaqueros who were involved in the . . . the incident where the gringos . . . the murderers . . . were punished, will accompany us in case the sheriff has returned and wishes to question them. Stoddard is a gringo, but a fair man."

Enrique stared at him. Jacques wanted to offer up faithful Rancho Del Robles Viejo vaqueros—men who had given their life's work to the rancho—to the gringos. "I have sent them away," Enrique snapped.

"You have what?" Jacques said, throwing his cloth napkin down.

"I have sent them away, all but Morengo who refused."

"Where, you muchacho *stupido.*"

"Jacques!" Angelina raised her voice.

"Into the mountains. Where they will be safe until *Padre* returns. He will know what to do."

"You are a fool, Enrique. A foolish boy who will bring

down this rancho. I pray your grandfather leaves this property in more capable hands."

"Such as yours, Uncle? I will rot in hell first."

"That can be arranged."

The argument went on until Angelina ran to her room, and Enrique stomped out into the night, leaving only Jacques to be attended to by the two Indian servant women.

At supper that night, Clint sat across from Davylou, the two of them the only ones at the second table. The first was filled with boarders, who talked loudly among themselves. But Davylou had no outside invitees, so her table was almost vacant, except for Clint.

She was strangely silent, which suited Clint fine, until after-dinner coffee was served.

"I heard you had a run-in with T.S. MacKendrick today?" she asked quietly.

"Hardly could be classified as a 'run-in,'" Clint said. "More like a small difference of opinion."

"Watch out for him, Clint. He's a hard man."

"I thought he was a friend of yours."

"He is, but I like you just fine, too, and would hate to see you join those two swinging from a rope."

Clint smiled wryly. "It's been tried before, Davylou. By a *bandito* called Cicatriz. I actually had the rope around my neck one time, innocent as a lamb, I assure you, and making my peace with the maker, and the horse was whipped and on his way to sending me . . . probably to Hades . . . but an old Californio don had a quick knife and sympathy for what's right. These Californios follow a hard path with their own law—"

"That's just it, Clint. The law that rules this land is not their law any longer."

"I don't disagree with that, Davylou. I just want what's

right, and sometimes even the law can be wrong. I've seen it so, more than once."

She had no answer for that, but gazed at him for a long while before speaking. "T.S. will use the law for his own end. He's a very cunning man. And most in this town will follow his lead."

Clint laughed. "Seems he has a more than passing interest in the widow Boxworth. That shows his good taste, but not his cunning. If he was so cunning he wouldn't allow you alone at the table with me, now that I'm beginning to feel myself."

Davylou laughed quietly. "You are feeling better, aren't you?"

"Up to snuff," he said. "Up to snuff."

"I don't want to break out the good brandy in front of all these other guests, Mr. Ryan, but I would like you to join me in my parlor so I can pour you a touch."

"And tell me more about T.S.?" Clint asked.

"If that's your favorite subject," Davylou said coyly.

"Hardly," Clint said, but it wasn't true. He was developing a real interest in T.S. MacKendrick and wondered to just what lengths he would go to get the Diego land, and water rights.

He followed Davylou Pearl Boxworth into her private parlor, the only room on the bottom floor of the house that was not open to the boarders.

Davylou closed the door behind them, and by the time Clint was seated, she had a snifter of ambrosia poured and in his hand. Soon after, a beautiful woman was loosening her collar stays and was sitting on the settee beside him.

Don Carlos awakened, feeling weaker than ever.

He decided he must go and place the trap, and at dusk did so. The light green weed he had spotted did turn out to be dove weed, and he gathered more than a handful of its tiny black seeds.

He was able to stay low in the chaparral to place the trap, and still have it in sight of the cave ledge.

Filling his stomach with the water from the seep, he was able to sleep on and off during the night, but awoke weaker than ever.

In the morning, he watched the quail work their way down the slope, and most of them passed the trap, but a pair found the seeds and followed the bait.

The basket trap, with a hand's-width trench dug sloping down and under the trap's edge, with seeds sprinkled down it and up inside the cage, and with stiff blades of grass shoved into the trench walls angling back so the quail could follow the trench in but could not come back against the angle of the grass, had worked as it had worked for hundreds of years. Once the birds started down the trench, following the seeds, they were committed.

Two fat valley quail called from inside the trap.

Now his problem was getting down and getting them, and getting back to the cave without being spotted, and building a fire. He could eat them raw; he had eaten worse in his day, but he felt he needed the nourishment and normality of hot food.

He lay back and thought of them roasting over a hot fire, and the mere thought gave him strength.

Gathering his old legs under him, he started out into the growing light. This time he was afraid to bend low and try to hide. He didn't have the strength and feared he might not be able to get up if he fell. Instead, he walked upright, taking his walking stick, working his way carefully, a step at a time down the embankment to the trap. Unconcerned about who might be watching, of how close the men from the camp might be.

He reached the cage and sank to his knees to retrieve the birds, but toppled over as he bent low and knocked the basket cage aside. So quick that he had no chance of catching one, they were out and away, the staccato beat of their wings an insult to all of his hard work.

He collapsed on his back, heartsick at losing the birds, watching his last chance at survival wing away. If he could get up, after he rested, he probably should try to work his way back to the gringo camp and give himself up.

At least he might get a half plate of frijoles.

If he could get up again.

Eleven

All Clint could think about was healing and getting the hell out of Los Angeles and back to Rancho Kaweah.

Davylou Boxworth, true to her word, had plied him with the finest of brandies and shown her hospitality in the most intimate way—a fact that Esperanza seemed more than aware of as Clint suddenly received no more special attention from the girl. And she once again called him Mr. Ryan.

He lounged about his room, reading the *Los Angeles Call* from cover to cover, and rested, only going down for breakfast and dinner. Davylou Pearl Boxworth treated him just as she would any other guest, with no acknowledgment of the intimacy they had shared just the night before. It seemed a bit strange to Clint, as if he had been there for her pleasure, not the other way around as most women he had known made him think. He chuckled at the thought, a new one to him. She was truly an independent woman, and he wondered whether he liked that or not. He decided he would reserve his decision.

One thing was for sure, Davylou took care of herself and asked nothing of any man.

Now he had to make up his mind about another matter. Would he stay here, stay out of harm's way, or go to the *bendición?* Somehow, he felt he was going into the dragon's lair if he did so. He owed the Diegos nothing. They had been hospitable, up until the time one of them shot him. That seemed to rather equal things out. He had nothing to gain by going to T.S. MacKendrick's home, even though he had been invited by the man at Davylou's supper table—and the man had not recanted the invitation. Still, he might be turned away at the door. He wouldn't be surprised if he was. He had been invited before he had had the falling-out with T.S. MacKendrick over the treatment of old Baltazar.

But he knew he was going. It sounded like it would be far too interesting to miss . . . far too interesting.

Don Carlos did not awake until the sun was high and beating down. It was already skillet hot; it would be the hottest day of the year, he thought, and the thought of the cattle on his ranchos came to him. Did they have enough water? Were the water holes full? Did those he had left at his ranchos remember to irrigate the vineyards and orchards?

Why was he worrying about those things? He was about to go to the Creator, where vineyards and orchards did not need watering, he was sure.

He feared trying to get up and make his way back to the cave. It was only twenty or so feet up the hill and twenty-five paces down the canyon from where he had slept, but he felt as if it might as well be a thousand miles.

Managing to sit up, he was startled as a ground squirrel scampered nearby, not more than a half-dozen feet away. Ah, if he could only catch even that little beast—then the Lord smiled on him, for on the trail of the squirrel, a fat four-foot-long rattlesnake slithered, unaware of the man who watched him, and certainly unaware of how starved that man was.

With dexterity and strength belying the fact he had been almost starved for a week, and without anything for two days, he moved quickly, lunging forward. Reaching almost as far as his stout walking stick would reach, he brought it down across the snake's back.

The reptile went into thrashing spasms, its rattle singing a death song for whoever was in reach of its fitful lunges, but it was inaccurate, for its back was broken.

Gaining confidence, Don Carlos brought the stick more precisely across the snake's head, then again, until the thrashing stopped.

Don Carlos smiled, raised his eyes, and said aloud, *"Gracias, mi Dios. Gracias."*

Using the flint, he cut the snake's head off and split it down the middle, gutting it. Then he carefully peeled the skin away. It took all of his energy to perform these chores, but he did so and draped the chicken-breast-white length of meat around his neck and struggled to his feet. The thought of cooking the snake drove him onward. He knew he must reach the cave, and he must gather some small dry limbs as he went. To cook out in the open, and risk the gringos' wrath, would be to defeat all he had done, all he wanted to do.

Thinking of his dead vaqueros and grandson gave him new strength.

One deliberate step at a time, he moved back toward the cave.

It took him over an hour, and he was sweating profusely when he finally settled himself down and carefully shaved some fine kindling from the sticks he had collected.

He skewered a six-inch piece of the snake on a branch, then set to striking flint against steel, until he had the shavings smoldering, blew on it until it flamed, then carefully fed other small branches until he had a very small fire. He looked over his shoulder at the cave entrance, pleased that the smoke seemed so diffused that it left no telltale trail.

The snake began to sizzle, and he began to hum.

He had outwitted the gringos again.

He would live, he would gain his revenge. He wished he had some salt.

Then he repeated an old proverb in a singsong voice: *"A buen hambre no hay mal pan,"* loosely translated as hunger is the best sauce.

* * *

The old don Vincente Mentiroso had been a fourth-generation Californio. His great-grandfather had received his land grant from the king of Spain, and the twenty thousand acres of Rancho Vista Grande was one of the finest in the Cahungas. The hacienda had been added to many times and now stretched over ten thousand square feet in the shape of an H, with a front plaza that could accommodate a dozen wagons and teams at a time in its circular drive, and a rear one for garden and entertainment.

And this evening, the front was full of fine carriages, and the rear of *gente de razón* and musicians.

Clint did not mention to Davylou or Esperanza that he was accepting MacKendrick's invitation, which had been granted before he had had the slight misunderstanding with the man—and was never rescinded. He waited until the others left; then he collected his things (for he had an inkling that he might not return) and placed a small pile of gold in the Chinese knickknack bowl to pay for his room and board. Saddling up Diablo, he followed the road west out of Pueblo de Los Angeles to Santa Monica harbor for three miles; then he turned north into Rancho Vista Grande and worked his way up into the hills another half mile, realizing why the rancho had been named as it was. It was truly a grand view, backed by the Cahunga Hills, with the Dominguez Hills to the south and the blue Pacific to the southwest.

When he reached the newly whitewashed hacienda with its clay tile roof—each tile formed over the thigh of the workman making it—he rode around to the rear and tied Diablo to a sandpaper oak, near where dozens of other vaquero mounts were tied. He removed and hung his spurs on the saddle, as the other vaqueros had done. It was immediately obvious to him that this was an affair of great Anglo influence, for at a true Californio event, the vaqueros would have remained mounted, sitting their horses on the edges of the festivities, vying for a place to best see the ladies, and only dismounting to eat or dance.

It was just dusk, and workmen were busily lighting *farolitos,* little lanterns, hundreds of them, along the lanes and lining the walls and fences—the whole hillside took on a festive air. Finely attired dons and doñas in velvets and silks circulated in the newly remodeled hacienda and its back patio, where an orchestra of three violins, a rare imported piano, a bass, and a viola entertained. The vaqueros, more than two hundred of them—dressed much as Clint was—gathered around a pit behind the separate *cocina* building, where two bullocks, four lambs, a dozen sandhill cranes, and as many peacocks, were being turned slowly as they basted in their own juices over pits of glowing coals. Dozens of quail, snipes, and ducks lay on grills, and great pots of pork-packed *chili verde* bubbled. Clint knew there would be beef and lamb heads buried in deep pits. Drippings sizzled on red-hot charcoal and wafted odors to make the mouth water. Smoke, steam, and enticing smells roiled from the *cocina* itself, where a dozen women slapped tortillas and stirred delicacies while others came and went with trays for those inside to nibble from.

The *aguardiente* flowed freely outside, and fine wines and champagnes inside. Clint found a plank bar set up near the pits with kegs of *aguardiente* and red wine, and filled a mug for himself, then wandered among the men, looking for some he might recognize.

It was only a moment before he saw Morengo and his *patrón,* Enrique Diego, talking with a group of vaqueros. Enrique was the only one dressed as if he should be inside with the *gente de razón.* Clint carried a small Allen's pepperbox stuffed in his belt inside his shirt, and noticed that all of the vaqueros seemed to be unarmed, with the exception of a few knives at their waists.

Without hesitation, Clint joined the group.

Morengo recognized him, but Enrique obviously did not,

as his gaze passed over the newcomer, then returned to the man to whom he spoke.

Morengo extended his hand, his speech still stilted but now understandable through a slightly open mouth. "Lazo. You seem to have recovered well."

"As have you, I'm glad to see."

Enrique stopped in midsentence and turned to face the man he had not spoken to since he had fired a lead ball into him. There was no anger in Enrique's eyes, but no fear, either. "I'm sorry, Señor Ryan, I did not recognize you." Enrique offered a nod of acknowledgment, but did not extend his hand.

"No reason you should," Clint said wryly. "You only met me for a short time and I was at a serious disadvantage while your vaqueros held my arms, then again while you were armed and I was not."

Enrique said nothing, but Clint could see he was shamed. "It has been a difficult time for the Diegos," he said quietly.

"I can understand that—"

"Possibly I should offer you my apologies . . . if you truly had nothing to do with my grandfather's abduction."

"How many times must I proclaim that? . . . Possibly I should accept your apology, if I thought it sincere," Clint said.

"Then I take you at your word and offer my hand, as well as my regards." Enrique stepped forward and extended his hand.

Clint seldom hesitated to take the hand of a man when it was offered in friendship, and he only hesitated a moment this time. He shook. "That's good enough for now, Diego, but I'm not sure it makes us even."

"That is for you to decide, Lazo, but I'm glad you seem well."

"I guess it is for me to decide, and I guess I'll reserve that right for a while."

"That, too, is for you to decide."

Clint offered his glass and toasted with the man. It was a

truce, if little else. Morengo slapped him on the back and guffawed. "Come," he said, "we need to refill our mugs."

Clint walked with them to the plank bar and topped his *aguardiente* off, slightly surprised that Enrique Diego was able to overlook what he had done with such aplomb—right or wrong, the young Californio had style. They made small talk for a while, and Enrique informed him that he and Morengo and the Frenchman, Jacques LaTour, were riding out at dawn to go back to Condor Canyon to hunt for his grandfather; then he excused himself to join the *gente de razón* in the hacienda.

As was always the case when more than two vaqueros got together and were not working cattle, the horse races began; the course, a rough one through the hills for almost a mile, lay lined with *farolitos*. Still, it was a dangerous ride in the dark. Clint had seen ranchos won and lost at these contests, but the betting here seemed to be limited to a few coins and fine woven headstalls and reins and romals—which was all many of the vaqueros owned. Then a contest of riding skills called *carrera del gallo,* the rooster pull, began. Roosters were buried up to their necks in a wide flat behind the *barbacoa* pits, and at full gallop the vaquero would swoop low out of the saddle and try to snatch the head off the chicken—the winner was awarded one of the buried, slow-roasted lamb's heads, *cordero cabazo.*

The tempo of the music increased, and the crowd gathered around the patio to observe the dancers who formed up under an *emramada,* arbor, erected over a well-packed dirt floor. Clint climbed to the top of a high wall enclosing the rear patio and sat with legs dangling, seeing Davylou, for the first time, dancing with the host, T.S. MacKendrick. She saw him on the wall and her look registered surprise. She whispered something to her dancing partner, who gave Clint a hard look, but continued with his dance. Also among the dancers were Esperanza and the Diego girls, Conce and Chita.

None of the women lacked for a dancing partner, as there were many more men in attendance than women. Esperanza,

Conce, and Chita, and many of the other younger women, were clad in bright-colored, full but low-cut gowns with layers of flounce over silk stockings and satin shoes. Esperanza, who was bare headed, sported a lace *rebozo,* which would be taken from about her slim waist and used as a head covering during the religious part of the festivities. Other women were dressed more conservatively in black, which demonstrated to all that they were wed. The Diego girls wore expensive, intricately carved tortoiseshell combs, which staked their hair in place, as well as a triangular black lace mantilla, which flowed down their slender backs. Both had pink pearl necklaces that hung well below their waists, and the jewelry swirled with abandon as they did. Esperanza could afford no mantilla, but rather had bright flowers pinned in her coal-black hair, which had been piled on her head.

The Californio girls, both señoritas and señoras, would slip away into groups to smoke long thin cigarettes, much to the disdain of the gringas, the Anglo women, who thought it a pagan habit at best, and a male one at worst.

More than once, Clint caught Esperanza's flashing eyes picking him out of the line of onlookers perched on the wall as she swirled and twirled, and he noted that she was the most graceful dancer of all the women.

Standing regally robed on the hacienda steps, attended by two simply frocked priests, was the bishop in a white-linen embroidered tunic and red-trimmed vestments. He had made a special trip up from San Diego to perform the hacienda's *bendición.* The hacienda housed its own chapel—now a lonely place with a gringo ranchero—as did all the regal homes of the Californios.

Clint climbed off the wall during a break in the music to refill his glass, and was surprised to find a group of a half-dozen uniformed California Guard dragoons at the kegs, freely partaking of MacKendrick's hospitality.

After filling his mug, Clint turned to them. "You fellows are with the guard?"

"That we be." A barrel-chested man, wearing sergeant's stripes, stepped forward, then placed his hands on his hips. "And what of it?"

"Not much," Clint said, not liking the man's manner, particularly after recognizing him as a fellow Irishman.

"An what does that suppose to mean, boyo?" he asked, sidling a little closer.

"It means, not much, bucko. You fellows are up from San Pedro?" Clint continued, wanting no trouble.

"That we are, fresh from a devil of a voyage down from San Francisco."

"I've made it many times, and it can be rough," Clint agreed, extending his hand. "I'm Clint Ryan."

"So ye are, and I'm Sean Flannagan. What brings you among these gentlefolk."

Clint smiled. "A fandango is not a shindy to be missed, not by any decent Irishman within a day's walk."

"Well, we rode. Maybe you and I will show these Mexe's real dancin' and do a bit of the cloggin' later. . . ." Clint laughed, and Flannagan continued. "Ye look more the Mexican yersef, Clint Ryan, if it weren't for the yellow in yer hair and eyes the color of the Emerald Isle hersef."

Clint knew the man was making fun of him, but he decided to let it go as the last thing he needed was a fistfight with a burly sergeant, and an Irish one at that. He offered his mug in toast, "To the Emerald Isle."

"To Ireland," the sergeant said, upending his mug.

"By God!" a voice rang behind Clint, and he turned to see Lieutenant Winchurch stride up. "I told you lads to take positions at the rear gates, not by the bloody bar." He slapped the mug out of the sergeant's hand, and Clint could see the hair stand up on the back of the big man's neck. Flannagan was on the verge of slapping back, and Clint knew it wouldn't be a clay mug, but rather the clean-shaven lieutenant's mug that he went after. However, the big Irishman collected himself just in time, glared for a moment, then turned to his men and pointed.

"You four take a position at the far gate. The rest of ye tag after me."

Clint watched them go, then turned to Winchurch. "You fellas made it back double time."

"Ryan, wasn't it?"

"Yes, Clint Ryan."

"When there's business to take care of you can count on the California Guard."

Clint almost laughed. The man sounded like a recruiting poster. "You're here after the men who lynched those two murderers?"

"That's our business, Ryan. You just stay clear of this."

"Not my problem," Clint agreed with an unconcerned shrug.

"Humph," the lieutenant managed, then spun on his heel and headed back around to the front of the hacienda.

Clint set the mug aside and strode into the patio, passing Sergeant Flannagan and a pair of his dragoons as he did so. The music and dancing had resumed, and he searched among the dancers for Enrique Diego, finally spotting him. He moved near him and grabbed his arm as he twirled by.

"Ryan—" he began, irritated at being stopped.

Clint drew him near. "There's a troop of dragoons here, claiming to be after those who hung the stage robbers."

"I should warn Morengo," Enrique said, starting to pull away.

"I think you should take warning yourself, Diego." As he said the words, he looked up to see MacKendrick, Captain Tabor, and Lieutenant Winchurch walk out of the hacienda and stand on a raised step that overlooked the dancers.

"What do you mean, Lazo?"

"I mean I think MacKendrick means to involve you in that lynching. If I were you—"

"Don Enrique Diego!" Tabor shouted out over the crowd,

and Clint could hear the music begin to fade and see Mac-Kendrick pointing fifty feet through the crowd to where he and Enrique stood. "There he is, with that bloody Ryan."

"See what I mean?" Clint asked, but Enrique Diego was already fading back into the crowd, made up of almost an equal number of Californios and Anglos. The Californios began to close in front of Enrique's retreat, keeping even Clint from following.

A group of dragoons fell in behind MacKendrick and Tabor as they charged into the crowd, with MacKendrick pointing and shouting, "Stop those men."

Esperanza stepped out of the crowd and pleaded with Clint. "Go from this, only trouble can come to you."

Clint nodded, thinking it was likely he would be tarred with the same brush MacKendrick was trying to use on Enrique, then charged into the crowd of Californios. He glanced back to see Esperanza, Conce, and Chita group together in front of the charging MacKendrick and dragoons, blocking their path with a fence of seeming frail femininity armored with wide skirts.

"Over the wall," Clint shouted as he caught up with Enrique and Morengo, "the gates are guarded."

Then bedlam broke out as a score of dragoons, rifles held across their chests, charged into the plaza from both gates leading out. The Californios and some of the Anglos took immediate offense at the intrusion, even by those who were now their own state troops, and a shoving match ensued.

Clint faded back against the wall as Enrique and Morengo mounted a thick wisteria and scaled it. He hesitated a moment, watching the rear and the growing confrontation as the girls blocked their retreat. Finally he spun and climbed to the top; in the distance he could see Enrique and Morengo making their way into the same stand of sandpaper oaks where Diablo was tied. Clint hurried after them but paused just as he passed the cooking pits, when he heard the sound of shots ring out from inside the patio. Things were really getting out of hand.

He grabbed a fat haunch of sandhill crane off a platter, got the evil eye from a woman carving it, and hurried on. He cinched, mounted, and rode out, gnawing the meat, following the sound of retreating hoofbeats.

In a quarter mile he caught up with them.

"It is only Lazo," he heard Enrique say to an alarmed Morengo.

He drew even with them.

"Thank you, Lazo," Enrique said. "It seems they did mean to make me answer for my men."

"Worse than that, I fear," Clint said. "MacKendrick claimed he saw you in town yesterday. He means to have you part of it, blamed for it . . . maybe hung for it."

"That cannot be gringo law?" Enrique blurted out, astonished.

"It can be, and probably is, for the men who lynched those ol' boys . . . and maybe you, if MacKendrick's lie holds and if you have the law against you."

"MacKendrick is a snake, inviting me into his home only to be setting me up for the gringo law." Enrique seethed in slow anger, contemplating what the man had done. Then his thoughts turned back to survival. "Then we should ride out in search of my grandfather this evening," he said thoughtfully, "before these gringos come in search of us."

"It would be just as well. I'd give them time to cool down before I faced them, and you should ride after your grandfather . . . only this time I'll ride with you."

"It will be a hard ride," Enrique said.

"One I have to make most of anyway," Clint offered. "It's time I headed for Rancho Kaweah."

"So we ride to the rancho, and then on to find Don Carlos!" Enrique declared, spurring his mount into a lope.

Old Mission San Buenaventura sat near the base of the mountain overlooking the Pacific. A half mile below Camino de Real, the old Spanish Highway of the King, ran nearer the beach, and alongside it sat the stage stop, the second two-story building in the group of two dozen mostly adobe hovels that stretched from the narrow, rutted road on down to the beach. Among those was the first two-story structure that had been built in the tiny pueblo. Built from boards brought from northern California by a coastal schooner and floated ashore, the Hakes Saloon and Hotel bragged of having the only rooms for rent between Santa Barbara and Santa Monica—and it did have six, all upstairs overlooking the saloon.

Ezra Hakes charged a dollar and a half a night for a one-quarter share of a bed in one of the tiny rooms, just big enough to squeeze by on either side of the bed. He normally got it without argument—the exception was the wild-looking redheaded man who introduced himself only as "Joe," and who offered Ezra a shiny $5 gold piece for a room to himself. Ezra started to tell him he could have it for much less if he was going to stay more than one night, but the man got irate before Ezra could get the words out of his mouth. Ezra was happy to oblige; his hotel wasn't full and he did not expect it to fill up. In fact, two of his rooms were unoccupied. He would have given the man a private for $2, had he asked, and had he not been such an ass.

When the man asked for a woman, Ezra told him he could oblige with a señorita for the night for $2.50, which the man happily paid in advance at the bar after downing a half-dozen shots of Tubourg's Old Malt, for which Ezra also overcharged him two bits a shot, getting a half dollar when he usually only got a quarter. And Juana, who lived nearby with her four children, usually got $1 a night, giving Ezra half that. Tonight he made a clear $2 profit on the woman's questionable charms.

At this rate Ezra could be on his way back to Philadelphia before the year was out. He wished that more of the men who wandered in looking like no-account drifters actually had a poke full of gold like this one must be toting.

Striker lay back in the bed, watching the plump Mexican

señora slowly undress. He had made a deal to sell his mount and the wheelhorse to the stupid hostler at the stage stop for $100 for the pair, which was cheap—but he could care less, for he had almost $5,000 of the California Coach Company's money in his bedroll. He laughed to himself for the tenth time since arriving in San Buenaventura. Selling the horses to the stage hostler—selling them back their own horses—had been the highlight of his almost two years in California, particularly when he had their money in his bedroll.

Tomorrow he would hire a packet to haul him out to the passing Pacific Mail Line steamship, and in ten days he would be sunning himself in Mazatlán with a pair of more shapely señoritas than this one.

He waved the girl, now immodestly clad only in her chemise, over to join him on the bed. He moved the shotgun he had taken from the stage guard off the bed to the floor. "Turn that lamp down," he commanded. "You are a fine-looking filly, Juana," he said hungrily. "A fine-looking filly."

Don Juan Diego and his vaqueros approached the saloon with care. To their surprise, they had tracked the duck-footed horse in the failing light all the way to the stage stop. It seemed like that should be the last place a stage robber would go. They had been equally surprised when the hostler told them that a stupid brindle-topped man had "sold" him the wheelhorse and another fair-to-middlin' bay gelding. Don Juan had to be told that the brindle-topped reference meant the man was a redhead.

The hostler figured buying the animals was a good way to keep the man in town—the wheelhorse was clearly marked with a C shoulder brand, signifying its ownership by the California Coach Company. Even without the brand, the hostler recognized the animal, having had it in the string for most of a year. The hostler was happy to tell the respectable-looking don that he had directed the man down the lane to Hakes Saloon and Hotel.

The deputy marshal was due back in town in a couple of

hours, having taken a day trip to Santa Barbara on the stage, and he would be interested to know that the redhead had possession of a wheelhorse taken during the recent stage holdup, and that the man carried a sawed-off Stevens double-barrel scattergun just like the one the murdered stage guard, Tommy LeRoy, had carried.

Don Juan thanked the man for the information. He told the hostler that he and his vaqueros were tracking the man and had their own agenda to keep with him. He assured the hostler the redhead would not be leaving town. He also promised the hostler that he would return the California Coach Company's $100 that the hostler had paid for the animals, or whatever the man had left, and inform the deputy, when he arrived, of what else the man might have in his possession.

He had two of his vaqueros at his side when he pushed through the saloon's door and surveyed the room—satisfying himself that no redheads were among its few customers. It was a pigsty of a place, with a month's worth of cigar butts and eggshells scattered over the floor. It reeked of cigar smoke and sweat.

A bald man stood behind the bar, waiting on two vaqueros and a man in a city suit who looked to be a drummer.

Don Juan Diego's two vaqueros spaced themselves at a wide distance apart as their *patrón* approached the bar.

He ordered three drinks, wishing he could have one for all of his vaqueros, but the other nine were spaced around the building, making sure that no one escaped.

But they could drink later, after business was attended to—after he beat answers out of this redheaded man; after he found out if he knew anything of the whereabouts of Don Carlos; after they readied him for the deputy sheriff, if they didn't kill him in the process.

As the bald man brought the don the drinks, he asked him in a low tone, "I seek a man with red hair. An Anglo, who arrived earlier today."

"Oh?" the man replied.

"Yes, I have reason to believe he is here."

Ezra Hakes was not in a hurry to lose the goose who kept laying the golden eggs, so he ignored the ranchero, shrugged his shoulders and scratched his shiny pate, and went on shining the mug. Then, on second thought, he decided this ranchero looked as if he might be another goose. "What do you want with this fella, and what's it worth?"

"I will pay," Don Juan said.

"Pay? How much, if I tell you what room?"

"That is answer enough, gringo." He turned and waved his vaqueros to the stairs.

"Now ya'll wait a minute," Ezra started to complain, but Don Juan brought up the shiny new Navy Colt revolver so the bald-headed Hakes could see it.

Don Juan's voice remained calm. "Clear these men out of here. I would not like them harmed."

Ezra did as he was told. "Come on, fellas," he said, waving them to follow him. "Bring yer drinks. There'll be one on the house when these fellas are through. Don't shoot up the place," he chastised as he led the others out the door.

A prudent man, Don Juan thought, joining his vaqueros on the narrow stairway leading up to the L-shaped landing above.

Slowly he moved up, reaching the top of the stairs.

He inched to the first door, tried it and found it unlocked, nodded to his vaqueros, and flung it open. The room lay empty.

At the next door, he could hear voices. Carefully, with his vaqueros at his rear, his Colt palmed and cocked, he flung the door open.

"What the hell?" one of the four men sharing the bed shouted, as all of them scrambled out of the sagging bed and climbed to their feet.

"If you are not criminals, you have nothing to fear," Don Juan said quietly. Two of them had been sleeping and were rubbing their eyes. Don Juan could barely see in the dim light, so he stepped in and pulled them, one at a time, into the light of the doorway. One man had sandy hair, but the others were dark.

"Damn, the *maldito* is not among them," he said to his vaqueros as he stepped back into the hallway. He counted the doors; two down, four to go.

He motioned them on.

Striker madly pulled his long underwear back up and got them half buttoned, then pulled on his pants. He saw he was never going to get his boots on in time, for he heard the men outside his door.

The woman started to say something, but he hushed her with a cold look. She climbed out of bed and stood behind him, eyes flared with fear.

Striker held his pepperbox in one hand and the sawed-off shotgun in the other. "Quiet," he instructed, cocking both weapons just in time.

The door slammed in and the doorway filled with a broad man. Instinctively, Striker fired both barrels, and the door emptied for a split second as the man careened back across the landing and crashed through the balustrades—his body spun out of sight, then landed below with a thump. Powder smoke hazed the room and scorched nostrils. Then the doorway filled again.

The woman began to scream as two men dropped to their knees in the opening, one on each side, and began firing. Flaming muzzle blasts lit the room like lightning strikes and reverberated like thunder.

Striker got off two shots from the pepperbox, even though the vaqueros' first bullet took him in the throat, passing through and striking the whore in the head, killing her instantly. She crashed back, arms flailing in a desperate effort to cheat death, sweeping the whale's-oil lamp off the tiny bedside table and sending it crashing to the floor. She did not suffer as it lit the chemise she wore and the bedclothes—for she was cold dead—then it flamed to the muslin curtains that covered the single tall window in the room.

Striker, blood pumping in squirts from his torn throat, fell to his knees, throwing aside the spent scattergun but firing the pepperbox as fast as he could pull the trigger, and the vaqueros traded more shots with him. This time two of the bullets took him in the chest, and he staggered back into the growing flames. He screamed a choked cry in agony, "Come on, you bloody soggers. *Yaee!*" Then he faded and died with his red hair aflame.

Others of Don Juan's vaqueros ran into the saloon to join in the fray, and instead they found themselves dragging their bloody, lifeless jefe out of harm's way. The two inside the upper, now shattered, balustrade, both slightly creased with hot lead, crouched against the wall and reloaded their weapons, not knowing that the redheaded man was out of the fight. By the time they again filled the doorway, the whole outside wall of the little room danced, enveloped in flame.

"*Bastardo,*" one of them screamed, and in frustration, he emptied his weapon into the chest of the burning corpse.

The two vaqueros spun and ran to the stairs, taking them three at a time.

By the time Ezra Hakes, screaming and yelling at the top of his lungs, could gather some townsfolk to fight the fire, it had covered the upper story and now snapped and popped, devouring the lower.

Several thousand dollars in gold coins, stored in Striker's bedroll and stuffed under the rickety bed, melted and collapsed along with Hakes Saloon and Hotel into blackened rubble.

The Rancho Del Robles Viejo vaqueros did not bother to help fight the fire. They were just as happy to see the wooden rat's nest burn. They loaded and tied their dead *patrón* across a saddle then, fading out of the firelight into the darkness, they began the long, slow ride home.

Twelve

Antonio Alverez reclined in a ladder-backed chair on the outside landing of the upper story of the building that was his office and home. Smoking, he watched the nighttime activity in the street below and thought. It was not a comfortable place for him, for the two-story clapboard building—two rooms up, two down—had been built by Anglos. He rented it, and he hated renting it, but it was in easy walking distance of the public buildings where he conducted much of his business, and it would have to do—for the time being.

He had been invited to the MacKendrick *bendición*, but he had not attended. He had been a longtime acquaintance of the Mentiroso family, and it galled him that this Anglo now owned their rancho, the hacienda where the three generations of the Mentiroso family had been raised.

Rather than prepare to attend, Antonio had spent the day in Conejo Canyon, one of the many on Rancho Del Robles Viejo. He had continued the business of overseeing—from the comfort of his buggy—the roundup of Rancho Del Robles Viejo cattle. And finding buyers. He had sent riders and contacted two who were making the rounds of the ranchos, and one was due up from San Juan Capistrano in a week and another over from San Bernardino. He had informed them it would be more than a week before he was ready to have them inspect the herd. He had almost five hundred head gathered and should have over a thousand by the time the buyers arrived.

He had done his duty, and Don Juan could not fault him when he returned. But Antonio was in no hurry for the buyers to arrive. The longer old Don Carlos remained gone, the better off it would be for *abogado* Antonio Alverez.

Clint, Morengo, and Enrique arrived at the rancho to find it empty. Don Juan and the vaqueros had not returned, and the servants told them there had been no word of them.

They got fresh horses—Clint's extra mount and mule had been put with the rancho remuda—and a few days' provisions. They rode on into the night until they were well up into the Tujungas and had pushed the animals to exhaustion. Camping where the horses could graze, with water at a tiny trickle, too, they awoke before the breaking dawn and were on the trail.

A low throbbing ache in his side remained Clint's constant companion, but the wound did not open. With the smooth gait of the big palomino stallion, he was easily able to keep up. He rode his second mount only when he knew Diablo was well winded, for the animal was not as smooth, and Clint tired more when astride him.

He knew he would have to be careful not to reopen the wound, to keep his wits and his capabilities about him. Not only did he have to ride with Enrique and Morengo, and come up against God knows what, but he had to continue on to Rancho Kaweah, through the San Joaquin Valley, where the dragoon captain told him there was an Indian uprising. And all this without the horses he had come to find.

So far, it hadn't proved to be the best trip—in fact, it was about the worst he had ever been on.

Now if he could bring this trip to an end without it becoming a total catastrophe.

The second night they made a dry camp, stopping when they could go no farther. They dropped the tack from the horses and hobbled them before they fell where they stood and slept.

By noon on the third day they reached the spot where the carving in the oak lamented Peter Lebec's fate. When Enrique told them it was only a few hours more, Clint insisted they rest and graze the animals and have a hot meal themselves. Enrique did not complain, as it seemed to Clint that he really hated the thought of going back to the spot where his brother and friends had been killed. He feared what he would find.

It was midafternoon, with weapons cleaned and checked, when they saddled up and headed west into the mountains, working their way toward Condor Canyon.

Conce and Chita, dressed in black, paced the floor, mourned, and worried. Never in their few years had things been in such disarray. The vaqueros had ridden in with their uncle, Don Juan, at noon; he now lay in the great room in a simple pine box strewn with flowers. A few of the rancho vaqueros sat outside the hacienda, smoking, wondering where the rest of the rancho's crew were. And they all wondered about Don Carlos.

And the worst of it, at least to the girls, was the absence of their mother and father—news had been brought to the girls early that morning that the gringo law had their parents under arrest.

The whole Californio community around Pueblo de Los Angeles was in shock. Don Jacques LaTour was being held as what the Anglos called an accomplice in the lynching of the murderers who had robbed the stage, and Doña Angelina Diego LaTour was under house arrest at the Boxworth Boardinghouse, the first time a woman had ever been held for any crime in the memory of any Californio. And the Californios did not as yet know of the death of Don Juan. That would add insult to injury.

The arrest of their parents had been at the order of the

California Guard, then confirmed by T.S. MacKendrick, and he now had the authority to do so.

On the morning following the *bendición,* the city fathers, mostly Anglos, had met and appointed T.S. as temporary alcalde—that, too, was a shock to the Californios. He was not among the most loved and respected Anglos by that segment of the community.

The pueblo was quietly seething, rising to the boiling point, ready to blow its lid.

T.S. and Oscar Bonny sat, each with a foot propped up on the leech barrel, sipping an afternoon lemonade.

"Things are happening in a hurry," Oscar said, his tone cautioning.

"It's time something happened around here," T.S. said, a sly smile on his face.

"Let's hope it all doesn't get out of hand. The Diegos are well loved—"

"Hell, Oscar, they'll be out of jail and back home soon. A little discomfort, and fear of the wrath of the law, may just encourage that whole bunch to pull up stakes. It's for the good of the whole town."

"Let's hope it works out that way," Oscar said, eyeing T.S. with a doubtful look.

"Those dragoons were a bit of a surprise, something I hadn't counted on," T.S. admitted, packing his pipe.

"They rode out after Don Enrique?"

"And Morengo, his man, and that Ryan fellow."

"That captain is a bit of an ass," Oscar said.

"He's all right. A bit too military for my taste, but he's turned out to be a help. The more we antagonize the Diegos. . . ."

"So long as that's as far as it goes. He doesn't seem to be the most logical sort."

"That, too, could be to the town's advantage," T.S. said, dragging deeply on the pipe.

"So what you're saying is that anything to the Diegos' disadvantage, is to the town's advantage?"

"So long as they won't turn loose of all that water, that's the case." T.S. took another thoughtful draw on the pipe, then continued, "You can't stand in the way of progress, Oscar."

Don Carlos had his strength back.

He sat in his cave, roasting the last two quail he had trapped, trying to make up his mind if it was time to try to hike out of this canyon.

Figuring he could walk right past the gringo camp in the darkness, now that they must be convinced he was either dead or long gone, he contemplated doing so.

But in his condition, climbing out of the canyon would be a difficult if not impossible task. What if he was only halfway out by dawn? They would see him on the barren canyon wall.

No, it was better to wait. Wait for his family, wait for Juan and Jacques. Where were they?

Where, in the name of *Dios*, were they?

Jory Mortenson would not allow any of the men out of camp. There had been too much dissension among them. He had seen the looks, he knew what the quiet grumbling was all about.

Since Courtney, the Englishman, returned and told his tale of Striker running off with the strongbox, and of the other men going separate ways—the men could talk of nothing but running for it.

In a way, Jory thought, that was fine with him. He had a decent stake already, from the man who had hired him to abduct old Don Carlos in the first place. And he still had the chance to collect the $10,000 ransom, if he played his cards right.

And he wondered if there was not another hole card in all this. How much would it be worth to the man who had paid him to abduct the old don, for him *not* to tell the Diegos. The man had his own secrets about why he wanted it done, and Jory was sure it was worth plenty to him to keep his plan just that, *a secret*.

Hell, he was a long way from being out of the race.

Tonight he would pack up and ride out without the others knowing, leaving the rest of these fools here to take the wrath of whoever might be on Courtney's trail.

If he could wrangle a way to get the ransom, then it would be all his.

To hell with the rest of this mangy lot, to hell with Striker, wherever he may be. And to hell with old Don Carlos. With any luck, the old greaser was at the bottom of some ravine, turning green, feeding his eyes to the crows, or in the belly of some old griz giving him indigestion.

The sun lay on the crown of the mountains to the west by the time the three riders, Clint, Morengo, and Enrique, reached the trail head at the top of Condor Canyon. Enrique waved them to a stop and walked his horse to the edge, then returned.

"They are brazen. I saw two of them riding in from across the canyon. I cannot believe they stayed in this place of death."

Clint cautioned, "Probably best we don't cross the horizon just yet. They saw you coming before—"

"It will be a tough trail in the dark," Enrique said.

"Not as tough as with a hundred bullets splattering around you."

"Es verdad," Enrique said, rubbing his chin.

Morengo, normally a quiet sort, offered, "They will have

a guard on this trail. I will go down on foot after dark and break his neck."

"Neither of us," Clint again cautioned, "are fit for close work. You can't take another shot to that jaw, and with this side wound I'm not fit for a fistfight."

"Then I must go," Enrique offered, and they all knew he was right.

Clint dismounted and walked carefully to the canyon's edge, staying low and in the cover of the buck brush. He studied it for a moment, then returned.

"They're making the evening fire down there. I can see where their camp must be from the smoke. We're all probably better off horseback, and if that bunch is the Blue Striper gang everyone's been talking about . . . we can sure as hell outride a bunch of *marineros.*"

"Your point, Lazo?" Enrique asked.

"Down the way there's a ravine, a few hundred yards up the canyon from their camp. I can't see it all from the edge, but the canyon turns some and I can see most of it, and it looks like we could slide the horses down there. With luck, we'll miss any sentries—I don't think they'll think anyone is crazy enough to try and come in from that direction. It's my guess they're watching the lower canyon, this trail, and that big cut heading west—then when we're on bottom, and if not discovered, we can decide what to do. But we'll never be able to come back up that way, so if we slide into the jaws of hell, there's no turning back and we'll have no choice but ride out through their camp."

Again Morengo spoke. "It would be foolhardy to charge into a camp of a dozen or more armed men. Better one of us slip into the camp in the dark, and try to free Don Carlos . . . if he lives."

"Agreed," Enrique said. "But we need to get to the bottom in order to do so. We will try Lazo's way. No matter what, we have to ride into their camp to find Don Carlos. I hate this trail . . . any other way. . . ." His eyes saddened; then he steeled his resolve and headed for his mount. He turned back for a moment, his eyes hard and cold as granite. "Then we come back to where we can take potshots at the camp, and kill as many of these so-called Blue Stripers as they have killed Rancho Del Robles Viejo men. All of them, with luck."

They mounted and began to work their way north, up canyon to the cut in the canyon wall Clint had seen.

The last light of day had faded by the time they reached the spot Clint had seen—they hoped it was the spot, for to start down anywhere else would mean sure death, at least for the horses. A man might climb out of the canyon, but a horse would never make it, except on the trail.

They tied their spare mounts back in the brush, then sat astride their selected animals and looked down into the dark hole in front of them.

If they survived this steep gash into the depth of Condor Canyon, then a band of killers awaited them.

Finally, after a moment of silence, Clint spoke without looking over. "Well, it was my idea, and this sumbitch ain't getting any easier by sittin' here dawdlin' at it."

He put his spurs to the big horse.

Without hesitation, Diablo sprang forward, but almost immediately stiffened his forelegs and planted them, sitting back on his haunches. Clint leaned so far back his back touched the big stallion's rump. In seconds they dropped several dozen yards, but the horse was still on its feet and Clint still in the saddle.

Diablo found a slightly flattened spot and stopped his descent. Clint dismounted to give the stallion a chance to breathe. He panted deeply and his chest heaved. Then Clint had to mount quickly and spur him again, as another rider was sliding into them.

Again Diablo jumped into the darkness, this section even steeper—rocks rolled away in front of them, a small landslide.

Clint knew the stallion was tiring, then felt the horse's forelegs give under him. Kicking free of the saddle, he was barely able to dismount before Diablo rolled to his side and disappeared from Clint's view. Clint sailed a few feet and landed in one of the few piles of brush in the steep ravine bottom.

He caught his breath, then kicked free of the brush and sat his own heels. Clambering down, he followed the horse's path, alternately rolling and sliding on his butt. He ran into the stallion in the darkness, the big animal on his knees, his chest heaving. Clint worked his way to the front of the stallion and recovered the reins. Again he could hear sounds behind him as the others followed, and rocks careened by him and into them, kicked up by his pursuers. He pulled Diablo to his feet, encouraging the big horse, wanting to move on before being pummeled to injury by the rocks from those above.

Considering leading the animal for a moment—then deciding not to as he would not fare well if caught under Diablo's weight or flailing hooves—Clint mounted once more, and again gave him the spurs.

He thought the worst was over, then Diablo stumbled again. Clint, this time, went over the animal's head, landing hard on his back on an uneven surface. He felt around and realized the ravine bottom was an escarpment of rubble, boulders, and rocks piled with equine-leg-breaking crevices between. He had to get Diablo out of this.

He led the horse back up the ravine a few feet, then worked his way to the side, Diablo slipping and clattering along behind.

He heard another rider across the steep ravine, then a horse scream a cry that sounded more like a mountain cat. Clint hoped the camp did not hear that mournful wail, or if so, did not recognize it as a horse.

Again they tried the descent, and this time only found their way impeded by brush. Clint broke through ahead of the horse and led him until they came to a flat—which Clint prayed was the canyon floor.

They must have descended two hundred yards; if so, this should be the bottom.

He stood quietly, letting both him and Diablo catch their breaths, searching down the canyon for signs of the camp. From his position, he could not see even the glow of a fire. Then he beat the dirt from his pants and shirt, spat it from his mouth, and cleaned out his ears and eyes with a finger.

From way down the canyon, he heard sounds of another rider, then behind him, Morengo stumbled up. He put his hands on his knees, his chest heaving, until he managed to straighten up again.

He whispered, "Lazo, you made it. *Caramba!* That was a ride."

"Not easy. Where's your horse?"

"Broke his leg between some rocks. I had to slit his throat to keep him from crying out."

"And Enrique?"

"I do not know."

"I heard another rider down the canyon. He must have come out there. Let's work our way down."

Then a whispered voice rasped nearby, "I am here. So we have two horses among us." He walked out of the darkness, leading his animal.

"Looks that way," Clint said.

"Soon we will have three," Morengo said. "I will go into their camp and look for Don Carlos, then steal a horse."

"Are you light of foot, Morengo?" Clint asked skeptically.

"As light as most."

"I'm lighter than most. I'll go in. You watch over your jefe."

"Let him go, Morengo," Enrique said. "He will have a better chance. He knows the way of the *marinero,* of the gringo."

"As you wish, jefe," Morengo said, but he was not happy with the decision.

"We will wait here for some moonlight. And for the camp to go dark," Clint said, walking over and stripping the tack from Diablo. He tied the big horse to the branch of some buck brush, while Enrique did the same, then found himself a comfortable spot and dropped to his back and rested.

Don Carlos had been dozing, waiting for darkness so he could go check his traps—he had a second one now—when he had heard the commotion not far from the mouth of his cave. Plus there was the voice of gringos speaking English, mixed with a little Spanish. They were far enough away that he could make none of it out clearly.

He moved to the mouth of the cave and carefully worked his way out on the ledge, listening for them to leave. But they did not.

Not being able to imagine why they did not ride on, he waited, wishing he could pounce down on them when they rode past, like he might have done when he was young. But he knew he could not, he could not even dare fling rocks down upon them.

He wished they would leave so he could check his traps—his cave smelled of roasted birds, and whetted his appetite. As hard as he listened, though, he could not hear the rattle of hooves on the rocks, nor as hard as he watched, he did not see the spark of horseshoes scraping the hard river rock of the canyon bottom.

Now he could not leave. He cursed the gringos and then dozed.

Clint waited until the sliver of moon was a quarter high in the east, over the rim of the canyon. Then he checked the two pepperboxes he carried, stuffed in his belt, and the ten-shot revolving Colt rifle. After that, he began to move quietly away.

"Good luck, Lazo," he heard Enrique whisper, but he did not answer.

The canyon narrowed when he had made only fifty yards. He stumbled on a river rock. He paused for a long while, unmoving, wondering just where the sentries might be. Hearing nothing, he set out again, trying to stay high enough up on the canyon side that he was in the buck brush, and hopefully as high as any sentries who might be watching. Suddenly he caught the odor of cooking. *Chickens? Hell, these men would be unlikely to have chickens in camp.* But he swore it smelled like roasted chickens.

He moved on, careful now, a step at a time.

Don Carlos, ever so slowly, eased his eyes over the rim of the ledge and watched the man below, carefully choosing every step, walking more like a thief in the night than one merely returning to camp.

Don Carlos was puzzled. The man drew even with the cave opening, only fifteen feet below and about a half dozen from the edge of the ledge. Don Carlos fingered a heavy flat rock, a foot in length and half that in depth. It must have weighed fifteen pounds.

Could he hit the man on the *cabeza* from where he rested— if he did so it would surely break the man's neck. Raise the rock over his head and fling it down upon the gringo. Then he caught a reflection off the conches lining the outside seam of the man's *calzones. Maybe the man is not a gringo, maybe he is a* paisano?

Should I call out to him? Don Carlos puzzled. *None of these* gringos *had worn the clothes of the vaquero.*

No, it is best to wait and see.

Then he thought again, *Ahora es cuando, yerbabuena, le has de dar sabor al caldo.* Strike while the iron is hot, so to speak. He stealthily got to his knees and lifted the rock overhead, gauging the distance.

Clint paused, hearing something. He cocked his head and listened, thought he could hear someone's breathing; then a white-footed mouse whistled loudly nearby.

Don Carlos quietly set the rock down again. This is foolish. *If he is a paisano, then I cannot fling this rock down on his head. He is here to help me. If he is not, he is up to some mischief. Let it be, maybe the gringos fight among themselves, if he is a gringo?*

That would be a good thing.

Clint moved on, and Don Carlos carefully worked his way back into the narrow cave opening.

Drawing near the camp, Clint made out the glow of the fire's embers, burnt down, and could make out no one sitting nearby. Carefully he scanned the hillside across the canyon. Surely, there would be a sentry there? But it was too dark to make one out. He found a spot and set the Colt rifle aside, checking its placement in a crevice twice as he moved away so he could recover it on the way out—or if he needed it in a running fight.

He heard a nicker from the remuda, then the answer of another horse in the string.

First he would stake out a horse, and at least get a bridle on him, then he would go in search of the old Californio. He remembered that he had never met Don Carlos. It would be a fine kettle of fish if he shook awake the wrong old man, who turned out to be some old Peruvian or Spanish sailor in cahoots with the Blue Stripers. But old Don Carlos should be dressed like a ranchero, not a *marinero*.

Clint inched his way among the horses, having to cross a small creek to do so, and picked one out. Saddles were lined up nearby and he made his way to them and pulled a bridle off a saddle horn, then back to a tall gray—at least he thought it a gray in the darkness—and bridled the animal, then pulled its lead rope from the tie line and led it a few feet, apart from the others, tying it to a river willow.

Now, he must find the old man.

He decided to survey the camp first, to see if the old man might not be tied up somewhere outside the tents. Carefully he circled the whole camp, then made a tighter circle, this time passing within a few feet of the larger tent, having to cross the creek twice. He moved in utter silence, taking the better part of an hour to make the two circles.

Nothing.

Then, as if he owned the place, he brazenly walked to the flap of the larger tent, a walled one almost fifteen feet long and ten wide, and quietly, but not stealthily, pulled the flap aside and stepped in. It was just too damned dark to see.

He worked his way back outside and to the embers, picked up a one-inch-thick branch and looked for something to wrap around it to create a torch—then he saw a container nearby, among some frying pans and pots that were upside down, near where the cook had made his cook fire apart from the bonfire of the men. Clint picked up the pot and smelled it. He was not surprised when he found it half filled with bacon grease. He dipped the branch in and got it soaked, then walked back to the embers and fed a few branches to the fire, got them flaming, then the end of the branch. While it was blazing, he walked back to the tent and pulled the flap aside.

Only three men were sleeping there. Over each one, in turn, he held the flaming firebrand. When he was satisfied Don Carlos was not among them, he headed back to the flap and reached for it.

"What the hell?" a voice called out behind him.

"Go back to sleep, sogger," Clint said.

"Ye'll burn the bloody place down," the sleepy voice complained.

"An' I'll step on yer bloody head, if I can't see where I'm steppin'," Clint said, lowering his voice an octave, then stepping outside.

He could hear the man grumble, but that was the extent of it. He moved to the other tent, having to cross the little creek again. Pausing in front of the flap, he pulled it aside, again quietly, but not stealthily.

The muzzle flash almost blinded him, and the ball cut the air so close that it passed through his shirt under his arm. He spun away, stumbling over a tent rope.

"By the gods," a man yelled. "You bloody bastards will not be having my gold."

Jory Mortenson had been getting dressed, ready to ride out of camp and leave it to the rest of the men. Let them be here when half of Pueblo de Los Angeles arrived—he wanted them here; maybe that would satisfy Courtney's pursuers, and he could get clean away. He was pulling on the second boot when he heard the commotion at the other tent. There was only one reason those bastards would be up at this time of night—it was too early to be changing the guard—and that was to be leaving themselves. He had heard the grumbling among them, or maybe they were coming to see what they could steal from him before they left.

He had moved away from his bedroll and crouched on the other side of the tent, waiting. And as he suspected, someone had tried to come in his tent. After he fired, he quickly reloaded the old .50-caliber pistol he carried—it would stop a man better than any of the newer smaller calibers—in addition to his Navy Colt. He checked his knife and, with one firearm in each hand, moved to the flap to see what damage he had done to the thief.

Clint had regained his composure and his feet, and was moving away in the darkness at a slow trot. The three men in the other tent swarmed out, blocking his path back to the horse. He switched directions, headed for his revolving Colt rifle, found it, and moved away. He was mad at himself for not getting a look inside the second tent, but whoever was there was damn sure not worried about whom he shot. Clint gathered up the rifle and moved away quickly, secure that the men moving around the camp could not hear him for their own noise.

It would be better to move quickly now, than after they had settled down.

Even if they suspected it was someone else in camp, he counted on them not following in the darkness—and he didn't much care if they did, now that he knew they were only four or five strong. Maybe that didn't count any who might be down the canyon on guard. But still, that didn't make it more than six or seven.

That was a damn sight better than a dozen.

The bad news was, they had them pinned in, for if they

went out on horseback, they had to come this way. And one of them would be riding double.

He was over a hundred yards up the canyon before the camp settled down.

Jory stood, Aston in hand, using it as a pointer. He faced the three men—Courtney, McGillicutty, and the cook Howard, who had run over from the other tent with their own hands filled with weapons. All three of them wore nothing but underwear. "Which one of you sneak thieves was it?"

The men looked at one another.

"Was it what?" McGillicutty asked.

"Which one of you tried to get into my poke?"

Howard, the slender cook, shook his head. "Some bloke tramped through our tent. I thought it was one of the boys up to take a leak. . . . But we was all there when the noise of yer yelling woke us. What 'appened?"

"It was a shot that woke you," McGillicutty said.

"I shot at someone trying to get in my tent," Jory growled.

"Well," Howard said, "t'wern't one of us. We was all in the tent and come running out when we heard you a'yellin' like a stuck pig."

Jory started to take a step to slap Howard with the Aston, then thought better of it. He calmed down. "Go back to sleep, it musta been the banshees."

The other two men, who had been out as guards, came running into camp from different directions. The four there held their guns at the ready, but seeing who it was, lowered them. They answered their questions and sent them back to their posts.

The three men scratched their heads, and other parts of their anatomy, then finally turned and headed back to their tent.

Jory decided to wait awhile, until the camp quieted, to go get a pair of the best horses and load up and ride out.

Whoever the hell that was at his tent flap, it wasn't one of his men—at least not one of the ones in camp. One of the guards could have come back and tried to get to his poke, but somehow he didn't think so. The man at the tent flap was a stranger, someone Jory didn't know. He was sure of it. That's why he had missed, surprised and shocked at not knowing just who the man was.

All the more reason to get the hell out of there before dawn.

Leave the rest of these soggers to get the wrath of whoever must have followed Courtney.

He would be gone with early light. He did not want to try the canyon trail in the absolute darkness. But it would still put him over the canyon rim before the camp was moving.

Gone to Los Angeles, gone to collect the ransom, gone to blackmail the man who had hired him.

Clint stumbled back into the clearing where Enrique and Morengo stood, guns in hand, waiting.

"What happened?" Enrique asked. "Are you hit?"

"No, and I don't think they follow, but no sign of Don Carlos," Clint said. "But they seem to be only a half dozen strong—if a couple were out on guard."

"But no Don Carlos," Enrique said with disappointment.

"I didn't get a look into the smaller tent, and got a face full of muzzle blast for my trying. He could be there."

"He did not yell out?" Enrique asked.

"No, he did not."

"He could have been gagged," a fourth voice said from the darkness.

The three of them grabbed for their guns and centered them on the figure that stepped out of the brush.

Thirteen

"Abuelo?" Enrique asked, stunned, as his grandfather, torn and tattered but seeming healthy, stepped casually from the brush.

"Jefe?" Morengo asked, sweeping his sombrero from his head.

"Sí," Don Carlos said, limping over to Clint. "And who is this hombre?"

"This is El Lazo, who has ridden with us to find you."

Clint extended his hand and received the bony but surprisingly strong one of the old man along with his polite nod.

"And where is *mi hijo,* my son, and my son-in-law, and the rest of my vaqueros?" Don Carlos asked, the irritation ringing in his voice.

Enrique looked a little sheepish. "Papa rides in search of some *banditos* who robbed the stage, and the rest of the vaqueros ride with him, *banditos* who he thought might be the ones who abducted you. And Don Jacques . . . he watches over the rancho." Enrique made an excuse for his uncle. Actually, they had had to leave him at the *bendición* when they fled from the dragoons.

"So my *nieto,* my grandson, and my *segundo,* and a stranger, are the only ones who search for their missing *patrón?"* the old man said, his voice weaker. "The rest of my family leads my vaqueros about the county, or rests at home?"

Enrique stepped forward. "Emilio and all the vaqueros came, but we were shot down like dogs. I was the only one—"

"This much I know," Don Carlos said. "I prayed you lived, and I did not see your mount among those the gringos brought back to camp. But I expected—"

"I'm sure," Morengo offered, "that Don Juan and Don Jacques do what they think is right."

"That is the question," Don Carlos said. "The question is, do they know what is right?" He shook his head sadly, then raised it with defiance in his eyes. "We still have the problem of getting out of here. There is only one way . . . through the enemy camp."

"And we have only two *caballos*," Morengo said. "The rest of the remuda await at the rim of the canyon."

"Then we must borrow a pair from the gringos," Don Carlos said, the old fire returning to his eyes. He nodded to Clint, "No offense meant, Señor Lazo."

"None taken," Clint said, knowing he was going to like this old man. "But we must have a plan, gentlemen, and we must move soon, before dawn."

"If we had horses," Enrique said, "we could charge through camp and be gone before they knew we were there, and be up the trail in the darkness."

"But we don't," Don Carlos said, "so first we must steal them."

"They may be waiting this time," Clint said. "I had a horse bridled and ready to ride, but could not get back to it. If they found him. . . ."

"Morengo," Enrique instructed, "you take Don Carlos on horseback, and stay as high on the cliff side, as far from the camp as you can . . . If that is all right with you?" he asked Clint, as it would put him afoot. Clint nodded—the old man needed a horse—and Enrique continued. "And Señor Ryan and I will go to the gringo horse string and steal a pair of animals. When we fire on the tents, you and Don Carlos ride for the trail."

"Sí," Morengo said, and Don Carlos shrugged his agreement.

Clint went for Diablo, and cinched him up and brought him over and helped the old man into the saddle and handed him one of his Allen's pepperboxes.

"Gracias," Don Carlos said, inspecting the weapon, then the horse. "This is a fine *caballo."*

"True. Treat him well, for we have far to go."

Don Carlos nodded, appreciating a man who appreciated fine horseflesh, then followed Morengo out of camp, staying as high on the canyon side as they could—still their path would take them within thirty paces of the tents. Clint and Enrique checked their weapons, then moved away on foot downslope into the brush.

As they neared the camp, the first gray light of dawn touched the east rim.

Jory Mortenson shook out the kinks of sitting and dozing in the corner of the tent, rather than lying in his bedroll. He had positioned the bedroll to look as though someone slept there, just in case whoever had tried to come into his tent returned, but he had not. Jory's caution had only earned him an uncomfortable hour.

He rolled his gold in his bedroll, almost twenty pounds of coins and a few pounds of flour, coffee, and jerked venison making a clumsy load, tied it tightly, and flung it over his shoulder. He carried a cap-and-ball musket and shoved his Aston in his belt on the side opposite his Navy Colt, and was ready to go.

Quietly he moved the tent flap aside and headed for the string.

Clint and Enrique reached a clump of brush near the horses and stilled for a moment to listen for any sounds of movement—and it was a good thing they did, for they heard footfalls. Clint could sense the tension in his companion and put a hand on his shoulder to calm him. They stayed in the brush and waited. The sky in the east was now glowing golden, but shadows still darkened the canyon floor.

A man moved among the horses, quietly saddling and bridling two of them. He tied a heavy bedroll in the saddle of one and made ready to mount the second. As he did so, he put his back to the men hiding in the brush. Clint stepped out and closed the few paces between them.

Jory Mortenson heard the approach and turned, pulling and cocking his Colt as he did so—but it never cleared his holster. Clint smashed him aside the head with the butt of the heavy Colt revolving rifle. Jory's thumb slipped from the hammer, and his Navy Colt discharged in the holster, creasing his thigh, but he was out cold from the blow and fell in a heap.

"The tents," Clint shouted behind him. He grabbed the reins of the horse Jory was about to mount as Enrique went for the other. Both men had the horses under control and were on their knees facing the tents, only yards away, with weapons ready by the time three men came running from the larger tent, weapons in hand.

Enrique fired, and the lead man went down. The others raised their weapons, and Clint, too, fired. His first shot took the second man in the chest and flung him back into the third, who shoved him aside. Before he could recover, though, Clint had rotated the chamber of the Colt and was ready to fire again. A sure shot to the chest put the third man on his back.

The scene quieted, with only the moaning of one of the men disturbing the stillness. Clint rotated the chamber again, tied the horse, then cocked the weapon and walked over to make sure the three were out of commission. Enrique's heavy caliber had killed the first man outright. Both of the men Clint had shot still lived, but one's whisper rattled with death, and the other was unconscious, a gaping wound in his chest, wheezing as he took his last breaths.

Clint used the barrel of the rifle to ease aside the tent flap, then spoke. "If you're in there, throw down your weapons and

come on out. There are several of us out here and we're going
to burn the camp."

He got no reply and moved on inside. In the darkness he
could not be sure, but he kicked around until he was positive
no one else was there.

As he rejoined Enrique, he heard rapid footfalls approaching from down the canyon. He and Enrique knelt to one knee
again and readied themselves.

"This time," Clint said quietly, "give the bastard a chance
to lay down his weapon."

"Like they gave my brother and vaqueros?" Enrique said,
without cutting his eyes away from the oncoming sound. But
just as the man came into view and Enrique shouldered his
weapon, another man galloped out of the darkness and drove
his horse into the running man, knocking his weapon flying,
and sending him sprawling, then again forcing the horse on
him. Morengo loosened his reata and caught the man as he
tried to flee. Then he dragged him, bouncing behind the horse,
back to the camp.

They waited only a moment, then heard another man call
out, "Hello, the camp."

"Come on in," Clint yelled. The man approached, his long
gun hanging at his side. He stopped short when he realized
something was seriously wrong. He made the slightest motion
to raise the weapon as Clint called out, "Lay it down—"

"Run," the man Morengo had lassoed shouted to his friend,
and Enrique fired his handgun point-blank into the chest of
the man in Morengo's lasso, silencing him forever.

"Wait!" the approaching man yelled, but did not drop his
weapon.

But Enrique flung his spent pistol aside and raised his long
gun to his shoulder and fired again, blowing the man backward,
his rifle spinning away, his arms windmilling. He slammed to
his back, curled into a fetal position, and did not move.

Clint shook his head, taken aback by the killing. Then a
moan came from where the rest of the horses were tied.

"You did not hit that one hard enough," Enrique said, reloading his long gun.

Clint moved over to where Jory Mortenson was regaining consciousness. "This one we'll keep," he said in a harsh tone to Enrique. He was sure the young man was readying his weapon to finish him off.

"Yes," another voice rang out as Don Carlos, astride Diablo, nudged the big horse into camp. "That one is the jefe of this band of *malditos*. He is the one who brought me here tied across the saddle like a sack of frijoles, and it would give me great pleasure to see him hang from the big oak in front of the hacienda at Rancho Del Robles Viejo."

Clint dragged Mortenson to his feet. "I might suggest we hand him over to Sheriff Stoddard and let the law handle him."

"We will discuss that on the return ride," Don Carlos said, and Clint nodded as he spun Mortenson around and tied him with a length of rawhide. He would not be returning with them, so he had said his bit on the matter. Mortenson would be their problem from here on.

While Clint bound Mortenson's hands and ankles well, Enrique and Morengo dragged the dead men away from the tents, then torched the canvas. It was full light by the time they had selected the best horses and cut the rest loose. The Californios mounted, but Clint hesitated. "There are men to bury here."

"My vaqueros and my grandson were left for the vultures," Don Carlos said. "Burying is too good for these *malditos*."

"And that shows you what kind of men they were," Clint said, walking over to where a few camp tools lay haphazardly. "We are not them," he said simply and picked up a shovel. Morengo looked from Clint to his two *patróns* and back again; then he dismounted and walked over and grabbed a second shovel.

Don Carlos looked to his grandson. "I am going to ride down the canyon and see if I can find your brother and the rest of my vaqueros. You may stay here if you wish."

"I will ride with you, Grandfather."

"Get a packhorse, *Nieto.*"

Morengo looked up from the hole he had started. "Jefe, I will go as soon as I finish this job. You should not—"

"This is a job for the Diegos," the old man said, and he gigged the horse forward.

"Then I will come," Morengo said and started for his horse.

"You stay and help Señor Ryan," Don Carlos commanded. "He is right, we are not them. It was only my anger and exhaustion talking." He motioned to his grandson to get a tarp that lay among the tools, and Morengo stepped over and grabbed it before Enrique could dismount, and handed it to him.

"*Vaya con Dios,*" Morengo said, returning to his work.

By the time they had finished the hard work of burying the five Blue Stripers, Don Carlos and Enrique returned. They said nothing—and did not have to, as their look said all—but led a pack animal with a long bundle wrapped and tied across the saddle.

Jory Mortenson also had said nothing during the burying of his men. He sat in the dirt, his hands tied behind him, his ankles bound, his camp smoldering in the background.

They gathered up the weapons and packed them and some of the better camp items, loaded and tied Mortenson into the saddle, then gathered up his bedroll. He hefted it and looked from man to man. "Feels like these old boys were doing real good in the robbery department," Clint said. He unrolled the bedroll and found Mortenson's stash. "There must be more'n a thousand dollars here . . ."

"Good," Don Carlos said. "It will go to the widows and orphans of the vaqueros they killed."

Clint shook his head in agreement as he rerolled the poke into the bedding and repacked it, then mounted up. Leading Mortenson tied on his horse, he headed up out of Condor Canyon. Neither Morengo nor Clint asked what the Diegos had found down the canyon, and neither Don Carlos nor Enrique offered the information.

They rode in silence, recovering the stock they had left at the canyon's rim, then on until late morning, when they reached the flat where Peter Lebec had met his end. They dismounted and watered the horses, each man lost in his own thoughts. Finally Clint mounted up.

"I will be leaving you now. It's time I headed home."

Enrique walked over and extended his hand. "We are in your debt, El Lazo."

"Not true, amigo," Clint said simply, "you would do the same, were the situation reversed." He shook hands with each man in turn, tipped his hat, and spun his horse, ready to lead his small string down into the San Joaquin Valley.

"That's far enough," a voice rang out of the brush.

Clint drew rein as a dozen California Guard dragoons stepped out of the river willows. Another half dozen moved into position fifty yards to the north, blocking Clint's retreat down the valley, as did another group an equal distance to the south.

Captain Tabor and Lieutenant Winchurch rode out of the heavy river willows and reined up next to the group of men and animals.

"Give up your weapons, gentlemen," Tabor commanded. "You're coming back to Los Angeles."

"Not me," Clint said defiantly, "I'm heading out to the north."

"Like hell, Ryan," Tabor said. "You're under arrest."

"For what?"

"For what and for as long as the California Guard damn well pleases, that's for what," Tabor said. Meanwhile, Clint was surrounded by a dozen dragoons, who stripped his weapons away.

"What is the meaning of this," Don Carlos demanded. "I have done nothing. I am the one wronged here."

Tabor glared at the old man. "Your men have taken the law

into their own hands. You're under arrest right along with them until the law has a chance to sort things out."

"The law! The gringo law does nothing but pester law-abiding Californios—"

To make his point, Tabor shoved the barrel of his rifle into the center of Don Carlos's chest, but Enrique flew out of the saddle, flinging himself, springing across the back of Morengo's horse and knocking Tabor from his mount. Three dragoons were on Enrique before he could pummel the man. They beat him into submission with gun butts. Morengo started out of the saddle, but had a half-dozen muzzles lay trained on him before he could move.

Tabor struggled to his feet, pointing an accusing finger at Don Carlos, who quivered in silent anger. "You'll button your lip, old man, or I'll carry you back bound and tied across a saddle." He turned to his men. "Chain this one, and the others if they give you any trouble."

All Clint could do was shake his head and clamp his jaw. It looked like he was heading back to Los Angeles.

"What's that god-awful stench?" Tabor asked.

"That's the dead grandson of Don Carlos," Clint said, motioning to the pack animal with the tarp-wrapped bundle across it.

"How did he die?" Tabor asked.

"That man, Mortenson, and the Blue Stripers killed him, days and days ago. Left him and a bunch of others they shot down out in the sun like carrion."

"Burying detail," the captain snapped.

"He's taking him back so the priest can speak over him," Clint said with quiet determination.

"The hell he is, we're not riding all the way back with that stink. Bury him," he commanded to a pair of his men, who tied bandannas over their faces, and went to lead the animal away.

"You will pay for this, gringo," Don Carlos said quietly.

"I told you to keep your mouth shut, old man," Tabor said,

remounting his horse. "Water your animals, men, it's a long way to the next creek." Tabor turned to his prisoners. "You Californios pride yourselves as being horsemen. You try and make a break for it, and you'll have two dozen rifles firing at your back. I'll not chain you, like I had to do this one"—he motioned to Enrique—"unless you give trouble, but I'll shoot you down like dogs if you try and run. Understand?"

The men all shook their heads in silence.

They rode out in a column of twos, with a dozen dragoons at their back and a dozen leading.

Antonio Alverez left the *juzgado,* the jail, which sat in a wing behind the public building. Old Sergio Canales, the only other Californio *abogado* in all of southern California, was not available. He had traveled to Sacramento where he petitioned the governor not to divide Los Angeles County as its eastern San Bernardino area residents wished. He was not available to respond to the LaTours' call for help, so they resorted to calling Alverez. He had just left his second meeting with Jacques LaTour and was on his way to see MacKendrick.

It gave him secret pleasure for the LaTours to have to rely on him. Jacques LaTour had always treated him like a second-class citizen, as had old Don Carlos, who only seemed to remember him as a thin, undernourished, runny-nosed *camposino.*

But all of that would soon change.

He knocked on the door of the alcalde's office, and was not surprised to see that MacKendrick had retained the same officious, little man as secretary who had served George Willington.

"The alcalde, please," Antonio asked.

"He is busy at the moment—" the secretary was interrupted by loud voices from the alcalde's office, then the sound of footfalls. The door swung open and Sheriff Stoddard stomped through.

The secretary glared after Stoddard as he left and slammed the outside door with vigor. Then he turned back to Antonio. "Have a seat and I'll see if Don MacKendrick can see you," the man said, his manner offensive as he looked down his narrow nose at Antonio. Antonio smiled at the reference to MacKendrick as "Don." It was interesting to note that he was taking on the customs of the Californios.

He passed through the inner door, then quickly returned. "He will see you," he said, sounding a little surprised.

Antonio entered, crossed the room, and stood before MacKendrick's desk. The wide-shouldered man studied some papers, then looked up, rose, and extended his hand.

"Señor Alverez," he said, and they shook. "Be seated . . . a cigar?"

"Why not," Antonio said, and fished one out of the humidor MacKendrick extended across the desk. The big man lit his own, then held the match for Antonio, who leaned across the desk. Then he sat, following MacKendrick's lead.

"Now, my friend, what brings you to the alcalde's office?"

Antonio was not quite ready to talk business. "You must be very busy, attending to the affairs of the city, as well as your drugstore?"

"I am very busy, so if you don't mind. . . . I understand you've been retained by the LaTours?"

"Yes, I have. I've come to request your indulgence to allow Señor and Señora LaTour to return to Rancho Del Robles Viejo, until this ridiculous trial is completed." He purposefully used an offensive manner.

"Ridiculous?" MacKendrick said, narrowing his eyes and leaning forward in his chair. "You're a man of the law, Señor Alverez. You know the seriousness of a charge of complicity in a murder."

"The LaTours are heirs to a great rancho, actually four ranchos, Señor MacKendrick, and are no risk to this court. They certainly will not flee the state, being landowners—"

"The hell they won't. They are not landowners, merely potential heirs. If old Don Carlos were here, he'd have them on the first ship out to protect his fledglings."

"Don Jacques is hardly a fledgling." Antonio took a deep draw on his cigar. "Then Señora LaTour . . . surely you will allow at least her to return to her hacienda?"

"Not on your life, Alverez. I've called for a bond of twenty-five thousand dollars, and if they post that bond, they are free to go out on bail until the trial. If not, they stay where they are. I've been lenient enough, allowing Señora LaTour to remain at Boxworth Boardinghouse—"

"Ridiculous is what the amount of the bail is, MacKendrick. Still, you know you would have an uprising on your hands if you attempted to jail her," Antonio said, clamping down on the cigar.

"Then let it come, Señor Alverez," MacKendrick said with a satisfied look. "If the local rabble want trouble, we can give it to them."

"You mean, Señor, if the Californios want justice, the Anglos will *not* give it to them." Antonio rose, and MacKendrick followed him to his feet.

"You'll have your day in court, *abogado*. I've got an arraignment scheduled in a week. You're an officer of the court, Alverez. If you foment civil disobedience, then you, too, can test our jail, and our 'ridiculous' legal system."

"I am not suggesting anything of the sort, MacKendrick—"

"Don't, 'cause to tell you the truth, I wouldn't mind seeing you spend a little time getting some humility."

Antonio studied him for a moment. "I will trust the law and my ability to give justice to Señor and Señora LaTour."

Antonio headed for the door and was stopped by MacKendrick's voice behind him. "Then again, if the Diegos decided to sell some water rights. . . ."

Turning, Antonio narrowed his eyes. "Then?"

"Then the city fathers might find some leniency."

"And who would be the buyer for these rights, Señor

MacKendrick? The city, or the city's druggist, T.S. MacKendrick?"

"It don't much matter, so long as the city has the use of the water."

"But I should bring any offer to sell directly to you?" Antonio asked, already knowing the answer.

"Of course you should, Antonio. And there would be a handsome commission in the transaction for the man who handled it."

"Of course," Antonio said, and opened the door.

As he walked out in the fresh air, he took a deep breath. He had done his duty, and the LaTours could not fault him. He had "tried" to get them free. And he had a few surprises in store for MacKendrick, who thought he had everything under control. The alcalde might benefit from the acquisition of the Diegos' water, but only as a partner. For it would be Antonio who brought the opportunity to him, and he would remain a partner.

Antonio had long ago come to the conclusion that if a man was to win in Anglo society, he must lie down with the Devil.

And he was prepared to do that—in fact, he already had.

Fourteen

With the threat of being placed in chains, as they kept Enrique for the first two days, the dragoons forced them to ride in silence during the three-and-a-half day trip back to Pueblo de Los Angeles.

They arrived in midafternoon, and Don Carlos, Enrique, and Morengo were placed in one cell, and Clint in the cell next to them, with, to Don Carlos's great surprise, Don Jacques LaTour. Jory Mortenson was put across the hall, in a cell to himself, as during the trip home it was clear to Captain Tabor that the Diegos would again handle the state's business if left within reach of the Blue Striper.

Sheriff Sam Stoddard locked them up, with T.S. MacKendrick, Tabor, and Winchurch looking on, but the sheriff managed to calm Don Carlos with a whispered, "I'll be back as soon as MacKendrick and these soldiers take their leave."

"I want my *abogado,* Don Sergio Canales," Don Carlos demanded, in a tone that rang through the flat iron bars of the small *juzgado.*

"Well, you're in luck. He came in on the Pacific Mail steamer yesterday," Stoddard said. "I'll send someone for him."

As soon as the sheriff and dragoons left the jail—in fact, the dragoons retraced their steps, heading out to the San Joaquin Valley—Don Carlos and the others in his cell crowded to the bars separating them from Jacques.

"What is happening?" Don Carlos demanded of his son-in-law.

All youth was gone from Jacques' face, and he was drawn and seemed grayer. He shook his head, in quiet anger. "I am glad to see you are all right, *Patrón* . . . but do you know that Don Juan is dead—"

"What? How?" Enrique asked, looking as if he'd been slapped upon hearing the news of his father's death. Don Carlos, too, paled.

"One of the men who robbed the stage," Jacques continued. "Don Carlos and a dozen of our vaqueros rode in pursuit of him, while others went after the other robbers. Don Juan thought these men would have knowledge of your whereabouts. Juan was killed by the man he pursued, who was killed in turn by our men.

"Then why are you here?" Don Carlos asked, but thought he knew the answer. Enrique had been able to tell him a few things during the trip back, including the incident at the MacKendrick *bendición*.

Jacques explained that he was being held as an accessory to the hanging of the robbers, as was Doña Angelina. Don Carlos and Enrique were outraged at this news.

"What has come of our beautiful California," Don Carlos said, shaking his head in sorrow.

"It ain't yer California," Jory Mortenson mocked from across the hallway.

Before they could respond, the door from the sheriff's office into the hallway between the cells opened, and Antonio Alverez strolled in, clad in a city suit, looking every bit the successful *abogado*.

Even Don Carlos, who had never had much use for Antonio, looked happy to see him. He moved to the bars and entreated him. "Can you get us out of here, Antonio?"

"I thought Sergio Canales was your *abogado,* Don Carlos?"

"He is, but—"

"I am here to see a Mr. Jory Mortenson, who has requested my assistance."

"You would help that scum?" Don Carlos asked, his look one of incredulity.

"You have an *abogado,* Don Carlos. I understand he has been sent for. And I have a profession, an obligation to help those in need, no matter if you think them scum." Antonio cut his eyes to Don Jacques. "I presume you will want the Diego family attorney, now that he has returned from Sacramento?"

"Yes, Antonio, you presume correctly. Send me your bill—"

"Trust me, Don Jacques, I will. Now, if you gentlemen will excuse me." He tipped his hat and moved down the bars until he was as far as he could get from the cell holding the Diegos and Morengo. He motioned to the man in the cell. "Señor Mortenson, I presume?" Jory Mortenson rose from his bunk and went to the bars, until his face was only inches from Antonio. They spoke in whispers.

"Traitor," Don Carlos said, loud enough that Antonio could hear him, but the attorney did not bother to turn or respond; he merely kept on with his council with the Blue Striper.

Don Antonio kept his back to the Diegos, trying his best to make sure they could hear nothing being said between him and Jory Mortenson.

"You've got to get me out of here, Alverez," Mortenson said in a low growl.

"This will not be easy," Antonio whispered. "And keep your voice down, or they will hear."

"The whole territory will hear if you don't get me out of here. They'll hear how you paid me to abduct the old man, how you wanted him gone for at least a month. They'll probably hang you higher than me, knowin' that."

"Keep your voice low, Mortenson. I said I would get you out and I will . . . but you have got to keep silent."

"Not in a week, not in a few days, Alverez. I want outta here now. They got my things, including the gold you paid me. I want it back and the rest of what you owe me, and I want out of here tonight."

"I can only get you out by legal means, and that will take days, at least. Getting the gold back may be impossible."

"Then replace it. Come tomorrow, if I wake up in this cell, I'll sing like a meadowlark, and you'll be right in here with me."

Antonio's look hardened. "Then you will never get out, Mortenson. You have got to give me some time."

"Tomorrow morning. You break me out tonight. To hell with legal means—"

"I cannot do that—"

"Tonight, Alverez, or the whole town will hear me singing in the morning."

Antonio took a deep breath, then moved even closer to the bars. "Be ready at midnight."

"Midnight," Mortenson confirmed. "Good. That's best for the both of us."

Antonio moved away from the bars, only to be stopped on his exit by Jacques. "What has come of the roundup of cattle that Don Juan entrusted to you?"

"We have over seven hundred head in Conejo Canyon, and the vaqueros are still working."

"And buyers. Do you have buyers?"

"What roundup?" Don Carlos asked.

"Momentito, Patrón," Jacques said. "Do you have buyers, Antonio?"

"I am meeting with them this afternoon. Even now, two different buyers are inspecting the cattle."

"But you will come here and check with us before you complete a sale . . . power of attorney or no power?"

"Of course, Don Jacques," Antonio said, smiling the smile of a man who clearly has the advantage of another, and was enjoying it.

As Antonio was leaving, he tipped his hat to Sheriff Stoddard, who was returning. Don Jacques quickly explained to Don Carlos the fact that Don Juan had given a power of attorney to Alverez to sell cattle, in order to raise money to pay the ransom demanded for his release, and that now the money might be needed for all of their defense. Don Carlos pondered this news as the sheriff walked straight to the Diegos' cell door, keys in hand.

"The rest of you step to the back of the cell. Don Carlos, come on. We're going to my office where we can talk."

They did as directed, and the sheriff let old Don Carlos out, then motioned him ahead. When they were seated in Stoddard's office, the sheriff offered him a cigar. Don Carlos took it, bit the end off, and with disdain, spat it on the floor, then accepted the sheriff's light. They both took a deep draw before Stoddard began.

"Don Carlos, you know I've always been an even-handed sort."

"That is true, Sheriff, but my family is being held for something others did . . . and more importantly, something that may have been against the gringo law, but as you and I both know, needed doing."

Stoddard shook his head. "That's neither here nor there, Don Carlos. My problem is T.S. MacKendrick. While I was gone looking for a bunch of holdup men, MacKendrick was appointed alcalde . . . only a temporary appointment, thank God, but appointed he was. I've got this man to contend with. It was MacKendrick who had your daughter and son-in-law arrested, it was he who involved these damned dragoons. Now we've got the state militia to contend with."

"And Sacramento," Don Carlos said, beginning to see that Stoddard was being a reasonable man, "has never been easy to deal with."

"True. Anyway, I would have handled this all differently. I would never have allowed the kind of bail MacKendrick set to be imposed on your family . . . at least I would have fought against it. But it's done, and ya'll are going to have to bear with it until the arraignment."

Don Carlos folded his arms. This was not news he wanted to hear. "And that will be when?"

"It is scheduled for Monday, three days. Can you keep something to yourself?"

"Of course, Sheriff Stoddard," Don Carlos agreed.

"I have sent for a district judge in San Diego, and if he doesn't arrive in time, I'll request a change of venue. Because of your water—"

"Water?" Don Carlos said, astonished.

"Because of the water on Rancho Del Robles Viejo, and the fact the city needs more of it, and that every businessman and highbinder in town would like to get his hands on it to sell it to the city, you're not likely to get a fair trial, particularly if T.S. MacKendrick has anything to do with it. And as acting alcalde, he has everything to do with it."

Don Carlos smoked his cigar and studied Sam Stoddard before he replied. He had never thought much about the man one way or the other, but now the gringo sheriff was gaining his respect. He knew the city wanted his water rights, but he had no idea to what extent. Had he known the retention of one hundred percent ownership of those rights would place his whole family in jeopardy, he would have thought long and hard about how much water the rancho really needed, and would have long ago negotiated a sale of the excess to the city. Now, it seemed too late for that. Unless he and his family was cleared of these ridiculous charges.

"Then, Sheriff Stoddard, I will remain in the *juzgado* until this arraignment?"

"And probably after that, if the district judge does not arrive until then. When he arrives, he will listen to reason and overrule MacKendrick and at least lower the bail to some reasonable amount so you and your family can go home to await a trial, if there is to be a trial . . . but until then. . . ."

"You realize my son lies in his coffin at my hacienda, awaiting a burial?"

"I realize that, Don Carlos. But I don't know what to do about it. I suggest you have your vaqueros pack him in salt and charcoal, and bring him in to the icehouse if you don't want him buried without your presence."

It took Don Carlos a long time to respond to that. "I appreciate your frankness and honesty, Señor Stoddard," Don Carlos said, extending his hand. "But this is a terrible travesty of justice. Terrible."

"I'm truly sorry, Don Carlos," Stoddard said, "but that's the way it is. I just wanted you to know that it wasn't of my making." He rose and shook hands with the old don. Then he escorted him to the door, and back to the cell. True to his word, Don Carlos said little to Enrique and Morengo about his visit with Sheriff Stoddard, but he did tell them to be prepared for at least a few days in jail. A few days that he knew might cost him the rancho, water rights and all. For there was still the unanswered question of the note. The note he had given to T.S. MacKendrick. The note that now must total many thousands of dollars. He must let this sale of cattle go through, if for that reason alone.

Old Sergio Canales arrived the last thing in the afternoon, and he, too, assured Don Carlos that nothing could be done to free them, short of paying the bail or waiting for the arraignment. And then, there was a good chance they would be held until trial. Don Sergio agreed to file a motion with MacKendrick and to send a copy to the district judge in San Diego, thus putting pressure on MacKendrick to do what they all agreed was proper. But the problem was, Sergio explained, that MacKendrick had a free hand in the matter, and even the district judge would not overrule him without being present and hearing testimony from all parties.

Still, Don Carlos could not believe that justice could be so blind. He put his faith in the district judge, and his ability to explain the situation to him. He spent the rest of the afternoon writing his own letter to the distant judge.

Finally Don Carlos retired to his bunk; he was very tired. He dozed, then snapped awake. It suddenly came to him. The note. That was the cause of all this. Probably the cause of his abduction in the first instance. Certainly, the cause of all the trouble that had come to his family.

Someone wanted to make sure he could not repay the note until the interest was so high no one could repay it, and his rancho would be foreclosed upon. And that someone could only be MacKendrick.

He called his family together and did not complain when Clint listened in as he explained his conclusion, and none of them refuted it.

They made a pact to get out of jail by any means, and to get to the district judge to plead their suspicions and their case. It was clear to all of them they would get no justice in Los Angeles—at least not while Thomas Salathiel MacKendrick had his own ax to grind. Clint listened with interest, but he accepted it when Don Carlos said it was not his problem, and that he should stay out of it.

Antonio Alverez returned to his office and met with the two buyers, each retreated to the anteroom of his office while he negotiated with the other. Finally he arrived at a price with one that the other would not meet. The $5 a head he got for seven hundred cattle would more than repay him for the money he had advanced Jory Mortenson for abducting old Don Carlos Diego—and legally he could keep it; he was within his rights. He could apply the proceeds to the note he held, to the note he bought from T.S. MacKendrick through that fat fool he had killed, Willington. He knew that Willington would have shot off his mouth about him being the one who bought the Diego note. And had that happened, his well-laid plans would have been for naught. The Diegos would have killed him, had he tried to collect the outrageous interest, for it would have been considered the ultimate affront—one Californio imposing the Anglo law to take advantage of another. Now no one knew who held the note. It was not as much as he hoped to get for the cattle, but it would have to do.

When he owned the rancho, he would get much, much more.

And now there was the matter of Jory Mortenson to take care of. If that came off without a hitch, then he could still come out of this thing whole, and with a considerable profit—the Diegos would be ruined, if he could hold onto the note long enough. He could leave Los Angeles with a tremendous profit, if everything came together exactly as it could, as it should.

Jory Mortenson was the only fly in the ointment.

* * *

By nightfall, Clint was pacing the floor. He paused to share a fine meal with the Diego girls. Conce and Chita had brought food into town as soon as they heard about the return of Enrique and their grandfather. Clint stayed out of the conversation when Don Carlos called the girls aside and spoke quietly to them.

Clint finished his meal, thanked the girls as they left, and resumed his pacing.

He hated being jailed. It had only happened to him one time before, for any amount of time, in Sacramento, and he had sworn then it would never happen again. And here he was, his rancho possibly in the middle of an Indian uprising, no productive business accomplished, and his freedom gone because of some trumped-up charges.

It was so much bunk. He decided that, like the Diegos, he would not wait for Los Angeles justice, if he had the chance to do otherwise. Like the Diegos, he would take any chance to get out of and as far from Los Angeles as he could. His Rancho Kaweah should be far enough. So far, Los Angeles justice seemed to be anything but.

Don Carlos lay quietly pondering in his bunk. He had instructed the girls to bring guns, hidden under their skirts, and the finest rancho riding stock, two horses for each man, when they returned the next afternoon with the evening meal. Tomorrow, if they escaped without incident, the others would ride out to find the district judge.

Once they were mounted, no one could catch his grandson and his *segundo*. He would not ride with them, but he would make the gringos think he did; he would return to Rancho Del Robles Viejo, where his vaqueros would protect him, and where he could hide where no one would find him—and where he could continue the business of raising the money to pay this damnable note.

He returned to his bunk and fell into a fitful sleep. He went to sleep hating T.S. MacKendrick.

Clint could not sleep at all. He arose and paced the floor,

thinking. If he escaped this jail, he would be a wanted man again, as he had been once before. He didn't like the thought, and he had done nothing to be here. Still, could he risk being at the mercy of T.S. MacKendrick and a Los Angeles court? No one had yet explained what he was being held for, or what he was charged with, if anything. He was in a quandary about attempting an escape, and he was sure Don Carlos was arranging one. He saw the wide eyes of the girls, Conce and Chita, as the old man pulled them aside and spoke with them. He would be surprised if something didn't happen this very night.

One thing he knew for sure, the Diegos had real trouble here. A good deal of the trouble was of their own making. He carried a Diego bullet in his side, and owed them nothing. He had already done more than he should. In fact, had he not gone on to Condor Canyon with them, he would be well on his way to Rancho Kaweah, where he should be. It was time he took care of himself and left the Diegos to take care of their own affairs.

He returned to his bunk and tried to sleep, but could not. Morengo snored like a bloated, bleating goat, and that didn't help. Finally he arose again and paced quietly. He could see Jory Mortenson sitting on his bunk, the light of his cigarette glowing in the darkness. Mortenson's cell, across the hall from the Diegos and the one shared by Clint and Jacques LaTour, was one of two on that side, and both of them had barred windows. The moon had arisen, and light flowed in from it and from a nearby window of the sheriff's office, where the building formed an L shape.

Clint leaned against the bars, watching the windows across the way, wishing he was out of this jail and on his way north, when he heard a hissing sound. He cocked his head and listened, and heard it again, coming from the window in Mortenson's cell.

Jory Mortenson rose quickly and placed his face up against the head-high windowsill. Clint's eyes widened as he saw the slim, angular face of Antonio Alverez flash in the window, then he flinched as the room flashed with a muzzle blast and reverberated with the roar of a big pistol.

Fifteen

Mortenson disappeared into the darkness of the cell, and the face appeared again, then disappeared as quickly. Clint was absolutely certain it had been Antonio Alverez.

The other men in the cells were on their feet as the door separating the hallway from the sheriff's office burst open, and the night guard ran in, carrying a pistol in one hand and a lantern in the other. "What the hell?" he yelled, panning the gun, beside the lantern, which he held at arm's length.

"Mortenson!" Clint said. "Someone shot him through the window." He wasn't ready to say that Antonio Alverez had shot his own client in the face at point-blank range—at least not until he thought it through. The guard hurried to the cell and held the lantern high. It was clear that Jory Mortenson was no longer any threat to the guard, as half the back of his head had been blown away.

"Sweet Jesus," the guard said, and ran from the room. It was only moments before the hallway began filling with spectators, including T.S. MacKendrick and Sheriff Sam Stoddard. Stoddard let Dr. Oscar Bonny into the cell when he arrived, but there was nothing the medico could do but pronounce the prisoner dead.

"Did you fellows see anything?" Stoddard asked, but Clint kept silent. He would keep his own counsel on this, at least until he had a chance to discuss it with Don Carlos.

Of one thing he was sure, Antonio Alverez was piss poor at client relations.

They removed the body and cleared out to the town's various cantinas and saloons; the cells lay dark and silent again. Clint called out to Don Carlos, and he, Morengo, and Enrique moved to the bars. Don Jacques also rose and joined them.

"What is it, Señor Ryan?" Don Carlos asked, his voice exhausted.

"Antonio Alverez, Mortenson's *abogado*—"

"Yes," Don Carlos snapped. "The *puerco abogado.*"

"Pig, maybe, killer for sure," Clint said.

"What?" Enrique, Don Carlos, and Jacques asked in unison.

"I saw him at the window. It was Antonio that killed Mortenson."

"Impossible," Jacques said, astounded. "He wouldn't have the *cojónes,* and why would he?"

"I don't know, Don Jacques," Clint said, "but it was him, sure as Mortenson's now cooling his heels at the undertaker."

"Could it be he was avenging Juan's death," Enrique said. "He was an amigo of my father's."

"Ha!" Don Carlos said with disgust. "Antonio Alverez is a friend of no man's. My son was a fool to trust him." His voice dropped as he pondered again. "It could only mean that Antonio is involved in this," Don Carlos said quietly, his mind working. "All of this, the note, my abduction. He must be working with MacKendrick."

"What are you talking about, Don Carlos?" Jacques asked.

"Yes, *Abuelo,* what?" Enrique asked, and Don Carlos began to explain the note, the abduction, his belief that T.S. MacKendrick was behind it all—at least his belief until now. Now he was again in a quandary.

He knew for a fact that Antonio Alverez and T.S. MacKendrick barely tolerated each other.

He shook his head in consternation. "We must get out of this jail, we must resolve this matter ourselves, we must not allow ourselves, our family, to be at the mercy of the Anglo court . . . not now. They may all be against us." At this point, he didn't even trust his own attorney, Sergio Canales.

Before T.S. MacKendrick could get the morning-coffee fire started, Oscar Bonny arrived. By the time he poured, they were already kicked back in the ladder-back chairs, each with a boot propped up on the leech barrel.

"So what's new, alcalde?" Bonny asked his old friend.

"Alcalde only at the whim of the council, thanks to you and the others. I don't think it'll hold past any elections, not unless we can keep our Californio brothers from voting. Seems I'm burning bridges right and left with those folks."

"You seem to be making hay while the sun shines." Oscar guffawed, then changed the subject. "How much is old Don Embustero into you for?" Bonny asked, always having coveted the Embustero rancho himself.

MacKendrick smiled. "Over a thousand. I've got one note churning away at ten percent per day for a thousand, and if the old fool keeps coming back to the trough, I'll soon have another. He's on a fast ride to hell, with the Devil on his tail."

"One of these days one of those hot-blooded rancheros is going to slit your gullet." Bonny leaned forward and held his cup out for T.S. to fill.

"They're going to have to be real fast or real quiet. Speaking of that, who do you suppose shot that Blue Striper last night?"

"I don't have the slightest idea, but whoever sure as hell didn't want to miss. They practically put the barrel in his eye before they pulled off. What a mess that was. That could happen to you, T.S., you keep pushing your luck."

"I swear, Oscar, I'm more worried about their women than the men. I had dinner at Davylou's last night, trying to pry a little information out of Angelina LaTour. Now there's a woman who'd like to split my gullet and pour hot oil down it."

"Like I said, you're pushing your luck." Oscar gave him a

doubtful look over his coffee, and they were both silent for a moment.

"I'd have quit," T.S. said, "had I been smart enough to hang onto that Diego note. I don't know what possessed me . . . hell, yes I do. I thought the old man had more cash money than he did, and could probably pay it off. I heard from Antonio Alverez that old Don Carlos was coming to town to pay the note off. I decided to sell when Willington came to me with an offer for twice the face value of the note. I thought it was a real ploy to get rid of it."

"Even you err once in a while," Oscar said with a chuckle.

"That's the last time," T.S. said thoughtfully. "I wonder who has that note now?"

Night had given him time to think.

Antonio paced his office, rethinking his plan. So long as the Diegos were in jail, they could do little to raise money for bail or to pay off his note. T.S. MacKendrick, without knowing it, was his staunchest ally. But he knew he could not keep the Diegos in jail. The district judge was a fair man, and he would eventually overrule MacKendrick's outrageous bail, and the Diegos would be free.

Dead, they could not raise any money. If old Don Carlos, Enrique, and LaTour were dead in an escape attempt, or even if they attempted escape and were captured, they would be held without bail.

So the solution to his problem was simple. Assure them they would have no chance in an Anglo court, and assist them in an escape.

An escape that he would thwart.

That would work to keep them until there was no hope of paying off his note. Particularly if they were dead.

He grabbed his hat, stepped out, and locked the door. Spinning on his heel, he set off for the jail.

The five prisoners were huddled together against the bars

in the rear of their cells when Antonio strode in—they quieted and parted immediately. Antonio approached the bars and called to Jacques LaTour. He thought he would have the best chance with Jacques of seeming sincere.

Jacques joined him, as did Enrique.

"I told you I was using Don Sergio—" Jacques began.

"That is fine. That is not why I have come."

The two men eyed him quizzically, and he continued. "There is something terribly amiss here in Los Angeles. It is a travesty what has been done to the Diegos, and to you and Señora LaTour."

"That is true," Jacques said, suspicious of what Antonio was saying, but interested nevertheless.

"Juan Diego was my dearest friend," Antonio continued.

Jacques eyed him carefully. Juan had been a friend to the man, but his dearest? "So?"

"So I want to help his family any way I can."

"So?" Jacques asked again.

"The Diegos cannot get fair treatment in Los Angeles. You must escape this jail."

"That would be foolish—" Jacques began. The last thing he wanted was any outside knowledge of their plans.

"Besides," Enrique interrupted, "we don't need your help in our plans."

Jacques gave the younger man a look that silenced him.

There was a clumsy silence, then Antonio smiled and spoke. "So you have plans—"

"Nothing of the sort," Jacques interrupted. "We will wait until we hear from the district judge."

"As you wish," Antonio said, "I only came to offer my help." Then he tipped his hat and left.

He paused at the deputy's desk. "Who has visited your prisoners?" he asked the man, who reclined with both feet up on the desk, cleaning his fingernails with a pocketknife.

"You and old man Canales, and those two good-lookin' daughters," the deputy said, hardly looking up.

"That is all?" Antonio demanded.

"That's the lot of it. Why?"

"It is not your affair," Antonio snapped and walked out. The man went back to cleaning his nails.

Antonio went straight to the small stable behind his office and harnessed his horse. In little more than an hour, he drew rein in front of Rancho Del Robles Viejo.

He knew that old don Sergio Canales would not have anything to do with any jail escape. He was a man who venerated the law. It could only be the girls. The girls were the key.

Conce greeted him at the door, a worried look on her face. "Don Antonio." She immediately tried to cover her concern. "It is a pleasure to see you. Don Juan is—"

"I did not come to view the body of my old friend," Antonio said. "I have come to help the living. Don Carlos sent me to help with the escape."

Conce seemed startled, as Don Carlos had been adamant in instructing the girls that they were to say nothing to anyone. In fact, he had made them swear on all they held holy. Chita entered the foyer as Conce stood in stunned silence.

"Chita," Antonio said, repeating his offer. "I have come to help plan the escape." The girls looked at each other, then back to the man who seemed to know all.

Finally Chita spoke. "Well, let us take tea on the patio, and we will see what each of us can do."

They retired to the patio where the servant woman brought them tea, and Chita explained the simple plan. The girls were to bring in supper, and for dessert, hidden under their full skirts, four Colt six-shooters.

Antonio listened intently, then nodded in agreement. "Sometimes the simple plans are the best. But a diversion would be in order. Something to draw the sheriff away from the jail, something to draw all the armed men away from the area of the jail, except, of course, for the jailer."

"What?" Conce asked, thinking it was a good idea.

"I don't know, but I will think on it. When do the men plan to attempt the escape?"

Chita answered. "When we have had time to get well clear of the jail, they will call the deputy in and force him to open the cell doors. We will have horses already waiting, brought in by some of our vaqueros and tied next door to the public building in front of O'Hanahan's Saloon."

"And out of town," Conce added, "will be four more horses. So each man will have a horse to ride and one to lead. No one will catch them if each has a spare mount."

"But only four?"

"Yes," Conce offered, "Don Carlos, our father, Enrique, and Morengo."

"No horse for Señor Ryan, the gringo?"

"He is not to be involved, we understand at his own wish," Chita said.

Antonio pondered this. The gringo was no threat to him. He had no interest in the affair, and only seemed to be caught up in it. If he died, he died, but it was no matter one way or the other. He could rot in jail, so much as Antonio cared.

"It is as good a plan as any," Antonio said, rising. "I will wait until I see you leave, then cross town and cause some kind of diversion, a fire or something. Don't wait, but leave quickly."

The girls rose and looked at him with appreciation. Antonio smiled, and smiled even broader inwardly. He would have his revenge on these Diegos, and with luck, the LaTour daughters would be the only ones left alive. They would both come crawling to him after this was over.

"Vaya con Dios," he said, and turned and left with a purposeful stride. He whipped up the buggy and left Rancho Del Robles Viejo at a canter, the dust flying behind.

In a little less than an hour, he drew rein in front of El Boticario's.

He tied the horse, its chest heaving from the fast trip, and hurried into the drugstore. A hired man was behind the counter. He directed him to the alcalde's office, and Antonio hurried out, leaving the horse tied. He walked to the public building and entered.

Irritated, he waited for the officious secretary to announce him, then entered T.S. MacKendrick's temporary office.

"What's on your mind, Antonio?" T.S. said, barely looking up.

"I have information that will benefit us both."

That got MacKendrick's attention, and he sat back in his chair. "Have a seat. Cigar?"

He handed the humidor over and Antonio took one. This time MacKendrick slid a silver cigar cutter across the desk. Antonio trimmed the end and accepted a light, then sat.

"So, what benefits me?" MacKendrick asked.

"You would like to get your hands on Diego water?"

"So would everybody."

"I will soon be in possession of Rancho Del Robles Viejo—"

"Hogwash," MacKendrick said with a sneer.

"True," Antonio countered. "I have a power of attorney from Don Juan Diego—"

"Don Juan is dead."

"And if you play your cards right, señor, so will be all of the other Diego men. And you could hold the option to one half . . . not all, but one half of the excess Diego water rights. You see, I own the unpaid note on Rancho Del Robles Viejo."

"You bastard! You lied to me about Don Carlos coming to pay his note . . . you're the one who bought it, knowing he couldn't pay it."

"I have watched you well, T.S., and learned. Learned that all is fair in Anglo business."

MacKendrick sat back in the chair and his eyes narrowed. He took a deep drag. Finally, he quietly chuckled for a moment, then spoke. "Tell me more, Don Antonio."

* * *

Clint was still in a quandary. Should he escape, or should he hang in and take his chances with the court? He had done nothing, except participate in getting the old man back, and a court could hardly hold that against him—still, he didn't like the way things happened in Los Angeles, and he sure as hell didn't want to be at the mercy of T.S. MacKendrick, the new alcalde.

He decided to play his hunches. His hunches had done okay by him for years, so he would listen to them now, and play whatever hand was dealt him.

Getting hoisted on the hangman's rope was not to his liking, but he did like and respect the old man Carlos and the vaquero Morengo, and he had even come to like the young hot-blooded Enrique. The man had proven his bravery time and again, even if he had a voracious appetite for revenge. If it had been Clint's brother and friends who had died under the guns of the Blue Stripers, maybe he would have been as bloodthirsty. Not having a brother, he had no way of judging.

Finally the girls arrived, dressed in their finest. To their dismay, the guard not only took great pains to search the food and containers, but joked—with a lecherous eye—about searching each of them. Then he did not leave them alone in the hallway to talk with their grandfather and cousin as he had the night before, but seemed to enjoy staying in sight of them—and staring at their every movement.

Eventually Conce was able to stand with her side to the bars, while Chita involved the man in flirting conversation, and the prisoners ate. Enrique sat against the bars on his bunk, and Chita boldly reached around behind her, as if she had her hands folded at her back, but actually hoisted her skirt, gathering it in her hands. Enrique was able to reach through the bars and free the Colts she had, one strapped to each stockinged thigh. Before she moved away, she said quietly, "Antonio is going to create a diversion across town in a few minutes—"

"Antonio knows?" Enrique said, cursing himself for arousing the *abogado's* curiosity.

"Yes, didn't you tell him?" Chita asked, looking perplexed. But the guard looked up, and she remained quiet.

Conce gave Enrique time to get the weapons hidden in his blanket, then walked the length of the two cells and stuck her lower lip out, pouting. "Chita, you are taking all the attention of this handsome man. You visit with Enrique and our *abuelo,* while I chat with the señor." Conce managed to lean on the jamb of the door between the cells and the jail office, making the deputy turn his back to the cells in order to talk with the eye-batting beauty. Chita was able to quickly pass the weapons to Enrique. In moments, the men had finished the meal and passed the utensils through to the girls, who took their leave with an exaggerated promise to return the next night.

Without the girls there, the guard quickly returned to his desk.

Enrique told the others what Chita had said about Antonio knowing and offering to set up a diversion across town. Don Carlos said they would wait for no diversion, and would go forward nevertheless. After all, Antonio was a Californio, and even though they doubted the sincerity of his offer of help, they did not believe him capable of any kind of treachery.

It was just full dark, with the saloon next door beginning to come to life with the sound of a pair of guitars and a piano, when Don Carlos called them together. "It is time," he said gravely. "I do not want anyone hurt. It would not go well for us if the guard or anyone is injured. The guard seems a fair man, and what is happening to us may not be of his causing, any more than it is the men on the street. We will lock him up and leave quietly. Four of us leaving will be too obvious. Enrique and I will wait for you and Morengo—"

"No!" Enrique insisted. "You two will go first, and Morengo and I will follow after you are mounted."

"Do not snap at your grandfather," Don Carlos chastised.

"I am not snapping, *Abuelo*. You have had enough over the last weeks. You will go first, and you will soon be home. Morengo will accompany you to be of service. The two of us," he spoke, nodding to his uncle, "will join up out of town and ride on to San Diego with your letter to the district judge."

"As you wish, Enrique. I am tired. Very tired."

"Then it is settled. Do not draw your weapons if anyone else is in the jail office, nor until the guard is well inside the hallway. Don Carlos, lay on the floor as we planned."

Don Carlos took his position on the floor near the front of the back cell; Clint walked back to his bunk, still undecided as to what he would do.

Jacques walked to the front of their cell, nearest the door to the jail office, and yelled. "Deputy. Quick, the old man is very ill."

Sixteen

In a moment, the deputy opened the door. "What are you belly achin' about?"

"Don Carlos is very sick. Hurry."

"So, he's sick," the deputy said, starting to close the door.

"My daughters will hate you if you let their grandfather fall ill."

The door opened again. The guard sighed deeply and walked through and to the rear cell of the two, now occupied by the prisoners. He bent to look at Don Carlos, who lay on his back, his eyes closed, holding his stomach with both hands, groaning softly.

Don Carlos opened his eyes and looked into the eyes of the deputy. "You have let your *cojónes* rule your small brain, gringo," Don Carlos said, a grin on his face.

The deputy looked up to see three guns drawn and centered on him. Soon, it was four, as Don Carlos got to his feet.

"Open the cell," Don Carlos demanded. The deputy looked sick, but complied. Enrique disarmed him, then snatched the large key ring from him and shoved him in the cell. He locked the door, then unlocked the cell holding Clint and Jacques.

Jacques exited quickly, and he and Morengo moved to the door separating the jail from the office and made sure no one else was there. Don Carlos and Enrique paused at the cell door, studying Clint who sat on his bunk.

"You are welcome to share our fate, El Lazo," Don Carlos said.

"No. Thanks, but no. I'll hang in here."

"Then," Enrique said, *"vaya con Dios,* Lazo."

"Hasta mañana," Don Carlos said with a wave, and with new-found vigor strode up to join the others. They hesitated in the jail office, lowering the lantern there so it was near dark in the room; then Don Carlos walked to the outside door and carefully opened it and eyed the street.

It was dark, with the exception of a pair of whale's-oil street-lamps and the lights of the establishments. Oddly, no one was on the street. Not a single soul.

"It is quiet, almost too quiet," Don Carlos said, "but we go." He stepped out in a normal stride, followed by Don Jacques. Enrique took up his position at the cracked door and watched as they strolled to the hitching post of the saloon next door. They mounted, and as instructed, Enrique and Morengo followed out and walked for the horses as Don Carlos and Don Jacques reined away.

The rooftops and windows exploded in gunfire.

Enrique scrambled back to the jail door and rolled inside. Morengo took two shots to the chest and fell to his knees, his Colts firing into the dirt street until another bullet ripped his neck and slammed him to the ground.

Don Jacques LaTour whipped his horse and rode a dozen paces at a gallop before the animal was killed under him and tumbled, slamming Jacques to the ground. He staggered to his feet, but was again blown almost as quickly to the ground by a pair of heavy slugs.

Don Carlos gave the spurs to his horse, and the animal took three gallant leaps, even though its chest and side had already been riddled with bullets. The horse stopped, stiff legged, and the shooting stopped at the same instant, for an instant. Long enough for the gringos lining the buildings to hear the old ranchero yell, *"Bastardos,"* and fire his Colt twice at the windows; then they resumed firing.

In moments, it was silent. Don Carlos Diego, like his son-in-law, Don Jacques, and his trusted vaquero Morengo, lay dead in the dirt street of Los Angeles.

Then the firing resumed. Enrique knocked a man down, shooting from the doorway. He could not see his grandfather from his position, or he probably would have run to his aid, only to be likewise shot down.

When the firing began, Clint bolted from the cell and into the office. The doorway, where Enrique knelt, exploded, splintered by the shots of the men across the street. Clint managed to drag Enrique away.

"Get back, it's sure death out there," he yelled to the wild-eyed vaquero.

"As *Dios* is my witness," Enrique said quietly and deliberately, "if they have killed my grandfather and my uncle, I will kill every gringo in Los Angeles."

"You'll not live to kill anyone if we don't get the hell out of here," Clint said, making up his mind in that instant that he was joining the escape. There was no mercy nor any justice in Los Angeles—he was heading for Rancho Kaweah.

Clint grabbed the ring of keys from Enrique, who still carried them, and crossed the room to a gun rack. He found the key to a padlock and removed his revolving Colt rifle, then opened a deep drawer in the desk and found his pistols. He also found a box of shells, and crouching, made his way to a small stove that had a cold coffeepot adorning its top. A few stray bullets still struck the front of the jail, and Clint stayed low as he crossed the room. He knocked the coffeepot aside and opened the lid to the stove and dropped the box of shells in, hoping against hope that there was enough fire—they were paper cartridges, and it would take little.

He killed the lantern the rest of the way, putting the room in complete darkness, then yelled, "Come on!" He and Enrique ran for the rear of the hallway between the cells, where a door led out to the back.

Pausing long enough to eye the night guard who shook the bars in anger, he snapped, "You keep your face shut or I'll blow it off." The man paled and backpedaled to a bunk. Clint had to fumble with the keys to the rear door, but finally got the lock turned just as the shells in the stove began to explode.

Kicking open the rear door, he dropped back and pressed against the bars, expecting a fusillade of shots to pepper the exit. But nothing came. He took a deep breath and dove through and into the shadows, staying flat against the building. He could hear the deputy screaming behind him, trying to tell the others that they were out the back, but the exploding shells in the office stove covered the sound of his voice, and belied the fact there was no one there doing the shooting.

All over the street in the front, men hunkered down with the onslaught of firing. Finally they began returning fire, then the shots slowed, then stopped altogether.

Finally someone yelled out, "They must all be dead," and men began filtering out of doorways and dropping down off rooftops.

When they finally raised the courage to shove their way into the sheriff's office, they were surprised to find no bodies. Then a disgusted yell came from the back. "They ran out the back, you damn fools, ten minutes ago."

T.S. MacKendrick entered the office in time to hear the yell. Antonio wanted nothing to do with stopping the escape. What would his fellow Californios think, if he were to participate in such an act. He stayed at the Parrot, sipping an *aguardiente,* cursing the Anglos who killed his friends.

MacKendrick, who had instructed the makeshift posse of townsmen not to fire unless fired upon, had actually fired the first shot himself, setting off the fusillade. Now, acting in his capacity as alcalde, he praised the men he'd collected from the saloons after sending Sheriff Stoddard out of town on a bogus errand. "You men did well; they brought it on themselves. They shouldn't have fired on us." Then he instructed them, "It's a hundred dollars each for the capture of these escapees. We can't have men thinking they can run from our jail. Dead or alive, men, dead or alive. Now find them."

The men filtered out and began a building-to-building search. Oscar Bonny arrived and began examining the men in the street, pronouncing each of them dead. He shook his head in disgust. He had liked old Don Carlos Diego, and the rest of the family. Even Jacques LaTour was all right, in his way.

MacKendrick walked to the center of the street and stood as Oscar pulled his coat off and dropped it over Don Carlos's face. He looked up and glared at his old friend, T.S. MacKendrick. "This your doin', T.S.?"

"It was nobody's 'doing,' Oscar. They were trying to escape our jail—"

"You've shot down three men in the street . . . men whose only crime was being suspected of being accessories, when you know damn well they weren't. If they attempted escape, it's because you set a bail no one in this town could make. Hell, if they shot the governor, the bloody bail wouldn't have been much more'n you set. That hanging just happened, and those bastards deserved it anyhows. You've gone too far this time, Thomas. Too goddamned far." Oscar stomped off, and T.S. stared after him. He would get over it, T.S. finally decided. By tomorrow, they would be propping their feet up on his leech barrel, as always.

Watching as men fanned out, up and down the street, Mac-Kendrick decided the alcalde had no business involving himself in a manhunt. He had more important business. Like a little poker at the Parrot. He hadn't been warming his big red chair there enough lately with all the business of being alcalde, as well as running the drugstore.

Let these other fools get shot running down that young hot-head, Enrique Diego, and the man from the San Joaquin, Ryan. Don Thomas Salathiel MacKendrick, alcalde of Pueblo de Los Angeles, was going to try on a whiskey, and hopefully, a little poker with old Don Embustero, if he was fool enough to come for another drenching.

Clint and Enrique had burst out of the jail to find only dark-ness.

"My horses are probably in the public house stable," Clint said, beginning to head across a vacant lot to that small outbuilding. Enrique followed, then pulled Clint up short. Five armed men, laughing and boisterous, came down between the public house and the nearby saloon. Clint and Enrique reversed their path and headed the other way, staying in an alley way behind the street's business buildings.

"I'm not leaving Los Angeles without my horse," Clint said quietly.

"I am not leaving without the head of Antonio Alverez," Enrique said, with quiet intensity. "Somehow, he was behind this. Otherwise, why would he have killed Mortenson?"

"I can't answer that, Enrique. But the whole town is probably looking for us," Clint said, trying to reason with the young Diego. "Leave Alverez to the law; you've got a rancho to worry about. And MacKendrick was only doing his job."

"The devil's work is what he did, and he, too, should pay. Those men outside the jail were laying in wait."

They moved three blocks away, then again heard men moving behind them.

"We've got to keep moving," Clint said, sensing Enrique's reluctance. "Where can we hide until these drunks wear out?"

"Esperanza," Enrique said.

"The Boxworth Boardinghouse?" Clint asked, surprised, for that seemed a little like going into the lion's lair. "Hell, that's next door to the Parrot, right in the middle of things."

"Yes. She has a room next to the stable. The best place to hide a tree is in the forest, and the last place they will look for us is next door to where the alcalde and those close to him frequent."

In moments they had crossed the main street and found their way to the rear of Davylou Boxworth's boardinghouse, and into the darkness of Esperanza's room.

"She will be finished inside soon, then she will come," Enrique said. "We wait."

Enrique took a seat on the only chair, and Clint collapsed onto the narrow bed. The room was well kept, as much as Clint could make out in the darkness. He was in a true quandary. Now he was a jail escapee, without a horse and without his poke, which Sheriff Stoddard had taken from the dragoons and stored in his office safe along with the money recovered from Mortenson. The money he could replace; Diablo was another matter.

He sighed deeply in the darkness. He had done it this time, but what other choice had he had? Had he stayed, it was likely those crazy drunks assembled outside would have shot him down for no reason. He had his guns; that was something. He closed his eyes and waited.

In less than an hour, Esperanza entered. Her eyes flared as she saw someone across her bed, and more so as Enrique stepped out from behind the door and covered her mouth from behind to quell her scream.

"It is Enrique Diego, and Lazo," he said quietly, close to her ear. She relaxed and he released her.

"They are searching the boardinghouse now. Four of them," she said. "Hide, and I will keep them from entering."

"So much for your tree in the forest theory," Clint said from his reclining position.

Enrique ignored him. "Where?" Enrique asked, and Clint rose to sit on the edge of the bed.

"Clint, under the bed," she commanded. "You behind the door." There was not room for both of them under the bed. Clint, a pistol in each hand, reluctantly complied, while Enrique did as he was directed, stepping behind the door, just as it rattled. Esperanza opened it a crack.

"What?" she said.

"Well, well, we got us a pretty little pepper," one of the Anglos outside said, trying to push the door open, but she resisted. "You got any company in there, señorita?"

"There is no one here. Leave me be."

"You want a little company, señorita?" the man said with a guffaw.

"Go away, before I scream and bring those from inside. I have a gun, señor," she lied, staying at the narrow crack in the barely opened door. But Enrique tapped the back of the door with the one he carried, making her statement believable.

"We're hunting for Enrique Diego," the man said, his voice hardening.

"There is no one here and I am not properly dressed. Go away before I scream. If Enrique comes, I will shoot him, as I'm about to shoot you."

"You scream all right, scream if you see Enrique Diego, understand?" he said. "That ol' boy and his jail-breakin' friend is worth a hundred dollars each of MacKendrick's money, and I aim to get it. Would you let me in if'n I had a hundred dollars, señorita?"

She slammed the door and latched it. The men outside laughed as they moved into the stable. They could be heard for a few moments as they poked and prodded. Then it was silent. Clint slid out from under the bed.

"Have you eaten?" Esperanza asked.

"Yes," Enrique said, then turned to Clint. "The girls, Conce and Chita, had horses hidden outside of town. Four of them. We must make our way there and get mounted." He turned back to Esperanza. "Have you heard anything?"

"Only that they shot down Don Jacques, and"—her voice caught before she continued—"and Don Carlos in the street."

Enrique was silent. He had hoped against hope that his grandfather and uncle might have lived though the vicious onslaught of lead.

"Who was behind this?"

"MacKendrick, of course," Esperanza said quietly. "But he is the law, Don Enrique. I fear I knew of most of this from the start," she said.

"What do you mean?" Enrique asked.

"Davylou Boxworth and your grandfather."

"What?" Enrique managed, astounded at the thought.

"He ate here many times, and Mrs. Boxworth encouraged him. I know she borrowed money from your grandfather. I fear he borrowed it from MacKendrick, only in order to lend it to her. I heard her and MacKendrick laughing about it, about old Don Carlos lending it to her without even getting a note signed, with her telling your grandfather she would pay it back in a few days—then telling him she could not. She claimed she needed it to pay off a note on the boardinghouse, but I know she owed nothing on it."

"I do not understand all of this," Enrique said, looking puzzled.

"She borrowed it, knowing your grandfather would do almost anything she asked. You see, old Don Carlos was invited into Davylou's parlor several times. He would have done anything for her. He put everything he owned in jeopardy in order to help her out."

"The old fool," Enrique said quietly.

"She lied to him." Esperanza defended Don Carlos. "He was very . . . very enamored with her. She could be a charming woman. The worst of it is that she gave the money right back to El Boticario, who Don Carlos borrowed it from in order to lend it to her. It was all a plot between MacKendrick and Mrs. Boxworth to get him to sign a note with high interest."

"Then they had him kidnapped—"

"No," Esperanza said. "They had nothing to do with that, at least they had no reason to have that done. MacKendrick sold the note at a fine profit, and brought Mrs. Boxworth half the profit, over two thousand dollars. Mrs. Boxworth was angry about him selling it. She said they could have had the whole rancho. But he said 'You can never go broke taking a profit.' Still, she was angry."

"How do you know all of this?" Clint asked.

"I listen," she said simply. "They think I am a stupid *camposina,* but I listen, and I know things. They talk, after much brandy, and they talk more loudly than they intend. And I come and go, serving."

"You should have come to me—" Enrique started to scold her.

She replied angrily, "Don Carlos was the father of my godfather. He swore me to silence about him seeing Mrs. Boxworth in the way he did. I could not betray him. But I did listen so I would know what was happening. I was going to him with the whole story, but he was abducted first. Then I didn't know what to do."

"So who bought the note?" Enrique asked.

"Even MacKendrick claimed not to know that," Esperanza said.

Enrique was silent for a long moment, then demanded, "Get the Boxworth woman out here."

It was Esperanza's turn to be silent for a moment. "I will lose my job, Don Enrique. I have told you all——"

"I want to talk with this evil woman."

"I'll get her out here," Clint said, standing face-to-face with Enrique. "But you'll not put a hand on any woman, Enrique, evil or not."

Enrique eyed him, the anger flaring in his eyes. "Get her out here, or I will go in there."

"Not until I have your word," Clint said quietly, but with finality. "And you're not going in there, so get that out of your mind."

Enrique stood glaring at Clint for a moment; then he relaxed. "I only want to get to the bottom of this."

"Your word!" Clint said.

"My word, Lazo. My word."

"Fine," Clint said as he disappeared out the door. In a moment, he was back with Davylou in tow. He ushered her in. It was obvious she was not pleased and had been lured out of her room under false pretenses.

"What's the meaning of this?" she demanded, seeing Enrique. "Esperanza, you——"

"She has nothing to do with this," Clint said. "We forced our way in here to hide from those drunks acting like a posse."

"I'm leaving," she said, turning. Clint pushed the door shut and leaned against it.

"Not until you tell Diego a few things," Clint said.

"Like who bought the note you tricked my grandfather into signing."

She was silent for a long moment.

"Just tell him the truth, Davylou," Clint said, "and you can go back. He's got no fight with you . . . so long as you tell the truth."

"I don't know who bought it. MacKendrick sold it through Willington, or at least claimed he did, and Willington is dead and can't tell you."

"What do you mean, claimed he did?" Enrique demanded, stepping closer so he was face-to-face with Davylou.

Clint laid a hand on his shoulder and gave him a not-so-gentle squeeze. "Let her talk, Enrique."

"I suspected that he didn't really sell it at all, merely told me he did and paid me off with two thousand dollars. He could have ended up with all of Rancho Del Robles Viejo—"

"So you thought he might have cheated you?" Clint asked, then laughed sardonically. "What a viper pit this place is."

"I don't know. I only know I was out of the deal."

"And I only know my grandfather, my father, my brother, my uncle, and my vaqueros are dead. All because of this treachery."

"None of that was my doing—"

"Bull!" Clint said. "I ought to let him have you."

Tears began to track her cheeks. "I didn't mean—"

"There is something you can do," Clint said.

"What?"

"Keep your mouth shut about us being here. Just go back to your room and go to bed."

"All right," she said, then hesitated. "Your aunt is inside, Enrique. You should go to her. She mourns her father and her husband."

"Not until this is over," Enrique said.

Davylou nodded her head, and turned, and Clint stood aside and let her out the door and closed it behind her, then turned back to Enrique. "MacKendrick is the only way we're going to get any answers."

"Then we find MacKendrick," Enrique said, as if they could walk down the street and knock on a door.

"He'll be at the Parrot," Clint said, "if he's not leading the search for us."

"MacKendrick is not the type to lead a search," Esperanza said. "He would leave that to who he considers lesser men."

"Then it's the Parrot, or Rancho Vista Grande," Clint said.

"I will go to the Parrot and see if he is there," Esperanza offered.

"This is no time for a señorita to be on the street," Clint cautioned.

"This is a special time, and it's only next door. I will be all right," she said, grabbing a shawl and hurrying to the door. "Wait here."

"You don't think Mrs. Boxworth—" Enrique cautioned, stopping her before she left.

"No," Clint assured them. "She'll go and lick her wounds. She's woman enough to spend some time thinking about what she has done. We'll be okay here for at least tonight. She'll stay busy with your aunt, appeasing her own conscience. Get right back here, Esperanza. If he's there, we wait for him to leave; if not, we'll find those horses and head for Rancho Vista Grande."

In moments, Esperanza was back. "He is not there. There was no one to play poker with; the gringos are all out hunting you two, and the Californios are all in their casas, angry at what has happened to Don Carlos."

"Then it's Rancho Vista Grande," Clint said. "But we wait until the drunks run out of steam and the streets are clear."

"I will wait one hour, no more," Enrique said.

It was already after midnight, so one hour was probably enough, Clint reasoned. He would have preferred two, but there was no holding this hot-blooded young Diego back. And besides, now that he had heard the whole story, his own blood ran hot. MacKendrick was no more the law than they were, no matter what his office. He used it for his own ends. Whatever Enrique had in mind for him would probably be fitting.

He sighed deeply. He had lived a good part of his life with a warrant out for him. It looked like it might just happen again.

By the time they left Esperanza's, the drunks had given up the hunt, and they escaped the town with little effort and found the four horses with little more.

With a spare mount each, they set out at a gallop for Rancho Vista Grande.

Seventeen

At a swift gallop, changing horses only once, they covered the three and a half miles to Rancho Vista Grande in less than a half hour.

Reining up, they dismounted in the scrub oak, a hundred yards from the hacienda, and moved forward through the brush. Neither of them was sure where MacKendrick's sleeping quarters were, but Enrique had been in the sprawling hacienda many times as a youth, when it belonged to the Mentirosos, and thought he knew. Quietly, pistols in hand, they slipped in the house and made their way down a long hallway to a massive carved door.

Enrique boldly shoved open the door, which creaked loudly, announcing their presence.

"Who's there?" MacKendrick's voice rang out of the darkness.

Enrique moved forward into the pitch-black room.

"I'd suggest you speak up," MacKendrick's voice announced again.

"Light your lamp," Enrique said, "and meet your death."

"Ha!" MacKendrick snapped with confidence. "You light it and we'll see who dies."

"Seems we have a standoff," Clint said.

"Ryan, is that you?" MacKendrick said. "Coming like a thief in the night. I'm not surprised."

"And Enrique Diego," Enrique said, his voice ringing with

anger and anguish. "I have come to make you pay for the death of my family."

"Let's go into the main room and I'll pour you some brandy and we'll talk about this," MacKendrick said.

"I do not drink with the Devil," Enrique snarled, then snapped off a shot at where he thought the voice came from. MacKendrick returned fire and Clint dove to the floor. But Enrique stood like a rock and fired again at the muzzle flash.

"This is crazy," MacKendrick said. "My ranch hands will be in soon, and you'll both die."

"You have men who will fight for you?" Enrique said. "I doubt it."

"MacKendrick," Clint said, "throw down your weapons and I'll talk Diego into taking you to San Diego to the district judge. He'll settle all this."

"No!" Enrique snapped before MacKendrick could reply. "He is going to die here. Here, and now." He snapped off another shot, and MacKendrick returned fire. Enrique stumbled backward, against the wall. Clint could hear him slip to the floor.

"Enrique?" Clint called out, but got no answer. "He's hit," Clint said. "Holster your weapon, MacKendrick, and I'll holster mine."

"How do I know that?" MacKendrick asked.

"I'm going to fetch a candle out of the hallway, MacKendrick. You might get me with a shot, but I swear I'll live long enough to fill you with enough lead to weigh you down all the way to Hell."

"Fetch it," MacKendrick said, and Clint did. He returned and lit a whale's-oil lamp on a bedside stand. Both men stood with guns in hand, Enrique sat silently with his back to the wall, his gun in a limp hand, his other hand across a wound in his gun-arm shoulder. He tried to lift the weapon, but Clint kicked it away. "We'll settle this another way," Clint said, tired of the killing.

"The gringo way," Enrique said, giving Clint a look of both anger and disappointment.

"Let's get him into the great room," MacKendrick said. "I've got a big table there and the light's better, and we can lay him out and treat that wound."

Clint exchanged glances with MacKendrick, then holstered his weapon. MacKendrick, dressed only in a nightshirt, shrugged his shoulders and set his aside on a chest of drawers. Together, he and Clint helped Enrique to his feet.

"Don't touch me." Enrique shook MacKendrick's help away, but accepted Clint's. They moved down the hallway, into the great room, where MacKendrick busied himself lighting lamps.

Enrique refused to lie on the table, so Clint inspected the wound while he sat in one of MacKenrick's high-back leather chairs, a dozen of which flanked the long table. "This didn't exit," Clint said. "He'll need a doctor."

"I'll send someone for Bonny," MacKendrick offered. "What the hell possessed you two to come here?"

"You tricked my grandfather into borrowing money so you could foreclose on the rancho," Enrique said, his voice growing stronger with his anger.

"Hell, I didn't make that old man borrow money. You Californios have got to learn—"

"You used a woman . . . Mrs. Boxworth—"

"I didn't ask them what they wanted the money for—"

Clint interrupted this time. "Davylou told us the whole thing."

"Nothing illegal about it," MacKendrick said as a servant woman and her husband appeared in the doorway leading out to the back of the hacienda. The old man held an ancient musket in his hands.

"Is everything all right, jefe?" the old man asked.

"It's fine. Bring us some coffee, viejos," MacKendrick commanded, and they disappeared. "As I said, it was all legal."

"Legal doesn't make it right," Clint said. Enrique was beginning to pale again.

"And wrong, in your point of view," MacKendrick said with a sly smile, "does not make it illegal. No court would hold me liable for anything I've done."

"How about abducting Don Carlos?" Clint asked.

"Not true," MacKendrick said. "I had no reason to. I didn't even own the note when Don Carlos was abducted. I had sold it."

"To whom?" Clint demanded.

"To an unknown party, at least then unknown."

"And who owns it, if you know now?"

"That's none of your damn business," MacKendrick said. The old woman returned with a pot of coffee and three cups. It was so strong, Clint knew it must have been on the fire most of the night. She poured, and Clint eyed the man.

"But you don't know, or won't tell?"

"That's right. I'll tell you what I will do. I'll have a buckboard harnessed and you can drive Diego into town to Oscar Bonny and see if he can get that slug out. Then I suggest you turn yourself into Stoddard. He should be back in town on the afternoon stage."

"No chance," Clint said. "But I will take your offer to drive him into town. That wound needs proper attention."

MacKendrick nodded and rose, turning toward the door out to the back. He took two steps before he stopped cold. Another man stepped into the room, holding a double-barreled shotgun waist high. Its barrels, shaking in the man's hands, were both leveled on MacKendrick's wide chest.

"Don Embustero?" MacKendrick asked, perplexed at seeing the man.

"Sí, señor. I have been waiting outside for you all evening, since I heard of Don Carlos, but I saw the others come in, and had hoped they would do my work for me. It seems they have failed."

"Your work."

"Sí, *bastardo*," the old man said, and both barrels flashed fire and the shotgun bucked in the old man's feeble hands. MacKendrick was lifted off his feet and blown backward. He landed and didn't move. Clint ducked, then came back as Don Embustero flung the weapon aside and stood looking at what he had wrought. He wrung his hands, looking satisfied.

Clint walked over and bent over MacKendrick, whose chest was a mess of a wound, but whose eyes were fluttering. "Was it Antonio Alverez who bought the note?"

"Go to Hell," MacKendrick managed in a hoarse whisper, just as blood began to trickle out of the corners of his mouth.

"Davylou told me she was in cahoots with Alverez and they bought the note from you when they knew for sure the old man couldn't pay it," Clint lied. "Was it Alverez?"

MacKendrick's eyes widened, and he managed to nod his head, just barely, but enough. Then he whispered, "He hired Mortenson, told me so himself," before his eyes widened and stared vacantly.

Clint straightened and walked over to Enrique. "It seems El Boticario' s ways caught up with him, without your help. Neither a borrower nor a lender be," Clint said. "He did manage a nod when I asked him about Antonio Alverez. It seems he now owns the note. He also whispered that it was Alverez who hired Mortenson. So that's why he killed him."

"I heard the *patrón* say it," the servant woman said, agreeing.

"Then I must kill the traitor, Alverez," Enrique said weakly, managing to get to his feet. "Bind this wound, and we ride back to Los Angeles." He turned to Don Embustero. "Thank you, old friend."

"El Boticario holds my note also," Don Embustero said. "I did it for myself and my family, as well as all Californios. I am old; it doesn't matter if I hang. I only wish I had never become involved with MacKendrick and his poker. . . ."

"He won't be collecting," Clint said.

"I would come to town with you," Don Embustero said,

"but I must stay here and hunt for my note, and destroy it, so my family will have something after the gringo law hangs me."

The old man and woman who were MacKendrick's servants had returned to the doorway when they heard the shot. The old man had his musket in hand again, but he set it aside when he heard Don Embustero speak of the note, and when he saw there was nothing to be done for his *patrón,* who lay dead on the floor.

But he did offer, "My señora and I will help you search, Don Embustero. I know where this pig of a *patrón* kept such things of value. But first I must harness the buckboard so—"

"No," Enrique said. "I can ride. We go now."

"Wait, Don Enrique. I must bind your wound," the old woman said, then hurried away and soon returned with lengths of clean cloth. She worked while Clint sipped the strong coffee, and Don Embustero sat with his head in his hands.

When she was finished, Enrique rose. *"Vaya con Dios,* Don Embustero," he said, managing to walk across the great room.

Clint tipped his hat to the three old people and followed. "Well, I might as well ride to Hell with you, I've tagged along this far."

The trip back to Los Angeles took much longer than the trip out, as they had to stop three times for Enrique to rest.

"It will be dawn soon," Clint said with some trepidation. "It won't do for us to be seen on the street."

"Then we will go straight to Alverez's. He lives over his office."

Antonio Alverez had never been an early riser, even as a young boy living with his grandfather, who had to toe him, and sometimes kick him, off his sleeping mat each morning. And this morning was no exception. But he was awake, too excited to sleep. He had watched while old Don Carlos and Don Jacques were shot down in the street, and had heard of the escape of the gringo Ryan and of Enrique Diego. But

Diego's fate was sealed. He was headed for a hangman's rope, as soon as the law caught up with him.

Then it was only the girls to deal with, two sisters—ignorant but beautiful—and a foreclosure in the gringo court—a court he knew well.

Then Rancho Del Robles Viejo would be his, and unlike the Diegos, he would sell to the best offer, then, maybe *Ciudad de Mexico*. But he would let the LaTour girls live with him, at least until the rancho was sold. That would be good, two beautiful half-French and half-Californio girls living with him. With him as *patrón*. He had signed over a one-half interest in one fourth of the water rights to MacKendrick, but that would pay in the long run, for MacKendrick would be his partner and would get the best possible deal from the city.

Clint and Enrique stood at the front door, in the light of a whale's-oil streetlamp. The door led to Antonio's first-floor office, but they found it well barred. They went to the rear, and it, too, was locked and barred. They tried each of the windows, but all were fastened tight. Antonio Alverez was a careful man.

The upstairs windows stood open, however.

"The last time you made a little too much noise, it got you shot," Clint cautioned, as he was afraid Enrique was considering slamming the door in.

"Yes, it did, and this shoulder will not work against that door, nonetheless. But I have another way."

"What?" Clint asked. And he watched with interest as Enrique returned to his horse and mounted, then loosened the reata, and uncoiled it one-handed. What the hell was the man up to? he wondered, then did not have a chance to stop him as he saw what it was.

Enrique tossed the loop over the lamppost, catching the loop tight just as it dropped past the fixture itself, high on the post; then he dallied around his horn and spurred the horse down the ten-foot-wide pathway between Antonio's office and the building next door. The reata drew taut and the lamppost snapped at the base, and the fixture, full of oil, slammed into the front wall of the Alverez building. In an instant, the flames spread across half the wall.

"Jesus, Enrique!" Clint said, watching helplessly as the fire caught, "there's nothing like keeping from drawing the town's attention." He returned to his own horse and mounted. Enrique recovered his reata and recoiled it as they sat and watched the flames grow. It was only moments before Antonio appeared at the upstairs window, shouting and screaming "Fire" at the top of his lungs.

Antonio turned from the window, dragging on his pants, wondering what of value he should take as he did so. He pulled a shirt on, then ran for the stairs without bothering with his boots. At the foot of the stairs, he was already repelled by the heat from the front wall of the building. He dropped low and took a deep breath, then headed for his desk. He fished the key out of his pocket and unlocked the file drawer and grabbed a small metal box residing there, then ran for the back of the building and threw the bar off the rear door.

Coughing, he stumbled from the building.

The loop dropped over his head before he knew anyone was there.

"Get the box, Lazo," Enrique called out, then spurred the horse. Clint dismounted and gathered up the box as Antonio Alverez bounced away at the end of Enrique's reata. He reined toward the street, then down it, passing running townsmen as Antonio screamed for all he was worth. Clint pounded along behind.

Finally, after Enrique dragged the man four blocks, Clint gigged the horse up beside Enrique's, and yelled, "You're going to kill him, amigo!"

"It is well!" Enrique said.

"It is not well!" Clint shouted over the pounding of the horse's hooves and the yelling of the man who bounced behind. "He should hang, after what he did! And he will, now that MacKendrick is dead."

"Stoddard is as bad!" Enrique shouted.

"Rein up a minute!"

"No!"

"Rein up a minute, and let's talk this out! If you don't agree, drag the bastard to San Bernardino for all I care!"

Enrique drew rein and they stopped at the east edge of town. Antonio moaned behind them, but made no attempt to loosen the loop. The sun was just beginning to gray the eastern sky, and the burning building lit the western half.

"You've got a big responsibility now, Enrique," Clint began. "You've got four ranchos to worry about—"

"If the gringo law does not take them from me."

"True, but it seems to me that's not a likelihood. I don't think Davylou Boxworth wants any more trouble. She said she gave the money right back to MacKendrick . . . all she has to say is that she paid him back for Don Carlos's loan. The loan was paid in full. And I'll bet you, she'll say it, and you know they'll believe her . . . she's one of them. Besides, the note is probably right here in this box, and we can put a match to it . . . before we take Alverez to Stoddard."

"Stoddard will arrest me."

"And probably me," Clint said, "but just until this thing is straightened out. Even Don Carlos said Stoddard was a fair man."

"That is true," Enrique agreed.

"You've got four generations of Diegos buried on Rancho Del Robles Viejo . . . you don't want to let all those ancestors down. And now your uncle and grandfather will join them. And your father has yet to be buried. You have much to do. Besides, we have to get that arm taken care of."

"And my cousins," Enrique said thoughtfully. "The girls could not handle. . . ." Clint could see he had Enrique going his way.

"Nor your aunt. She needs you now, more than ever."

Enrique nodded in agreement.

Clint continued. "Then we take Alverez back to the jail and turn ourselves in. You've had enough revenge. Killing him would be too easy. Let him sweat out the hangman's rope, then you can bring the ladies in to watch him do the blind-folded jig."

"Agreed," Enrique said, suddenly looking exhausted.

Clint started to dismount.

"No, Lazo. I drag him back."

"You'll kill him; then he won't suffer waiting for the rope."

"I will drag him very slowly."

Clint sighed deeply, but kept his seat.

"But you may dismount for one reason," Enrique said.

"What's that?"

"To burn that damnable note."

Clint managed to open the box and fish out two folded parchments.

He studied one in the growing light, then handed it to Enrique. "Your grandfather's note." Then he read the other. "A copy of a bill of sale. Antonio gave an interest in the water rights to MacKendrick." He handed that one over also. As they clomped along, Enrique tore them into tiny pieces and let them drift away on the breeze.

"Will it end now, Lazo?" Enrique asked as they neared the public buildings.

"It has ended, Enrique. Enough is enough."

They reined up in front of the sheriff's office and found the door locked. Antonio groaned in the street, unmoving at the end of the reata.

Clint and Enrique sat on the step of the sheriff's office. They watched the dawn.

It was going to be a clean, new day.

Visit L.J. Martin on his Web site: www.ljmartin.com

William W. Johnstone
The *Mountain Man* Series